P9-BAW-134

Lora Leigh's novels are:

"TITILLATING."
—*Publishers Weekly*

"SIZZLING HOT."
—*Fresh Fiction*

"INTENSE AND BLAZING HOT."
—*RRTErotic*

"WONDERFULLY DELICIOUS . . . TRULY DECADENT."
—*Romance Junkies*

ALSO BY LORA LEIGH

Rugged Texas Cowboy

LORA LEIGH

collision point

St. Martin's Paperbacks

This is a work of fiction. All of the characters, organizations, and events portrayed in this novel are either products of the author's imagination or are used fictitiously.

COLLISION POINT

Copyright © 2018 by Lora Leigh.

All rights reserved.

For information address St. Martin's Press, 175 Fifth Avenue, New York, NY 10010.

ISBN: 978-1-250-11032-9

Our books may be purchased in bulk for promotional, educational, or business use. Please contact your local bookseller or the Macmillan Corporate and Premium Sales Department at 1-800-221-7945, ext. 5442, or by e-mail at MacmillanSpecialMarkets@macmillan.com.

Printed in the United States of America

St. Martin's Paperbacks edition / March 2018

St. Martin's Paperbacks are published by St. Martin's Press, 175 Fifth Avenue, New York, NY 10010.

10   9   8   7   6   5   4   3   2

Memories can whisper of a child's laughter, a mother's advice, a father's strong embrace. They can recall a song, a teenage crush, the whisper of the soul's greatest desire.

They warm cold bleak nights, bring hope, strength, or a rueful smile.

They remind us that we make mistakes when we're certain we're right, and that even when we're right, we can still be wrong.

They are tears, heartache, passionate kisses and sighs in the dark, parking on a deserted lane, or an argument brewing from unrequited love.

They are the culmination of our lives, our promises and our passions. Our hopes, dreams, and failures, stored forever where we can but close our eyes and access them at will.

They are a gift. They are a curse.

They are who we are, and they're what created us.

And sometimes, they are magic . . . .

For the memories

Because death has taken you and there's no bringing you back.

Because all the tears, the fears, the hopes, and the dreams can never recreate what's been forever lost.

For the memories, because without them,

where would I be?

For my grandbaby, Manny—we miss you . . .

foreword

The Legend of Irish Eyes

Irish eyes see through eyes not their own, feel with a heart outside their chest. Wild Irish Eyes. When you love, love well and love true and take care, because those Irish Eyes are windows into not just your own soul, but the soul of the one you love. Don't lose that heart, for you lose a part of your soul when you do. The legacy of those eyes will ensure it. And if you lose that soul yours clings to, you can't leave the places where your memories are best. To leave would be to leave the comfort of the soul that even in death, your own will always cling to.

There are layers to life. Nothing is as we think. There are always layers and layers, shades of gray and shades of black or white. You have to find out why, not see what. Those layers are always shifting, always moving, and always revealing layers you never knew waited below. Remember that there's always what you don't know and what you don't see. And love doesn't always do what we think it should.

                            Grandpops Malone

prologue

"What took you so long?" The words rasped from the young woman's swollen, split, and bleeding lips.

The beauty she had been weeks before was marred by the heavy fists that had landed repeatedly on her fragile face.

Her once long, inky black hair was chopped off to only the few inches that covered her scalp, and the clothes she wore were stained with far too much blood.

Riordan "Rory" Malone could feel the rage crawling up his back and moving steadily to explode at the base of his skull as he crouched in front of her, his palm cupping her cheek with a ghostly touch. Just enough to feel the warmth of her, to assure himself she was actually there, she was actually alive.

"Your father," he muttered, finally answering her as his brother, Noah, swept the bright pinpoint of light off her fragile body. "He had me locked in a cell until he could get a team together."

"Liar," she whispered as she tried to smile.

He wished he was lying.

That was exactly what Ivan Resnova had done.

"I wouldn't lie to you, baby," he reminded her.

How many times had he promised he'd never lie to her, and still, she refused to trust him?

"What happened when you left, Riordan? Why did you leave me?" Pain and tears filled her voice, making him crazy. The sound clawed at his chest, tore at the control he'd fought for over the years. "Why didn't you tell me goodbye?"

"Because it wasn't goodbye." The light paused, high on her legs, pulling his attention to the blood heavily staining the light-colored denim.

God help him, what had they done to her?

"Amara, I'm going to have to move you." Lifting his gaze to the shattered blue of her eyes he steeled himself for the pain he knew he was going to cause her. "Tell me what hurts worse."

He knew the breaks, the wounds, but he needed her talking, needed her focused.

"Broken ankle," she said. "At least one broken rib, and they broke my wrist to make certain I couldn't get up the ladder." Her gaze moved to the crudely built ladder extending from the trapdoor in the floor above. "Get out of here, Riordan. Please. You know it's a trap. Get out now."

He knew a lot of things, just as he knew there were men positioned outside to ensure their exit.

"As soon as I have you ready to transport. Now, rein in that sailor's tongue of yours while we secure these breaks. Remember, your daddy's on the link. We don't want to upset him by letting him hear what a wicked tongue you have."

Panic flashed in her expression, in her eyes. Yeah, she knew her father and she knew exactly what the sound of her curses, or her screams, would do to him.

What they had already done to him.

"He should be arrested." It was her favorite curse where her father was concerned.

He heard the love in the accusation though, the belief that her father was far better than others believed, more honorable than others saw.

"Do something about it then." As Noah arranged the supplies he needed, Riordan stared down at her, forcing himself to hold back the agony he could feel threatening to explode past his control as her head settled weakly against the side of his arm. A whimper escaped her lips as Noah secured her wrist first. "If you can beat me to it."

He was going to bust every tooth Ivan Resnova possessed in that arrogant head of his, then he was going to rip his damn dick off.

Amara caught his wrist, distressed, her face pale, her blue-gray eyes filled with pain. "Don't hurt him. Swear it, Riordan. Don't hurt him."

She was too pale, there was too much blood, and it terrified him.

"Then live," he snapped, nose to nose with her, ignoring the fear in her eyes. "Live or I swear to God, Amara, I'll make him pay, personally." And he was capable of doing it. "Now, we're going to do this, baby so we can haul your butt out of here," he encouraged her, feeling the ragged pain burning his guts at Noah's signal that they had to secure her ribs next.

Behind him, Micah and Nik caught the metal life basket being lowered into the cavern. Even secured in the basket, her trip up would be painful—and there was no way to make it easier.

"Not going to happen." She sighed as though resigned to that fact. "There's no way you can get me out, whether you bind these breaks or not."

He almost laughed at the certainty in her tone.

"Have a little faith in me for once." He ignored the bitter slash of memory that assured him just how little faith she did have in him.

"It's not a lack of faith in you," she told him, her voice weary as she lifted her head, allowing him to ease the torn material of her shirt above her ribs so Noah could tape the area of the break. "I know what you're facing. Get your men out of here. . . . You get out of here. I won't let you die for me—"

"Shut up," he snapped, "We're going out together, stubborn-ass, or neither of us will go out. Take your pick."

Even as he spoke, he considered and weighed options, forcing himself to ignore her pain-filled, smothered sobs.

Her strangled cries destroyed him. The sharp, ragged scream she cut off the second it left her lips had a curse slipping free.

He'd once thought nothing could have been worse than hearing his sister-in-law Bella's screams of grief when his brother had been reported dead years before. The agony of holding Bella and dealing with both their grief at the same time was marked as the most painful period of his life.

This surpassed it.

How had he managed to let this woman get so close to him in such a short amount of time? So close that the need to murder the men who had done this to her was burning inside him like an inferno threatening to rage out of control. Threatening to destroy the man he had been and leaving in its wake nothing but pure fury and the soul of a man laid bare.

The agonizing pain had her crying out, even knowing the raw, ragged fury that would be consuming her father if he was truly listening through the link the agents wore.

Riordan and an agent tried to secure the breaks and stabilize them as much as possible, but movement was still the enemy. Movement, and fear. She knew the men who beat her were expecting a rescue force. She'd told Riordan they were expecting her father to send someone after her, they'd be waiting.

They wanted her to suffer . . .

"Almost there, baby," he assured her as he moved up the ladder, staying next to her as the basket they'd secured her in was hauled up the expanse of the cavern she'd been thrown into.

"They're waiting," she whispered again, pain and fear building in her mind, through her senses. "They're waiting."

"We have friends waiting topside as well," he promised her. "You remember Noah, right? His men are up there just waiting for some dumb-ass to stick his head out."

His voice was calm. So calm and so confident.

And she did remember Noah. Remembered the man Riordan introduced as a good friend, as well as the three others who hadn't been introduced at all when she'd caught them meeting with Riordan and her father in the Resnova penthouse months before.

They were hard, dangerous men, she'd seen that immediately. But they weren't inhuman. They weren't immortal.

"Don't die for me." She couldn't let him do that. She couldn't allow that to happen.

A sob tore from her and immediately sent a wave of agony tearing through her mind as the broken rib protested the movement. The haze of white-hot agony raced through her, stealing her breath, and for a moment, her very senses.

Dead men . . .

They were dead men . . .

"Easy, baby. Easy. Here we go. Let's get you out of here . . ." It was his voice that drew her back from the darkness waiting to take her, from the soul-shattering knowledge that the enemy was waiting.

"Copters moving in," reported one of the men suddenly surrounding her, his tone dark, steel-hard. "Evac in three."

It was going to happen, she could feel it.

"Riordan, leave . . ." she gasped, feeling the basket level, looking up into the dark, shadowed faces of the two men supporting it as Riordan and the other agents surrounded them, covering them.

"Copter in sight," Riordan stated as the sound of blades beating in the air could be heard in the distance.

It was coming.

"Get him out . . ." She stared at the shadowed face of the man at her feet. "You have to stop this." Blue eyes stared back at her. Eyes like Riordan's. Eyes that bore into hers. "You have to—"

"Riordan, take the basket," the shadow snapped, the authority and clear command in his voice causing the others to tense, to watch the night more closely.

"Copter's landing," Riordan growled. "No time. Move out. Now."

The first shot was fired.

"Now! Move out!"

They were running for the helicopter, racing for it, fireflies filling the darkness, the sharp explosions echoing around her as she fought to keep her eyes on Riordan.

"Go! Go!" The shadow holding the bottom of the basket pushed it to another of the dark shapes firing back as she watched Riordan fall.

"No! Riordan!" She fought against the pain, struggled against the restraints holding her in the basket.

"Get her out—" He was almost on his feet, almost, when he suddenly stiffened, his back bowing before a shadow caught him, threw him over his shoulder and ran.

They were all running, racing . . .

"We're losing him. . . . We're losing him! . . ." A voice shouted out as the helicopter was lifting off, banking and shooting across the sky. "Goddammit, Micah, do something. Rory . . . Rory, don't you do it, damn you. . . . Don't you fuckin' die on me . . ."

She felt him.

Amara swore she felt his heart stop, felt him give up and leave her. She felt him die and she wanted nothing more . . .

. . . than to die with him.

"Don't leave me . . ." she whispered, giving in to the darkness, to the comforting embrace of nothing. "Please, don't leave me . . ."

chapter one

Six months later

She'd been told that West Texas in the spring wasn't much different from West Texas in the fall, but as Amara Resnova pulled in the driveway of the small house outside Alpin, she felt she had to disagree with that summation.

Stretched out in front of the house with its wraparound porch was a lush green valley fed by a lazily running stream winding through it. Sunlight speared from the cloudless blue sky, bright and warm, spreading its heat in a comforting embrace.

And the charming little house sat just beneath the warming sunlight. Spreading out in front of it was the picturesque valley; behind it, the normal West Texas part-grass, part-scrub, potential-desert landscape that never failed to amaze her.

On a rising knoll stood a lone tree, thickly branched and heavily leafed, shading what appeared to be a small cemetery. Rather than looking desolate and lonely, that little plot of land with its surrounding black iron fence, appeared instead to keep watch over the land below it. As though those buried there kept a gentle eye on those who came after them.

As isolated as the property was, it should have appeared stark. Instead, an air of contentment and peace lay over it. As though the land, the house, the vibrant green of the valley, and the cemetery that overlooked it all, knew all there was about life and love and had locked all those secrets within it to sustain it.

Drawing in a deep breath to steady herself against the fears she hadn't been able to push behind her even in such a lovely setting, Amara turned off the engine, forced her hands not to shake, and opened the door before stepping into the warmth that filled the valley.

It wasn't a blazing heat, but rather a gentle wave that filled the air and wafted around her. And in it there was a strange sense of familiarity. A "been there before" feeling that had her heart racing, her mouth drying as she stared around and drew in the sights and whispered sounds of a land as yet untouched by civilized life.

Here, a person could see the stars at night rather than the city lights. The sound of the lonely coyote rather than the rush of traffic. Peace rather than a hectic race.

Here, perhaps, she could find some answers. And maybe there was a chance to find everything she'd lost.

Tugging the hem of her tank, she straightened it over the band of her jeans beneath the light denim jacket she wore as she walked slowly from the car to the stone path that led to the porch. The thick carpet of grass stretched from the valley to surround the house, but she'd noticed as she parked that it became sparser at the back. As though that carpet of green with its lazy stream could only struggle so far to embrace the weathered home.

The dark blue pickup parked at the side of the house attested that someone lived there. And she knew the vehicle belonged to the man those in town called Grandpops Malone.

Riordan Malone Sr. was grandfather to Riordan Malone the younger, she'd been told, when she stopped at the gas station and auto repair garage outside town that bore the name MALONE AND BLAKE—SERVICE AND REPAIR. There, she'd learned Riordan the younger was part owner but currently out at his "grandpops'" place.

Riordan.

That name haunted her dreams, her fantasies. Though the man in those dreams wasn't an old man. The one who came to her in those nightly images was tall, strong, impossibly sexy.

As Amara forced herself to walk to the porch, she looked around, searching for the face, listening for the voice of a man she knew only in those dreams. The man she'd escaped her father's protection to go search for.

Was he friend or foe?

Even she couldn't answer that question, not fully. But for some reason, she couldn't seem to help the need to learn which he would be.

As her foot lifted to the first step, the front door creaked, causing her to pause, to wait with bated breath as it slowly opened to reveal an aged, gray-haired gentleman she suspected was Riordan Sr., Grandpops.

In his worn loose jeans, well-washed white shirt with sleeves folded neatly back below his elbows, scuffed leather boots, and with that serene expression, the man

looked as old and wise as the mountains themselves.
And there was no doubt he was just as damn stubborn.

"Well, hello there." The smile that lifted the corners
of his mouth was reflected in his dark blue eyes. "Can I
help ya, young lady?"

There was a whisper of a lyrical accent. Irish. Just a
whisper though, not the full, male lilt she sometimes
heard in memories that never fully revealed themselves.

"I'm looking . . ." She swallowed nervously. "I'm
looking for Riordan Malone."

His head tilted to the side, his thick graying hair
neatly trimmed but giving a hint of the rogue he must
have been in his youth.

"I'd say you're looking for my grandson rather than
myself," he said gently. "He should be along in a bit. His
da just called to say he's done stole that wild pony again
and headed this way." A chuckle filled the air. "Come
along up to the porch and sit with me till he arrives. That
wild beast always gives a show when he comes barreling
through the valley."

Moving gingerly up the steps to the porch, she followed him to the comfortable-looking cushioned rock-
ers that faced the valley.

"Does he steal ponies often?" She frowned as she sat
down, feeling more off balance than she'd felt in her
life—which was saying something considering the past
six months.

"Just that wild-assed black son of a satan that took a
liking to him." He grinned back at her, his gnarled hands
gripping the arms of the rocker loosely. "His da threat-
ens to kill the beast every time Riordan takes it out. He
swears it's gonna kill the boy."

Boy.

That didn't sound like the man she was searching for. But, everything she learned assured her this was the one place she was certain to find him.

"Ahh, here he comes now." Fondness filled the old man's tone as he motioned to the valley.

He appeared at first as no more than a storm of dust rising beyond the verdant green of the valley.

Amara watched, her heart racing as that trail of dust grew steadily closer.

It was an imposing sight, she had to admit.

A sensual, exhilarating sight.

The horse, black as midnight, neck extended, flying across the deserted landscape, was enough to hold the eye. But the sight of the man, bent low to the horse's neck, black hair flying back from his face, riding without a saddle, was a bit more than simply imposing.

It was exhilarating.

Imposing and savage and wildly erotic.

Amara could feel her body responding to the sight, weakening, filling with a sensual lassitude she couldn't combat.

"Be watching this now. That horse loves ta take him on a wild ride he does," Grandpops said softly.

The horse flew over a gully as though he had wings, before jumping the stream, neck and legs extended as it went airborne for precious seconds. The animal then took a series of fences as though they were nothing, and as she stared, she felt she knew how those women felt from centuries past as they watched a conquering warrior bearing down on them.

When the horse flew over the fence that enclosed the

house yard, Amara was certain there was no way it could pull up before slamming headfirst into the porch itself.

With no more than a few yards to spare, the beast came up on his hind legs, a triumphant equine scream filling the air before landing again and prancing about with pure high-spirited joy before finally settling.

And Riordan sat firm on the animal's back the whole time, holding onto the horse's mane rather than a bridle, thighs gripping the animal's heaving sides as he stared at her with blazing, furious blue eyes before turning them on his grandfather.

The younger Riordan dismounted smoothly, the soles of his moccasined feet hitting the ground as he slapped the beast on the rump. It came up on its hind legs once more in another display of savage beauty as it reared up, pawed the air, then shot off back the way it came the second it landed.

Flying like the wind, strong legs launching it over the fence, the gully, then the stream before a trail of dust followed it around the bend of the mountain.

So much beauty, she thought. A display of savage male temper and strength, and no less showed in Riordan's expression as he propped his hands on his lean waist and glared up at her where she sat next to his grandfather on the porch.

Well-worn denim encased his hips and legs, and the moccasins that covered his feet weren't fringed or fancy, just well made. A black T-shirt stretched across a broad chest, emphasizing his muscular abs and making her fingers itch to remove it.

Yes, this was him. The savage who invaded her

dreams, the fury who slashed at her nightmares. Vivid sapphire eyes, daunting features, proud, imposing. A man who knew his own demons as well as those that inhabited other men. Or women.

She rose slowly to her feet, aware of Riordan's "grandpops" as he sat comfortably in his rocker, watching in interest.

"What the fuck are you doing here?" the words that passed from his lips caused her to flinch; their icy tone caused her heart to sink.

The tender tone, the edge of lust and hunger she'd dreamed of, was nowhere in sight.

His gaze raked over her and there was none of the sensual promise she's seen in his eyes when he'd invaded her dreams, none of the dominant sensualist who tormented her with his touch in her fantasies.

She hadn't expected this. This wild fury and enraged demand. He didn't seem the least bit glad to see her, she had to admit. What made her think he would be? she wondered.

Was she wrong? Did she not know him?

She was certain she had to have known him, certain that somehow, someway, they must have meant something to each other. Could she have been so wrong?

"Riordan!" Grandpops' surprised tone had a grimace contorting Riordan's face.

Evidently the grandfather thought little of the grandson's language.

"Grandpops, perhaps you should go back to Grant's." He turned to his grandfather, his voice firm. "Noah, Sabella, and the babies will be there in a bit."

Grandpops continued to glower at him.

"I'm certain I can handle whatever language he wants to use, Mr. Malone," she assured the older man. "I'm not exactly a stranger to it these days."

Her father cursed more often, brooded more often, and Amara knew the situation she'd found herself in was weighing on him. If she didn't do something, didn't fix things, then she was terrified of what may happen. Of what her father would do to fix things himself.

"But can his grandmother?" The old man sounded disappointed rather than angry. "Remember whose home your using that language in, boy."

Rising from his chair, Grandpops moved to the steps stiffly and made his way down, casting his grandson yet another warning glare.

"Drive carefully, Grandpops. No more racing with those Brickford boys," Riordan stated as his grandfather passed by.

And Amara could have sworn she saw a gleeful grin tease at the older man's lips. But he merely grunted as he passed.

A few moments later the truck started, and they watched Grandpops ease around the circular drive and onto the road that led to the small valley.

The silence that stretched between them was heavy— with his anger and her uncertainty.

As the truck took the curve around the rising hill, she turned back to Riordan and tucked her hands into the pockets of her light jacket, her fingers curling into fists.

She'd faked the last six months with friends and most of her family. Taking cues from her father and his assistant Nikolai, she'd smiled and faked her way through every damn meeting and gathering she'd been forced to attend until she slipped silently from her father's estate the week before and, in essence, ran away from home.

Not that he was letting her run without giving chase. He and his men weren't far behind her and she knew it. They'd almost caught up with her the night before, outside Houston. If she didn't do something, if she didn't find a way to eliminate the threat shadowing her, then her poppa could do something she may not be able to live with. And it was that decision that sent her running to Alpine and the man who shadowed her dreams.

She was here now. She'd found the man she'd gone searching for, and she knew the days of lying and pretending to be who she'd been six months before were over.

She lifted her head, straightened her shoulders, and stared up at him in determination.

"Whatever I did to you, I'm sorry," she told him, miserably aware that if she'd offended him in the past, angered him, then there was the possibility it couldn't be fixed with an apology. She hadn't been the nicest person she could have been in the past.

His eyes narrowed on her before once again moving to sweep over the landscape. There was a tension that surrounded him, a steady watchfulness she'd noticed her father and Ilya always carried as well. That prepared and ready-for-action thing strong men always seemed to carry with them.

"Go home, Amara," he told her when those brilliant eyes turned back to her. "Go back to daddy. This is no place for you."

He knew her. He was angry, but for a second, she

swore she saw something more in that flash of heat in his expression.

"No. Riordan, please." He couldn't make her leave. Not yet, not until he knew what was coming, because what was coming didn't affect just her. She could sense it, her dreams assured her of it.

Turning, Riordan dismissed her just that easily and strode up the steps to the porch, leaving her to stand alone as the storm door slammed behind his retreating back.

Alone.

Strange, but this feeling of "alone" didn't seem nearly as unfamiliar as it should have.

Inhaling deeply, she followed him rather than doing as ordered. Not that she often did as she was ordered. That was probably how she found herself where she was now. Opening the door quietly, she stepped into the house, her gaze taking in the homey atmosphere of the large living area.

A comfortable leather couch, recliner, and matching chairs were grouped around a cold fireplace. The mantle held a variety of family pictures that she would have loved to have time to check out. The wood floor was smooth, aged with a sheen of time and caring.

There were more family pictures in frames on the wall, many appeared old and passed down through the years, the frames lovingly polished, the photos a bit faded from time.

As she stepped into the room, Riordan watched her silently, leaning against the wide doorframe into the kitchen, his arms crossed over his broad chest as he simply stared at her, his expression still and remote.

"What the hell are you doing here?" he asked, that rumble of his deep voice sending a stroke of sensation up her spine.

What was she doing here?

Trying to survive, to live.

"I need your help." She had to force herself to say the words, and still they came out as barely more than a whisper. "Please, Riordan. I need your help."

Six months.

For six bloody months this damn woman had tormented his dreams while asleep and his thoughts while awake. He'd given his life for her on a dark, blood-filled night, then again on an operating table, only to be told she never wanted to see him again when he'd been released. And now, two months after he'd returned to Texas, here she was.

Son of a bitch. Just when he thought he could get through a night without being tormented by her, she just showed up out of the blue. And it was all he could do not to touch her, to jerk her to him and show her exactly what she was dealing with in coming to him.

But, she'd been his weakness from the moment he'd met her, hadn't she? From the second his gaze touched hers, she'd been the one woman he couldn't get out his head. And God knew he'd fought it.

Tiny and delicate, she made a man want to wrap her in cotton and hide her away from the world. Resilient, stubborn, and independent, she made a man realize fast that she wouldn't allow him to do so.

Her once-long, straight silky black hair was shorter now, courtesy of her abductors. At first jagged and close to her scalp, it had grown a good six inches or so and feathered around her delicate face becomingly. Piercing gray-blue eyes stared back at him, somberly.

Frightened.

Riordan straightened from the doorframe, his eyes narrowing on her. That was fear in her eyes, along with the uncertainty and the heat he always saw there.

"You need my help?" he couldn't help the mockery that tinged his voice simply because it flooded every corner of his mind. "Strange, two months ago you never wanted to see my damn lying ass again. What changed?"

What had changed? For a moment, that question had her pausing.

God, if only she could tell him. She was damned if she knew herself what had changed. All she knew was that now, six months after she'd awakened, she was unable to remember what had happened or who had abducted her or what they had wanted. The nightmares had grown worse, the sense of imminent danger and panic that fueled them had become overwhelming. In each one, this man stood with his hand outstretched, his voice whispering to her, urging her to find him. To come to him.

She swallowed tightly, uncertain what to say, how to explain. She didn't trust him, not by any means. But she didn't trust anyone now. She didn't know who to trust.

"I'm sorry." But she was damned if she could remember telling him he wasn't wanted.

No doubt she'd had a good reason. Savagely hewn, rough and sexy, and a cowboy to boot. No doubt he had a wandering eye and hands that had no idea how to be faithful. The one type of man she despised. But personal

fidelity and the ability to protect weren't always intimately acquainted, she'd since learned. The man who
cheated on his wife and walked away from his children
could also be the very man willing to give his life for
that same woman, or those children.

Men had never made sense to her, even from an early
age. But she didn't need him to make sense to her, she
needed him to fulfill the promise he made in her dreams
and help her figure out who was determined to see her
dead and why she was so certain it was someone she
knew and loved.

"You're sorry?" he snorted, flashing her a look filled
with disgust. "Fine, go home and be sorry there. I don't
have time for it here."

The panic was beginning to build inside her chest. It
thundered through her veins and raced to her heart. If
he made her leave, if he threw her out and forced her to
run again, she was going to die, and she knew it.

"You promised you'd help me," she snapped, her tone
more demanding than she would like despite her uncertainty and the fact that the words tore from her almost
involuntarily. "You swore it. You can't renege now."

Had he really promised, or had she just dreamed it?
Was the memory of that dark little hole and the pain that
filled her just another nightmare? Had he really been
there, swearing he'd always save her, or had she just
imagined it?

"Did I now?" Softly voiced, the question held that bit
of Irish sexy, lyrical sound that she often heard in those
fantasy dreams filled with pleasure rather than pain.
"And when did that happen?"

She shook her head. Memory or nightmare?

"You swore you'd always be there if I needed you." She fought to believe it was memory. "All I had to do was reach out to you. Well, dammit, I'm reaching out. Do you want me to beg too?"

She could see his hand outstretched, his expression somber, demanding. He wouldn't come to her, she had to go to him.

Riordan felt as though his world had narrowed, that nothing existed but this moment, this woman, and the dreams that had haunted him. Dreams of her cries, her pleas that he come to her. And no matter how desperately he tried to reach her, she was always but a touch away. No matter how often he'd urged her to take his hand, to come to him, just reach out to him, she never did.

The dreams had become so insistent over the months, he'd actually contacted his former security team members who still worked for her father to check up on her.

All was well, he'd been told. Princess Resnova was still the princess, and the czar still protected her like the cherished daughter she would always be. And still, he dreamed, reached out to her, and urged her to take his hand.

I'll always be here for you. Just reach out to me.

He hadn't told her that, he'd whispered those words in a dream.

And son of a bitch if that wasn't enough to make a man force himself not to shake in his boots.

"Why?" he demanded. "Why the hell do you need me when your father has over fifty protection agents, and every damn one of them is on call in case they're needed to protect you? What the fuck do you need with me?"

Damn her. She'd waited six months to come to him. She'd let him lie in a hospital out of the country, half alive for weeks, and hadn't once called or reached out him. Why the hell was she short circuiting his brain now?

"I need you to help me," she whispered again. "I need someone I can trust with my life, Riordan, before I die because I don't know anymore who's a friend and who's the enemy. But *you* might know. I need someone I can trust to watch my back while I figure out who the hell is trying to kill me and why."

Kill her?

According to every source he had in her father's organization, she was safe. The men at the farmhouse where they'd found her were all killed. The bodyguard they'd identified as being behind the abduction and her beating was dead as well.

"Your father's men can protect you." God help him. If he even tried, he'd get them both killed—because he wouldn't be able to stay out of her bed.

She was shaking her head even as he spoke. "I don't trust them. I don't trust anyone." Desperation filled her expression now. "You don't understand, Riordan. All I have are these crazy dreams of you. Every nightmare I have you're at my back, protecting me. That's all I have because I don't remember what happened before my abduction or the abduction itself. I've lost a year of my life and I don't know why and I damn sure can't force those memories back," she cried out, fury filling her tone. "All I have are the nightmares and dreams, and the only person I can see, the only person I can trust in them is you. And by God, I want to know why."

She faced him, fists clenched, anger flushing her face,

but that was heat in her eyes. It wasn't just nightmares she had, it wasn't simply dreams.

It was this bond he could sense between them even as she stared back at him, furious, frightened.

And he'd waited long enough.

Taking the steps that separated them, he jerked her into his arms, his lips stilling her cries, his arms tightening around her, holding her to him.

Her lips parted in shock, and he took full advantage of it. He tasted her. Lips and tongue possessed her kiss, and he let his senses grow drunk on her.

Because somehow, someway, she'd shared not just her dreams with him, but those incredibly erotic fantasies that filled his head as well.

And now, he wanted a taste of all that passion, that feminine hunger and need he hadn't nearly had enough of before her abduction.

Then they could discuss the rest.

chapter two

It was a kiss ripped from her darkest dreams, her most sensual fantasies. A melding of lips and tongues and a heated pleasure she couldn't deny herself.

Hunger poured from Riordan, rocked her to her core, and spurred her own.

It didn't feel like a stranger kissing her. This wasn't a stranger, it was a lover she'd known before, if only in her dreams. Shuddering, trembling, she met the kiss, anxiety and emotions surging inside her that she had no idea how to identify yet.

Leaning closer he pressed her against the wall, his hard chest against her breasts, sensitizing the already tender nipples as his mouth ravaged hers. Stole her breath, her will to fight, and pulled her into a vortex of such sensual pleasure, she didn't have the strength to pull away from him. She whimpered against the demanding thrust of his tongue, moaned as his knee pushed between her legs, his thigh angling against her sex and creating a friction so delicious she felt weakened by it.

This was what she dreamt of. His lips grinding against her, thrusting between her lips, tasting him as he tasted her and growing drunk on the pleasure.

She was on her tiptoes, fighting to get closer, to draw him to her. Her hands gripped his shoulders, feeling the muscles beneath bunch and tighten as he lifted her closer, allowing her to ride his thigh with erotic need as her clit swelled and throbbed with increasing sensitivity.

What was he doing to her? How was he doing it? She couldn't remember a time, except in those erotic dreams of him, that her senses had come alive like this. That so much pleasure had flooded her body, rushed through her mind. As though every cell was poised to explode with exquisite agony.

The shock of his lips pulling back, releasing her, had an instant denial rocking her.

"No," the soft cry tore from her as her hands tightened on his shoulders, her fingers digging into his muscles through the material. "Not yet."

Powerful fingers gripped her hair, holding her head back, forcing her to open her eyes, to stare up at him.

"I'm going to end up fucking you against the wall in my grandpops' home if we're not damn careful here." Rather than releasing her, his head lowered, his lips going to her neck in a heated caress before his teeth raked the sensitive skin with erotic intent.

Her lashes drifted closed, pleasure swirling through her as each touch of his lips against her neck, each rake of his teeth pulled a moan from her that she was helpless against. Each sensation left her intoxicated on each bit of pleasure and aching for more.

Just as she was ready to beg, he stilled before pulling himself from her with a muttered curse.

Forcing her eyes open, she watched as he kept his back to her and pushed his fingers through his overly long hair before gripping the back of his neck.

"You're as fucking dangerous to my self-control as you were before your father fired me," he muttered, the anger in his tone impossible to miss.

Her father had fired him?

She fought to push the pleasure, the hunger and need aside at that comment.

When had her father fired him? Hell, when had her father hired him?

It had to have been in the year she'd forgotten. Months of memories that tormented her in her dreams and her nightmares, and brought her awake screaming or sobbing in loss.

"I was your bodyguard." He turned on her, the words shocking her. "I headed a four-man team as well as your cousins Elizaveta and Grisha, until three days before your abduction when your father sent me to England."

She felt something—knowledge, aching loss—shift inside her.

She didn't doubt him. Her father had always been prone to sending away any bodyguard she seemed to be getting close to.

"You said he fired you?" she whispered.

Mocking censure filled his expression. "I might have

loosened a few of his teeth before I went out with the extraction team." His lip curled in a sneer. "I take that back, I know I loosened those bitches." Pure furious pleasure filled his gaze at the words.

"You argued before you went out after me?" She could only shake her head in confusion. "Why?"

She didn't know. But then, she hadn't asked her father why he'd left after she'd realized who he was. She hadn't asked anyone, she'd simply begun searching her father's employee database first.

"Why?" he murmured as he watched her closely, those intense blue eyes focused completely on her. "You don't know?"

"I told you I didn't. Didn't you hear me earlier or were you too focused on pushing me against the wall for a quick little groping session first?" Shooting him a disgusted look, she pushed her hands into the pockets of her jacket and stepped away from the wall. "Didn't you hear me?"

Oh, he'd heard her.

Watching her, Riordan could feel that little internal alarm going off, warning him that, number one, she wasn't lying. And number two, this was possibly a hell of a lot more serious than she was telling him.

"What makes you think someone's trying to kill you?" He watched her closely, tracking her as she paced to the door and stared out at the valley below.

Her shoulders lifted defensively for a second before a heavy sigh left her lips. "I've been staying at the estate in Colorado since I left the hospital." She turned back to him, rubbing at her arms as she faced him, making him ache to hold her. "Three months later the brakes went out on my car while I was on the more mountainous roads into Aspen; then someone broke into my hotel room when I should have been asleep, but I was staying in Elizaveta's room, which I rarely do. And I was nearly run over crossing the street in Aspen last month." For a moment, uncertainty and confusion flashed across her expression. "Poppa thinks they are random events."

Ivan suddenly believed in random events? Since when, by God?

"If you've lost your memory of the year before your abduction, then why are you here?" Why come to him after throwing him out of her life as she had just before her abduction?

"I told you." That fear in her face was killing him. "I have nightmares . . ." Her voice lowered to a mere whisper on that final word, then with a deep breath, became firmer. "In those dreams, you're always there. You keep me safe. You tell me you'll always keep me safe." She swallowed, hesitated. "Were we lovers?"

His jaw tightened as he held back every curse he needed to rain down on Ivan.

"We were," he growled. "For a while."

"For a while," she repeated softly. "What happened?"

What *had* happened? He suspected Ivan had happened, but he'd never known for certain.

"I have no idea," he told her, keeping his voice cool, unconcerned. "I was due to leave for England for several weeks for an extraction your father needed me on. You decided to break off the relationship."

There wasn't a glimmer of knowledge, just that damn confusion that filled her gray-blue eyes.

"Did Poppa know we were involved?" she asked, her hands pushing into the pockets of her jacket once again.

That was one of Amara's "things" when dealing with a personal situation she was having trouble with. If she had pockets, she made use of them.

"Not that I'm aware of it," he assured her mockingly. "That was one of the things we argued over. You didn't want him to know."

Yeah, wouldn't do for the little Irish bastard she was fucking to mess up his daughter's pristine reputation, now would it?

She frowned at that, as though she wasn't certain it was the truth. But then, she hadn't exactly put much faith in him when they'd been together, had she?

"I'm sorry for that," she stated, the weariness in her voice tugging at him, making him want to take it back, to reassure her, to take the fear and the regret from her expression. "When I asked Poppa if I had a lover, he seemed so shocked, that I was certain I had to be wrong. I didn't know I could be so deceptive."

And it was obvious the knowledge wasn't sitting well with her.

"Your father tends to fire men who become interested in you," he growled. "You didn't seem to believe I didn't give a damn if he fired me. I didn't work for him for the money to begin with."

The money was okay, but he had his own money. Money left to him from an inheritance his grandmother Erin had set aside for her grandchildren on her death as well as money his father—as much as Riordan hated calling him that—deposited monthly into an account that Riordan never touched. The money he made in contract work for his brother, Noah Blake, was building nicely as well. Soon, it might actually exceed the other accounts.

He'd never hurt for money, he just preferred to make his own way, to do what he did best—until the last six months. Hell, he'd just regained his full strength two months earlier after taking three bullets and spending two months recuperating from surgery he nearly hadn't come back from.

"Poppa can be . . . protective," she sighed, and he heard her complete weariness in it. "He's very difficult, but I'm sure you know that."

"Beside the point." He shook his head, realizing they were getting off track. "Did you mention your search for me to him?"

If he found out Ivan had stood in her way . . .

"I didn't tell anyone." She shook her head quickly. "Once I found you in the employee database I just left and came looking for you." She turned back to the door. "Poppa's men were following me though. Elizaveta and Grisha nearly caught me last night. I've driven straight through from Poppa's estate, hoping I could keep them from knowing where I was going until I could speak to you." She bit her lip for a moment. "Hoping I could convince you to protect me."

"Your father's men are experienced. The best in the business," he reminded her. "I won't go back to being your dirty little secret, Amara."

Evidently, that little piece of information didn't sit well with her.

"I don't know who to trust anymore." Her voice

seemed to hitch as though she were holding back a cry. "I don't know which way to turn. If it's money . . ."

"I might be an Irish bastard, but trust me sweetheart, I'm too damn Irish to hide who and what I am. And if I came back, I'd be returning to your bed as well. And you can keep your goddamn money," he snarled, restraining the need to find Ivan and knock the hell out of him. Again. "The last thing I'd take from a Resnova now, is their damn money."

She flinched, her shoulders tensing at the sound of his voice and the anger that filled it.

She hadn't seen this anger in her dreams. He'd been protective, hard sometimes, definitely dominant sexually, but he hadn't been angry.

"So, all you want is a ready fuck?" she snapped back, hating the habit she had of becoming defensive.

"Your mouth is going to get you fucked," he bit out, the lust that filled his gaze intensifying as he pointed his finger toward her with such arrogance it made her teeth clench. "Being in your bed was damn satisfying, Amara. Watch it that you don't end up in my bed before you leave here."

And she knew if he touched her again, kissed her again, she'd not deny him. He'd already proven that.

"So, to convince you to protect me, I have to let you into my bed?" She definitely wanted clarification here.

The smile that curled his lip had her heart racing, her sex dripping. She was going to have to change her damn panties at this rate.

"No, you don't *have* to let me do a damn thing but protect you," he murmured. "You just have to be able to say no. Think you can do that?"

The challenge was one that had her eyes narrowing, her fists clenching in her pockets.

"Watch it Riordan, you might lose that cold little heart of yours. What then?" she asked instead.

The smile deepened. "Or you might lose yours. Trust me, Amara. You never knew the man I really was when we were together before, but by God you will now. So be very damn sure you want me back in that bed of yours. Because baby, I'll make sure you don't have the energy to throw me out of it again."

She rolled her eyes, knowing it wasn't exactly the smartest way to meet his challenge.

"Keep telling yourself that." She shrugged. "As long as you come back. As long as you help me find out who still wants me dead sometime before they actually kill me."

Oh, he'd figure that one out. He'd do that whether he was in her bed or not. He might be damn pissed with her, she might have taken a chunk of his pride last year, but he'd never let anyone hurt her. Not as long as he had enough breath in his body to stop it.

Nodding, he pulled his cell phone from the holder on his belt and keyed in a message to his brother. Short. A numeric code that Noah would know was serious. He and another agent he worked with would be there before the hour was out.

"I'm sending you back to your father. You'll have a protection detail shadowing you. Let Elizaveta and Grisha find you in New Mexico." Stalking to the bookcase on the other side of the room, he pulled his electronic pad free before motioning her to the couch.

Pulling up a map, he pushed the pad into her hands.

"Here." He pointed to the town on the map. "Get a room, stay till you're found by them." The resort was known for its secure premises and for its focus on keeping high-profile guests protected at all times. "You won't see them, but there will be a team protecting you. Let Elizaveta and Grisha take you back to the estate. I still have an agent there I trust to keep you safe until I arrive."

She stared at the map before lifting her eyes to meet his. "And after you arrive?"

After he arrived? Well, then things would get damn interesting.

"The agent will let you know when I'm close." Pulling up the notepad, he typed in a code. "Memorize those numbers. When he makes contact with you, he'll give you that code before he tells you what I have planned. Agreed?"

"Why can't you go with me?" The fear in her voice nearly had him changing his mind.

God, he wanted to go with her. He wanted to be with her every second to ensure no danger, whether by accident or design, touched her.

"Because if someone is trying to kill you, they'll be more on guard if they know you've contacted me first," he warned her. "I'm not returning as your bodyguard. I'm coming back to claim my lover. An enemy will expect me to be distracted. They won't expect what I'll have planned."

She nodded, albeit it slowly.

"You'll make sure I'm protected until you're there?" She was trying to hide it, but he could hear the fear and uncertainty.

"I swear it. You have to trust me this time, Amara, or you'll put both of us in danger. No matter what I do, what I tell you to do, you have to trust me." Anything less could see them both dead. And Riordan decided months before that dead wasn't what he wanted.

"Very well," she murmured. "I trust you."

That trust was in her gaze, something that hadn't been there before the abduction. Before she lost that year of her life.

"Get ready to go." Moving abruptly, he paced to the window and glanced down the winding road that led to the house. "Company will be here soon. You'll meet the men that I'll send to follow you, then you'll leave. Agreed?"

"Agreed." She watched him, the bleak shadows in her eyes reminding him that the trust, the faith she was putting in him, had nothing to do with their past, but with whatever dreams she'd had of him in the past months.

"Get ready then. I can see their dust." His brother was racing to him, no doubt his father, and his uncle and other "help" as well. There was more than one vehicle barreling its way there. He turned back to her, keeping his gaze hard, his voice firm. "Whatever I tell you to do, do it when you're told. Don't hesitate. Not even for a second."

"I'm not a moron, I understood the first time." She rose quickly to her feet and squared her shoulders in determination. "I said I would do it."

Because she wanted to live.

Because now she trusted him when she hadn't before. Son of a bitch, it was enough to make him want to drag her to his bed then and there.

Because he knew Amara. While she might do as she was told this time, the next time could very well be another matter.

Standing at the window, Riordan watched as Amara's rented car sped back down the road escorted by the four men Noah had brought with him, two leading, two following.

It was a damn good thing Ivan Resnova was a person of some importance to the Elite Ops that his brother directed there in Alpine. The highly covert, highly classified investigative and strike team had worked with Ivan before and they'd been part of the force that extracted Amara out of that damned hole she'd been thrown into.

Now, they'd protect her until he could make certain everything was in place.

"You should have gone with her. We could have still run the op without suspicion," his brother commented behind him. "You didn't have to be so damned stubborn, Riordan."

Riordan. He'd been Rory until the year Nathan returned as Noah, the year Riordan had nearly died trying to protect Sabella, Noah's wife. When he'd come out of the hospital, the nickname had dropped and he'd become Riordan.

"Her father and whoever's behind this would be forewarned." He turned back to Noah slowly. "There's been three attempts on her since she returned to Colorado after leaving the hospital and her father's claiming coincidence. Someone close to him is obviously filling his head with fairy tales. Or he's making them up himself."

Ivan Resnova believed in Santa a hell of a lot more than he believed in coincidence.

"Doesn't sound like Ivan," Noah agreed as he paced to the window and watched the trail of dust as the vehicles neared the main road.

"No. It doesn't." Riordan grimaced, then sighed heavily. "She's forgotten the year I was with her, Noah. Doesn't remember a damned thing."

Telling his brother that one was hard, he admitted silently. The dent to his ego was ignored but there were other implications.

"Yet she still found you," Noah murmured, still watching the scenery. "How did that happen?"

Reaching back to rub at the back of his neck, he bit off a curse before glaring at his brother.

"She has nightmares. Dreams . . ."

"Have you found your way, Riordan?" Noah asked softly. "That's what Grandpops claimed when you came back from the hospital. That you'd found your way, and you were fighting it."

Found his way. Found the woman that he'd let into his soul.

Son of a bitch, how had it happened? There was no doubt it had, he just hadn't quite figured out how.

"Maybe," he murmured, not quite ready to discuss something he hadn't really believed in until now.

"Hmmm," Noah murmured in response. "There are no maybes, baby brother, not with a Malone. Remember that. It is, or it isn't. We don't do in-betweens. None at all."

Clapping him on the shoulder, Noah turned and made his way to the kitchen and the stew Grandpops had made that morning. Yet Riordan couldn't take his eyes from the rapidly dwindling dust trail and the knowledge that once again, he'd let Amara go.

And he swore to himself, he'd let her go for the last time.

chapter three

Five days later

There was a storm coming.

Even if the weather channel hadn't predicted a coming snowstorm, Amara would have known. She could feel it in the air, that crisp, icy bite that assured her the land was preparing itself for winter's fury.

There were only a few clouds on the horizon, the sky still held that chilly blue that marked the spring season in the mountains of Colorado. A week at the most, she thought, then it would hit.

She rubbed at the chill in her arms despite her warm, soft, cream-colored cashmere sweater and black slacks. A fire blazed in the fireplace, crackling merrily over the heavy logs the butler had added minutes before. Warmth spilled into the room, even washed over her, though she couldn't stop the shiver that worked over her.

She couldn't seem to get warm. Even before winter had hit the mountains, this chill had held her in its grip.

And now that winter was fully bearing down, she felt that chill deeper than ever.

"Miss Amara, Mr. Ivan asked to see you in his office," the butler, Alexi, informed her politely as he stepped into the room.

Mr. Ivan "asked" to see her.

She sighed at the careful phrasing. Her father "demanded her presence" was more like it. And she had a feeling she knew why.

"How loud is Poppa screaming, Alexi?" She forced a grin to her lips as he grimaced ever so slightly.

"He was actually quite calm," the butler warned her as he pushed his hands into the pockets of his dark slacks and shrugged his shoulders beneath the white shirt he wore. "Deliberately so, I believe."

Uh-oh. That definitely didn't sound good. Poppa was rarely deliberately calm.

"Guess that rules out lunch first," she teased, feeling little of the amusement she tried to show.

"Perhaps afterwards as well, miss," he guessed with a quirk of his lips.

He was well used to her and her father's fierce arguments by now.

"I doubt afterwards," she told him, striding to the doorway where he stood. "The good women of the Easter Committee are due in about twenty minutes. Cook should have a small buffet set up in the meeting room. See that they're shown there if I haven't returned."

The last thing she needed was to have something go wrong with this damn luncheon. She'd worked her ass off to make certain everything was perfect.

He nodded sharply. "I'll check and ensure all is ready for them as well."

Passing him, she wondered why the hell her father had called her to his office. They'd barely spoken for days. After years of bitching over the fact she had gone to law school rather than marrying some big strong goon he approved of, he was bitching now because she hadn't returned to classes. As though he gave a damn about that degree. And after her little disappearance the week before, he was really going ballistic on her.

Making her way to the opposite wing of the house, she entered the reception area and gave her father's assistant, Ilya, a questioning look.

Tall, good-looking in a rough sort of way, and far easier-going than her father, Ilya had been friends with Ivan Resnova since they were boys. He'd also been at her father's side just as long, taking care of whatever he needed him to do.

"I hear Poppa's deliberately calm today, Ilya," she commented, tucking her cold hands beneath the loose sleeves of her sweater. "What did I do this time?"

Looking up from the laptop, he grinned back at her, causing the dragon tattoo on the side of his face to shift lazily. Pale green eyes lit with amusement as a smile tugged at his lips. "To my knowledge, nothing since that unscheduled stop you demanded at the coffee shop the other day," he chuckled. "But I believe the two of you covered that in your last screaming match. He's still bitching about your jaunt to New Mexico, but not as loudly as before. Unless you've done something since those two events that I'm unaware of?"

Well, anything was possible, wasn't it?

"I thought it best to give him a rest. His blood pressure, you know?" Shooting him a rueful look, she nodded at the door. "Should I go in, or do I have to twiddle my thumbs and wait for him to give me permission."

Ilya shook his head, his grin widening. "Go on in, he's waiting for you."

Stepping to the double doors, she gave the silent security agent who opened them before stepping back a polite smile then walked into the office.

"You wanted to see me?" she asked as she moved toward her father's desk.

Her father stood up from the desk, as did the man sitting in front of it.

Riordan's grandfather.

Grandpops Malone was acting for all the world like the innocent old man she was certain he wanted everyone to believe he was. Unfortunately, that devilish gleam in his eyes hinted otherwise.

Leaning negligently against the wall, one leather boot crossed over the ankle of the other, was Riordan. Easily as tall as her father, his thick black hair fell straight with a silky, raven's-wing sheen. In his well-worn denim and a dark gray shirt, the sleeves of which were rolled to his elbows, he didn't even pretend to be anything less than the powerful male animal he was. Darkly tanned flesh and sapphire eyes that held hers, locked her to him. Had she always found them so mesmerizing, so hard to break free of?

She knew the second she saw him that he was furious. It was there in the gleam of battle in his eyes, the tension that filled his powerfully corded body. And he was possibly angrier now than he had been when she met with him in Texas. A meeting she wasn't to even let her father know about.

Keeping secrets from Poppa had never been easy, but she'd learned a few tricks over the years. This time, she had to employ every damn one of them.

She was unaware she stood still, silent, as she stared back at him, her heart beating sluggishly, arousal and fear kept carefully masked. God how she had prayed she wasn't making a mistake.

Since she'd seen him the week before, the erotic dreams had grown more frequent, more erotic. Now, she awoke sweating from arousal rather than fear and that was a bit disconcerting at three in the morning.

"Amara?" There was an edge of concern her father's voice.

She had to force herself to turn to him, to focus on him rather than on Riordan. But even then, she was careful to keep him in her periphery.

"Gentlemen, my daughter Amara," her father introduced her, his gaze holding hers as he watched her worriedly. "Amara, meet Rory Malone Sr. and his grandson Riordan."

"Hello," she directed her greeting to both men, but couldn't bring herself to meet the Riordans' gaze again for fear of giving herself away. And he'd been quite specific in the fact that she couldn't give herself away.

"It's a pleasure, lass," the Irish in the grandfather's voice was unmistakable. "And I'm certain it is for ma Riordan there as well. I tried to teach the lad manners but he slips a time or two and becomes a bit mute."

Riordan's lips quirked a bit mockingly. They were

perfect male lips, the lower curve slightly fuller, sensual. Kissable. The first thing a woman thought about when she saw lips like those was feeling them against hers in hungry demand.

That fact that she knew that hungry demand wasn't helping her equilibrium at all.

"Hello, Amara," he said, the roughened sound of his voice stroking over her senses and dragging her gaze back to his, locking it there, holding her.

"Do I know you?" the question fell from her lips, as it did with most everyone she met these days. But her father couldn't know the truth. He couldn't know that she'd met with Riordan less than a week ago.

The tension seemed to increase in the room, becoming heavier, rife with too much unsaid.

"Do you think you've met him?" her father snapped and his tone of voice was that soft, dangerous pitch that was a warning in and of itself.

"Who knows these days, Poppa," she sighed. "He seems familiar."

Now, that was a hell of an understatement.

Dammit. She knew he would be difficult about this. Her gaze slid to Riordan's once again and the brooding intensity in it only made her heart beat faster.

His gaze slid over her, from head to toe, leaving a lingering warmth in its wake that had her flushing.

She felt off balance, uncertain and nervous beneath that particular look with her father present. It was nerve-wracking, staring into those eyes and feeling as though he was touching her.

Dragging her gaze from his once again, she turned

to her father as she swallowed tightly, fighting a sense of unreality that seemed to take hold of her.

"Alexi said you needed to see me?" She couldn't shake the feeling that there was something she should know, or should question of these two men. "The Easter Committee should be arriving soon and I need to be there."

Why she needed to be there, she still wasn't certain. Her father asked her to oversee his commitment to the charity, and now the women that were part of it refused to let her simply sit and watch.

Her father slid Riordan Malone a dark look at that point. One she followed and watched as Riordan arched one brow mockingly.

She needed to stay calm, composed. No one, especially her poppa could know just how well she'd become reacquainted with her mostly forgotten former lover.

"I wanted you to meet Riordan and his grandfather," her father finally answered. "Riordan will be taking the position as head of your personal security as of today. His grandfather is here in an advisory position. It was merely a formality, sweetheart."

There was an air of expectation in the air as he made his little announcement. Amara narrowed her eyes and met his navy blue gaze as this little meeting suddenly made sense. What he was up to she wasn't certain, but she knew Riordan had no intentions of coming in as her bodyguard.

"What about Elizaveta and Grisha?" she asked, knowing they had taken over command of her security.

Elizaveta and her brother Grisha had been with her

since they were teenagers. Ivan's first cousins had come from Russia with them and other than the time they'd spent away training as security agents, had been by her side.

They'd been away six months ago, when she'd been abducted.

"Elizaveta and Grisha will stay in place. Your father has obviously misunderstood our previous meeting, Amara. I'm not here as your bodyguard. Now tell me, do you remember me or not?" Riordan asked the question as he shifted and straightened from his position against the wall.

Standing, feet braced apart, he was taller than she'd first guessed. Six-two at least, leanly muscular, and arrogant as hell.

That arrogance was going to cause her father to kill him.

"Elizaveta and Grisha stay with me, no matter their ability to work with anyone else." The words passed her lips sharply. "And should I know you?"

Okay, so that wasn't what she was supposed to say, but it was that damn arrogance where her cousins were concerned.

His brow arched at the demand.

"Tsk-tsk. Tell the truth now," he murmured, a vein of amusement sliding through that dark, roughened tone, as well as one of warning.

Her eyes narrowed on him, her fingers forming fists beneath the sleeves of her sweater.

"You look familiar." She pushed between clenched teeth.

Still, not exactly what he'd ordered her to say. But he

was really starting to piss her off. She'd waited five days for this idiotic farce? He could have just met secretly with her father and informed him of their plans. That would have worked far better than this.

She turned to her father, her arms crossing beneath her breasts as she suddenly caught a shift in his gaze. Or had they already discussed it.

"Just familiar?" Riordan asked, mocking her now.

This was going to be harder than she'd first imagined.

"Maybe more than a little?" she still hedged.

"Goddamn it, Amara, he says the two of you were lovers," her father burst out angrily then. "Is it true?"

Was it true? It was, she knew it was, yet all she had were the dreams, not actual memories of the events that drew them together, that ended with him in her bed.

"Probably," she snapped back. "Maybe. You could say I've had a flash of a memory here and there about it."

Men.

This was insane. How had she known she should have fought Riordan where this was concerned? She could have just told Poppa she remembered a lover and wanted him to find Riordan. Anything but this.

"A flash of memory?" That tone could be deadly. "Did you remember he was one of your bodyguards before the abduction as well?"

Okay, maybe Poppa didn't know, or didn't suspect this ruse for what it was. He was furious now. The only rule he had in regards to any relationship she may have formed was that she didn't form it with one of her bodyguards.

Rather than answering, she crossed her arms beneath her breasts and faced him with silent anger. If he thought he was going to take her to task for ignoring that little demand, then he could reconsider the option.

"Your point being?" she finally asked him coolly. "Considering bodyguards were all I had a chance to get to know, it perhaps seemed the better option. I'm not exactly a teenager nor am I without the needs other women have. And I'm perfectly capable of choosing my own friends, not to mention my lovers."

She could have sworn he paled just the slightest bit and muttered a curse even she rarely allowed past her lips.

"That was uncalled for Ivan," Riordan informed him as he stepped from the wall. "You should have known I'd be back eventually. Did you really think I'd allow one little argument with her to keep me away after her recovery?"

"I don't recall asking you," her poppa all but snarled. "You knew the rules as well. You weren't to touch her."

She rolled her eyes at that one. "Poppa, I'm not one of your paintings or expensive statues," she informed him. "And I like to think any man I cared for would be strong enough not to feel compelled to obey your every whim, but mine."

She was certain Riordan obeyed no one's whims. The mocking grin that threatened to curl his lips assured her he wasn't in the least bit tempted to do so. Unless it suited his purpose.

Sitting back in his seat, her father's gaze went between her and Riordan before his expression hardened. "Fine, he can return when your memory has returned. At least I'll be reasonably confident that you know what you're doing. And his grandfather can go with him." His hand flipped toward the door in a mocking invitation to leave. Amara could feel the anger building and see the potential rising for another screaming match at a time when she needed to remain calm. She would not go into that meeting with those damn women right after another confrontation with him, no matter his anger.

She looked down at the nails of one hand for long seconds, smoothing the pad of her thumb over her index finger. "Poppa," she finally murmured gently without looking at him. "Would you please call Mother?"

A tense silence met her request. Her parents couldn't exist in the same country comfortably, but her father would never deny her if she wanted her mother there. Lifting her gaze to see his dark look, she glanced at the desk phone then back to him.

"Why?" he all but growled.

"Please tell her I've changed my mind and I'd enjoy having her here for Easter after all." She smiled brightly. "The more the merrier. And perhaps while she's here, she can convince you of all the reasons you don't want to make this decision for me. Considering the fact that each dream I have of him assures me that we cared for each other, they also assure me that he was very protective of me. All things considered, one would think you wouldn't fight this near so hard."

"There is no proof of a threat, Amara," he assured her again.

There was no proof? Since when did her poppa need proof?

"If Riordan leaves, Mother will be on the next flight out of Russia. I'll make certain of it," she informed him. "I may even decide to return with her when she leaves. Think about that. Because I assure you, I'm not joking. Now, I have one of your little pet committee demons to deal with. We can discuss this further, if needed, at a later date."

Turning on her heel she stalked from the room, her head held high, very well aware that Riordan didn't take his eyes off her until she closed the door behind her with a snap.

She could feel her stomach pitching, panic edging at her mind. Because she knew him, his expressions and his phrases. There was no proof of a threat. He didn't believe in proof any more than he believed in random acts of violence against her. No, her father knew something. Something he wasn't telling her, and that was terrifying.

The only thing that could make him say that phrase— there is no proof of a threat—in that way was his definite belief that there *was* a threat. And he feared Riordan would compound it to where she'd fear that without him she'd die. For a woman who had tried very hard to not make waves throughout her life, she was suddenly churning them up in a way she feared would drown her.

As the door closed behind her, Riordan turned his attention to her father, his temper simmering. He'd known Ivan would fight this, but still, it pissed him the hell off. As Grandpops rose and walked to the door, Riordan moved to the front of the desk, placed his palms carefully on the polished wood, and leaned closer.

"You've done everything you could to keep me away from her and it ends now. By God, stop playing your games with her or she'll disappear, Ivan." The snarl that curled his lips wasn't quite voluntary. "I'll make damn sure of it. Just as I'll make damn sure you never fucking find her if you force me to make that choice."

And he'd do it. Ivan knew he'd do it and he knew Riordan had the resources to ensure she stayed hidden. Ivan had used every trick possible to keep them apart, and the games were going to end. Now.

"You're going to destroy her heart," Ivan muttered.

"I'd like to think that if I were a father, I'd consider a broken heart fair exchange," he snarled. "But my relationship with her is none of your damned business from here on out. Remember that one. Or I'll remind you."

Pulling back, he turned and stalked from the office, knowing exactly where he was going and what awaited him. Behind him, he heard the door close, and he was all too aware that his grandpops was still in that office.

Hell . . . he almost felt sorry for Ivan now.

chapter four

The committee meeting went more or less how Amara expected it. Phoebe Adelbarre did her very best to completely take over the meeting, including every decision concerning the final details of their annual Easter charity ball. The dozen other women there went from feelings of frustration to resignation where that battle was concerned.

By the end of the two-hour lunch Amara felt as though she'd been through a minor war, and she wasn't certain if she'd won or lost. One day, she promised herself, she was going to manage to outmaneuver the Adelbarre matron if it killed her.

As she completed her notes on the meeting and finished up her to-do list, she laid aside her tablet and propped her elbow up on the small table. The maids had finished cleaning the meeting room nearly thirty minutes earlier, and Cook had taken away the last of the food from the lunch meeting.

Pushing her fingers through the shortened strands of her hair, she paused.

Six months ago, her hair had flowed thick and straight to the middle of her back. Now, it was no more than six or eight inches long, the back of it barely covering her nape. Rather than a heavy, straight ribbon, it was now a cap of lush curls.

Whoever had abducted her had not just nearly beaten her to death but had hacked her hair almost to her scalp. She pulled at the curls again, her eyes closing as a wave of pain and fear washed over her. Her breath hitched on a smothered sob and once again a sense of grief assailed her.

What had they done to her?

She couldn't remember the abduction any more than she could remember the year before it had happened, except for bits and pieces of inconsequential memories and those too-damn-erotic dreams. Eleven and a half months of her life were missing and she couldn't find a reason why. All she knew was the hollow grief she couldn't seem to shake.

"You look like you need a drink."

Her eyes opened in time to see the shot of whiskey the broad, sun-bronzed hand placed before her as Riordan straddled the opposite café chair he'd turned so he could place his arms across its low back.

Her gaze went back to the shot glass.

"Five o-clock somewhere, right?" she sighed before lifting the glass and taking the liquid in one swallow.

Heat spilled from her throat to her stomach, where it pooled then spread through her senses in a rush of warmth.

For a second, just a second, the cold chill she'd lived with for the past six months eased beneath the fiery lash of the liquor.

"What was it?" She stared at the empty shot glass before lifting her eyes to him, watching as his lips quirked in amusement.

"The finest Irish spirits made," he confided, lowering his voice. "You can't even buy anything that smooth."

She set the glass on the table, then folded her arms, resting them in front of it as she stared back at him curiously. "So, you make your own?" Why wasn't she surprised?

"Hell no." He grinned, his deep blue eyes almost glowing in amusement as he made the admission. "I believe that might still be a shade illegal in the quantity I'd need. Cousins in Ireland make it. They've made it the same way for generations. They send their American cousins a couple of cases a year just for the hell of it."

She doubted it was just for the hell of it and wondered what the cousins got in exchange.

"It's good." She had to compliment him as the warmth lingered through her senses.

"Grandpops keeps a bottle in his work shed and sneaks out every evening for a sip or two. Says it keeps him young." Fondness touched his expression, softened it. "He still acts as though he's hiding it from my grandmother, too, even though she's been gone for a lot of years."

"From what little I've seen, I have to agree something has." Brushing back a curl that fell over her forehead, she looked down at her tablet, then turned her head to look out the window.

His eyes kept drawing her, holding her. It was uncomfortable. It tugged at that darkness in her mind and made her ache.

"Grandpops will be eighty-five in a few months." His statement had her staring back at him in shock. "Go figure." He chuckled. "Still drives himself everywhere he goes, unless I'm in the vehicle with him. He likes to speed."

She shook her head in amazement before staring down at the table once again, uncertainty filling her.

"Poppa's very angry. Perhaps Grandpops should return home," she told him, lifting her head to stare back at him. "This is no place for a man his age."

His brow lifted with deliberate mockery.

Dammit, she hated people who could do that on demand.

"*You* tell Grandpops to leave," he suggested with the air of a man who was tired of arguing about it. "He insists on being here, and I know Grandpops. He is one stubborn man."

It seemed it ran in the family.

"Poppa says there's no threat." She felt like boxing her father's ears some days. "The abduction was six months ago. The rescue team killed the men who took me. Perhaps I'm just being paranoid." She wanted to believe that. She really did.

She'd been at the estate since her release from the hospital. Six months filled with recuperating, nightmares, and fear. But there had been no threats against her. Just odd events.

Her eyes narrowed on him as he just stared back at her, his gaze somber, heavy.

"Has there been a threat that Poppa hasn't told me about? Did he tell you anything?" She forced herself to ask the question.

Surely, he would tell her. He wouldn't hold something like that back from her, would he?

"Other than I had no right to be here?" he snorted, a mocking curve to his lips. "There hasn't been an additional threat that I'm aware of, but I believe he doesn't consider the threat over. Until we know why and who, we can't assume the danger has passed. And apparently, no one knows the answer to that but you," he told her softly. "Do you remember the abduction?"

She considered refusing to answer. For a moment, she braced herself to jerk to her feet and stalk away from him. The air of familiarity, a certain knowledge in his expression, and a gleam of male hunger in those blue eyes stopped her.

She shook her head. "Nothing." She didn't even remember her nightmares unless Riordan was in them. "All I remember is you."

Inhaling deeply, she fought back the fear, the panic, as well as the arousal. That wasn't going to help her, it would only make it impossible to think.

There wasn't an additional threat, she told herself, so there was no reason to panic

"Your father says you still have nightmares?" he questioned her again.

The roughened edge of his voice, that sinful sound, shouldn't be discussing death, it should be whispering erotic phrases and sexually explicit demands, she thought inanely.

For a second, she could feel a rising anger toward him but didn't know why.

"I never remember the nightmares." She reached for the shot glass and began rolling it between her fingers as she stared into it.

She didn't remember the images that brought her awake screaming, but she remembered the grief. The terrible heaviness in her chest, the knowledge that she'd lost something that left her broken inside.

"Have you wondered why?" he asked her.

Her gaze shot back to his, the anger she always fought at the thought of those nightmares rising inside her.

"What do you think, Riordan?" she snapped. "Do you think I just flit through my day without wondering what the hell happened? That I don't care that I lost a year of my life or why I lost it?" Anger tore at her. "Do you think I don't care about the men who risked their lives to rescue me?"

She came to her feet so fast that the chair she was sitting in nearly toppled over. She hadn't realized she was shaking—whether from anger or fear, she didn't know.

Echoes of grief and pain, fear . . . *We're losing him!*

Choking back her tears, she fought to hold onto her sanity. That single cry, harsh, filled with fury, was all she remembered. But her father assured her no one had died. They hadn't lost anyone.

But would he tell her the truth? He'd always fought to protect her, not just from danger but from the truth of whatever his life and his business truly was, but would he lie to her about that?

Riordan rose as well, his expression tight as he watched her closely, his gaze brooding, suspicious.

"You've stopped the sessions with the therapist your father hired. You refuse to discuss it with anyone. I think you don't want to remember," he accused her, standing there, staring at her as though she should be spouting information like a damn robot.

"You're crazy!" The cry was ripped from her. How dare he say something like that to her. She didn't want to remember? "Do you think I enjoy missing a year of my life? That I don't want to know who stole that time from me or why?"

"No. I don't believe you do," he said bluntly, the arrogance and complete certainty in his expression infuriating her. "And it makes me wonder why you bothered to even remember me in your dreams."

She could only stare at him furiously, her fingers curling into fists to keep from slapping that knowing look from his face.

"And I believe you need to go to hell!" She was so furious she was shaking, torn between clawing his eyes out and . . .

She took a hasty step back as she realized she was reaching for him and didn't even know why. Not that it mattered, because as she reached out, he finished the move and jerked her into his arms.

"I lived in hell for six fucking months, calling this house, being told you weren't taking my calls," he snapped, one hand burying in the back of her hair, his head lowering until his lips brushed hers. "And by God I'm not waiting any longer."

She was burning for him. Her breasts ached, her nipples hardened until they were little points trying to push through the material covering them.

His knee slid between her legs, his thigh settling against the sensitive flesh between her thighs and exciting the little bud of her clit.

"Riordan . . ." Just that fast, she was weak, arousal burning through her, ripping past her defenses.

Staring up at him, his eyes darkening, the sapphire deepening, she knew whatever he wanted in that moment, she'd willingly give him.

"Amara," he whispered against her lips, caressing them, teasing her before smoothing across her cheek to her ear.

Once there, he nipped at the lobe, stroked over it with his tongue, then caught it between his teeth to worry it with a sensual, highly erotic grip.

"What did I do to you in your dreams, Amara? Did I let you run from me? Or did I show you all the reasons you didn't want to run?"

Before she could answer him, his lips were taking her. He was voracious in his demand. Hungry, determined. He nipped at her lips, then his tongue soothed the slight pain. A second later it pushed past her lips in demand, sweeping over hers, sweeping aside any objections, any fears.

There was no fear here, no panic, just complete pleasure. She moaned at the heat and demanding possession as his hand gripped her head, holding her still as his lips slanted over hers and the kiss deepened.

"Damn, what you do to me." He jerked back, the

graveled sound of his voice sending a rush of heat straight to her vagina. "Oh baby, I love getting drunk on the taste of you."

Her lips parted, a plea for more on them when he drew back, releasing her slowly.

What could she say? Do? She wanted more, craved more, and if she stood there another second, she'd be begging for more.

Swinging away from him, she hurried from the room, desperate to escape, to get as far away from him as possible. Him and whatever it was he was doing to her. Whatever he was doing to make the darkness claw at her mind and her own screams echo in her head. She was crazy to have done this. She should have never gone looking for him or allowed him to kiss her. And all she wanted now was more, the dominance and the sheer erotic thrill only he could give her.

And that terrified her almost as much as the nightmares and the danger she knew had returned.

Riordan wanted to hit something.

It was all he could do to smother the curses that rose to his lips and threatened to slip free, let alone keep from putting his fist through a wall. To keep from following her.

If he followed, he was going to take her, though, and damned if he had the control to go easy on her. He wanted to push her against a wall and take her like a fucking animal. Hear the cries of pleasure, the pleas he knew that would spill from her lips as she begged for more.

And he had too much to do before he could allow

himself the time for that. Too many things to put in place, to ensure her protection.

"Son of a fucker," he snarled, swinging around to stare through the window into the bleak winter landscape as his hands went to his hips.

Hanging his head, he stared at the floor, the stone floor with its swirled green-to-gray pattern.

God, the pain in her eyes when she'd reached for him. The fear.

He couldn't follow her, couldn't ease her needs or the horrors that haunted her nightmares. Because God forbid if she knew what she was to him, what she meant to him.

"It's too soon, Riordan," Grandpops said quietly behind him, his voice filled with compassion, with far too much knowledge.

Too soon. It was too soon to tell her, too soon to explain why she only remembered him in her dreams, in the fantasies that filled her. That tormented him.

"You didn't see her eyes, Grandpops." He pushed his fingers through his hair and clenched his teeth as the anger threatened to overwhelm him. "I should have been there when she woke in the hospital. I should have been beside her . . ."

He should have fought harder . . .

"Kinda hard to do when you're fighting to live," his grandfather snorted, that shade of Irish in his voice heavier than normal. "Noah's worried ya came too soon the way it is. Says ya lied 'bout the doctor releasin' ya back last month."

Noah worried like a damn mother hen.

"I didn't lie." He met the older man's look in the

window. "I wouldn't have returned if I wasn't strong enough to protect her. I would have made sure of it."

Grandpops snorted at that, his gaze shadowed with disbelief. "Ya would have come to her on yer deathbed if ya coulda."

He couldn't argue with that. Hell, he'd tried to come to her as he lay half dead. A bullet to the chest, one to his side, and one to his lower back had nearly done him in. For a month, the doctors weren't certain they'd keep him out of a wheelchair, let alone whether he'd be strong enough to return to any kind of heavy work.

He hadn't had a choice but to get back in shape, to rebuild his strength and pass the physical requirements. He'd known. A part of him had known that this wasn't over. Not his relationship with her, or the danger edging closer once again.

"I nearly lost her," he said quietly. "I shouldn't have waited for her to find me. I should have returned to her instead."

His damnable pride had held him back. He'd called, only to be told she refused to talk to him by whichever servant answered the phone. And he'd refused to call Ivan. The son of a bitch had been part of the reason he and Amara had argued the night before he flew to England.

"She came far closer to losin' ya, boy." The rough growl in his grandfather's voice reminded Riordan that Amara wouldn't have been the only one who would have felt that loss. "We all did. And those are days I'm not wantin' to revisit."

"I'm fine." Riordan shook his head, dropping his hands from his hips, and turned to face the man who had been both grandfather and father all his life. "Noah worries like a mother hen since the babies started coming."

As always, the subject of his great-grandchildren distracted his grandpops.

"Aye, little Noah's hopin' for a brother this time. Says he needs help in keepin' up with our wee Erin and Aislinn." Amusement filled his grandpops' face. "Bella said she dreads to see the boy's face should the little one be a girl."

Noah Jr. was far too much like his father. He was already searching among his young friends for help in keeping his sisters out of trouble as they grew up. At seven, he was intense, far too responsible for his age, and more like the man Noah Blake had been before his "death" than a child should be.

"Yeah well, his dad isn't much better," Riordan snorted.

Noah was already beside himself over his daughter's girlish ways. At five, Erin was a little fashionista with a style that hinted at the little hellion she was going to become, and she was cute as a button to boot. Two years younger, Aislinn was determined to run beside Noah Jr. every step he took and fight every battle her brother took as his. She was a tomboy in lace and pretty dresses with a smile so charming it was damn hard to tell her no.

Their father was already trying to figure out how he was going to keep the boys away from his sweet little girls, though it would be a decade at least before he was going to have to actually deal with it.

"You'll be the same." His father slapped his shoulder as he started back at him somberly. "One day, boy, you'll be a da yourself. You'll be as bad or near worse than our Noah."

He couldn't allow himself to think that far, not until he'd ensured Amara's future. He hadn't protected her properly and someone had nearly taken her from him—he couldn't allow it to happen again. He wouldn't allow it to happen again.

"I have to go, Grandpops, I have to meet with River and Tobias, make certain they have the electronic security upgraded and hooked into Noah's operations center." He had to get a minute to himself, to think, to get used to the fact that he wasn't going to pick up where he and Amara had left off. He was going to be starting again.

And he knew Amara.

It wasn't going to be easy.

"Riordan." His grandfather stopped him as he moved to turn away. "She's scared of whatever it is that haunts her in those memories she hides from. Remember that when you're pushin' her. Sometimes, as my Erin told me often, a woman needs more than words to convince her of the why of needin' to do something."

Riordan could only nod sharply, a concession to his grandpops' wisdom and the fact that the old man sometimes knew things he shouldn't. But the knowledge that she'd forgotten him was eating at his control, eating at his patience. She belonged to him, and she didn't even remember it.

chapter five

Amara had known her Poppa wasn't finished with their argument from the day before. Meetings that day, as well as the next morning, kept him away from the house, but her poppa could be amazingly patient sometimes.

It was just his way. He refused to give up or give in and he was going to make this as difficult as possible even as he gave in.

He was waiting for her as she entered her room after dinner that next evening, standing before the gas fireplace, arms crossed over his chest, a scowl on his face. Yep, he looked ready for a fight, and she just wasn't in the mood.

Not that it ever mattered. Her father had a way of antagonizing even the most patient of people. It was that arrogance and confidence he had that he always knew best.

"Everything okay, Poppa?" she asked as they faced each other now.

She'd at least try to be civil about this.

"Where did you go last week when you ran from the estate?" Suspicion laced his tone. "Where did you find me?" she asked in return, glaring at him. "You chased me down like a little child, Poppa. Did it occur to you that I'm no longer a teenager?"

It hadn't, of course. Her father refused to believe his little girl had grown up. She'd known that for years, but the knowledge that someone seriously wanted her dead bad enough to come after her a second time, had the need to consider her father's feelings on this dimming by the day.

"Why do you insist on making that statement?" Frustration filled his tone now. "I don't treat you like a child, Amara. But only a child would run away as you did."

"Of course you do, Poppa," she disagreed, fighting back the pain at the thought. "You refuse to tell me a single detail about the investigation into my abduction. Your own agents are not allowed to discuss it with me. I'm not permitted to make a decision outside this estate without Elizaveta and Grisha contacting you first. And you believe you can choose my lovers for me?" Her voice rose as she ticked off each offense. "What is that, if not treating me as a child?" Fury pulsed through her. "You knew he was my lover and you lied to me when I asked you if I had one. You lied to me, Poppa."

That was the gravest insult of all.

"I did not," he snapped, frowning back at her. "I didn't know you were sleeping with that little bastard. I only knew you paid him far too much attention." Disgust marked his gaze then. "And he refused every assignment possible in those last months that would take him away from you. I feared a relationship would develop."

She rolled her eyes again and gave a disgusted shake of her head. "Perhaps you enjoy lying to yourself then," she told him.

Her father was more calculating, more perceptive than that. It wouldn't have been possible for her to hide a lover from him.

"Amara." He was obviously making an effort to rein in his legendary temper. "You don't know the type of man he is."

Oh, she had a feeling she knew exactly what kind of man Riordan was, whether she wanted to acknowledge it or not.

"Obviously, at least subconsciously I do," she bit out, the placating tone grating on her patience. "You perhaps don't know me as well as you thought you did. I won't be forced to be a child all my life. Please. Stay out of this thing with me and Riordan, or I truly will go back to Russia with Mother."

Her mother was just as arrogant and hard as her father, but at least she never expected Amara to remain a virgin until her death. And her stepfather, a gentle, quiet-natured man, never tried to tell her what to do. Her mother wouldn't have allowed it if he did.

"Your mother makes you crazy," he reminded her. "You can barely tolerate her for more than a week and that husband of hers is like an overload of sweets. He gives me a toothache."

Sometimes, that was no more than the truth.

"I'd rather tolerate her insanity and his over-niceness

than your controlling machinations," she assured him, inserting a confidence she simply didn't feel. "You can't convince me you didn't at least suspect Riordan was my lover. Or that you wouldn't have known that if I was . . ." She inhaled, fighting back her own emotions. "If we were lovers, Poppa, then you know, I loved him."

The dreams, the feeling of something lost within her life, the hunger for something she couldn't name. The moment she saw Riordan, all that had stilled within her.

"When did you become so damn stubborn?" he muttered, his expression anything but pleased. "I know you weren't like this before that little—"

"Don't." Her hand lifted, her finger pointing to him demandingly. "Call him a little bastard again and you won't like the consequences."

She surprised even herself with that demand.

"For God's sake," he snapped as though mortally offended. "I meant nothing by it. A general insult." He shrugged as though it didn't matter.

"You weren't married to my mother," she reminded him. "Would you allow anyone to call me a bastard? Even 'generally'? Just back off, Poppa. Let me have this. Let me decide for myself what I want, and who I want. It should never have been your decision to begin with."

She prayed she wasn't making a mistake. Riordan was every bit as protective and arrogant as her father. But at least he was willing to work with her, to tell her the truth of whatever danger faced her. He'd proven that both before his return to the estate, as well as now.

She could only pray that trend continued.

"When you finally grow tired of the little prick, let me know," he growled, glaring back at her. "I'll take great delight in getting rid of his ass."

With that, he all but stomped to the door, jerked it open, and left the room.

At least he didn't slam the door closed. Not that it would have bothered her if he had.

"Interesting."

Swinging around, she faced Riordan as he opened the connecting door between their rooms.

If there had been mockery, or any snide amusement in his expression, she could have thrown him out, could have fought this insane reaction to him.

Instead, her heart raced at the sight of him, freshly showered, his black hair gleaming with dampness, his chest and feet bare, unbelted jeans settled low on his hips.

And he was aroused.

The proof of it showed beneath the denim. Impressively aroused.

God help her. How was she supposed to deny herself this man?

"And what did you find so interesting?" she demanded, fighting with everything she had to keep from touching him.

Hell, to keep from begging him to touch her. She wanted his touch so bad it was all she could do not to beg.

"You finally learned how to stand up to your father," he stated, closing the connecting door behind him and moving further into the room. "You didn't seem to have a handle on that last year."

She narrowed her eyes at him.

"It's all according to what he's trying to deny me. A man who had been your lover before the loss of your memories is a pretty big thing."

"But not the lover while he's in your bed?" He nodded as though he understood when she knew differently. "That's rather interesting as well."

"Most likely, I didn't want to deal with his interference," she muttered. "He can be nosy."

Riordan snorted at that before moving to the sofa and the electronic notebook, which she only then noticed had been placed on the couch. Picking up the device, he opened it, snapped the keyboard in place, then settled into the cushions facing the fire as he turned it on.

"What are you doing?" What the hell was wrong with his bedroom?

"Spending the evening with my lover," he stated a little absently, his attention on the device's screen. "I ordered your tea for you by the way. Along with coffee for myself and some of those pastries Cook had this afternoon. David should have it here soon."

The night houseman, David, was a distant cousin. He spoiled them horribly. If she dared enter the kitchen for a snack or hot drink at night, he'd chide her terribly for it and fix it himself before bringing it up to her.

She normally spent the evening in her room working on the charities she'd promised her father she'd keep track of, and the details for the spring ball. But she knew there wasn't a chance in hell that she could work with him sitting there. Bare-chested. Aroused.

She just wanted to jump his bones.

This was a mess. She should have known better. She did know better, but the minute she saw him, she lost precious brain cells evidently.

A light knock at the door had her swinging around. Before she could move, Riordan was on his feet and opening the door enough to assure himself it was David.

"It's nice to see you again, Mr. Malone." The houseman's smile of greeting had Amara frowning at him.

David never smiled at her like that.

"You too, David. You fix that coffee?" he asked.

"Yes sir." David's dark head nodded. "It's so fresh it may even deserve a date."

The two men chuckled, though Amara saw little humor in it. She was simply too aggravated by men in general at this point.

David placed the tray, loaded with coffee, tea, and pastries, on the low coffee table.

"Good night, Mr. Malone. Amara." He nodded before stepping back and leaving the room.

As the door closed, Riordan was there to lock it securely before returning to his seat and his precious pastries.

"Come on, baby, might as well join me." He grinned over at her. "Or we could go on to bed?"

Amusement gleamed in his eyes.

She was a second from agreeing to the second suggestion before common sense snapped back into place and she moved slowly to the chair next to the couch.

She was in so much trouble here, she admitted. More

trouble than she ever imagined. He hadn't joined her the previous night at all, though she'd expected him to. It seemed tonight he was about to rectify that.

His grandpops had once told him that women were like the weather, Riordan thought, as he kept Amara in his peripheral.

Mercurial, ever-changing, and more fascinating by the day. Of course, as a boy, Riordan had scoffed at such things. Grandpops had only laughed and gave him a warning: The sky can be picture perfect, a clear blue so bright it hurt a man's eyes. The breeze light, barely stirring the air. Until the storm cleared the mountains.

Between one blink and the next it was upon you, flashing with fury, drenching the land with its tears and its strength. And before a man knew what hit him, it was steaming and sultry with the promise of her pleasure.

That's what Amara reminded him of. The sultry heat after a midnight thunderstorm, full of promise and life. His own, perfect little storm, he'd once called her.

Relaxing back in the cushions of the couch as he ran through the encrypted files he was receiving from Ivan's computer, he had to admit, if she had any idea he was running every damned employee, associate, and cousin she'd came in contact with for the past two years, she'd be like that storm.

As he worked, she did the same on whatever committee plans her father had given her to keep her busy. After several hours she rose and retreated to the bathroom. The sound of the shower had his cock throbbing, his body tense with need.

Keeping his hands to himself was becoming damned hard and as the evening lengthened, the thought of crawling into that bed beside her had him fighting for control.

Six months.

Closing out the program he was working on, Riordan leaned back on the couch and stared broodingly at the flames in the fireplace.

Six months since he had held her in the darkness of the night, felt her deep, relaxed breathing, and knew she slept safe within his arms.

Admitting how he'd missed her, needed her, hadn't been hard. He'd become accustomed to both in that shadow-sleep they'd kept him in while he was in the hospital.

There, he'd felt her, touched her, and it hadn't felt as though it were a dream. Her warmth, the silken feel of her skin had been as real as the prick of the needles in his arm.

Reaching up, he rubbed against his chest, thankful she'd dimmed the lights after her father left, before she realized he was watching her. The scars were shadowed by the hair on his chest, not as apparent as they could have been. The bullet that had lodged too damned close to his heart hadn't been difficult to remove or cause extensive scarring.

The one to his back was a different story entirely, as well as the one to the back of his leg. He was damned lucky he was walking.

Hell, it was a miracle he was alive.

No . . . don't leave me . . . He could still hear her voice as he had the moment he felt his heart stop. He'd heard her, past death, he'd heard that whisper. It had followed him. He was damned if he remembered another thing but the sound of her voice, his desperation to find her in the darkness.

To not leave her.

Hell of a thing for a man who had sworn to never love in such a way.

Malone men didn't just love, they were cursed, or gifted as his grandpops claimed, to share a bond that bound them forever to the ones they loved. To see through their eyes, their dreams.

And if the object of that love loved them as well, then the bond went both ways.

As it did with his brother and sister-in-law.

He could still remember Bella's screams as she awoke from her nightmares during those horrible years they'd believed Noah, or Nathan as he had been, was dead. She'd be hysterical, claiming her husband was being tortured, he was alive, he needed her. At times, she'd swear blood covered her hands.

With Noah's return, Riordan realized those horrific nightmares Bella had had were based in truth. The hell Noah had lived through to come back to his family had been inhuman.

The sound of the shower turning off had his gaze narrowing on the flames flickering in the hearth and his cock throbbing with imperative need.

She'd come looking for him, he reminded himself. If she'd dreamed of him, then she would have to know, or at least suspect, the type of man he was. The type of lover he had been.

If she didn't, she was damned sure getting ready to.

* * *

He was waiting for her when she came out of the bathroom. What had made her imagine he wouldn't be? Other than the fact that he had mostly avoided her the night before, that is.

"I'm going to bed," she told him as she approached the couch where he lay back against the arm, watching her. Firelight flickered over the hard muscles and tough, sun-bronzed flesh.

"It's early yet." The graveled tone had a shiver racing up her back.

"I have meetings . . ." She swallowed with difficulty as he scratched lazily at his chest, his lashes lowering with drowsy sexuality over his eyes.

"Come here, Amara." Softly voiced, it was still a demand that rocked her to her core. Because she couldn't deny him. She didn't want to deny him.

Now, she was breathless. She felt drawn, ensnared. Her breathing was harder, heavier, her breasts rising and falling with her hard breaths as they swelled beneath the light cotton shirt she wore with her loose pajama bottoms.

Her nipples were spike hard, too sensitive. Her entire body was too sensitive. And the hunger in his expression assured her whatever relationship they'd had before, he intended to have again.

She'd been certain she could resist him. As he rose from the couch, she told herself she would resist him.

"It's late . . ." She would have stepped back, if he hadn't reached her first, one hand settling at her hip, the other threading through the hair at the back of her head.

"Not too late," he assured her, the look on his face brooding and far too sexy.

Hunger filled the sapphire depths of his eyes, lustful, intent, and she felt powerless in the face of it.

Then his lips touched hers, a slow, almost gentle caress against her lips. And she wanted more. For one insane minute all she wanted was more of him. Harder kisses, hotter kisses. That complete possession she'd dreamed of. As good as it felt, it wasn't this gentleness she wanted. She wanted to be wild with him. Wanted him as untamed and ravenous as she dreamed of him being.

"Tell me what you want, baby," he whispered against her lips, watching her, mesmerizing her. "All you have to do is ask for it. Or do you want to take it?"

His voice, his expression, was knowing. He knew what she wanted.

"If you need instruction, then perhaps my dreams were just wishful thinking."

She had time for a breath, a single breath before her senses exploded with pleasure, with Riordan.

He took the kiss. His lips slanted over hers, his tongue pushing past, tasting her, owning her, then igniting a hunger she knew shouldn't have surprised her.

As he devoured her kiss, he swung her up in his arms, turned with her above him, laid back on the couch, draping her thighs over his, pulling her to him until her nipples were cushioned by the wide contours of his chest.

She felt his cock between her thighs, pressing, grinding against her sex as his lips and tongue continued to drive her insane with need.

She met his kiss, fed from the savagery of each stroke

of his tongue against hers, and let him drag her into a swirling, white-hot pleasure unlike anything she'd dreamed.

His lips pulled back from hers, his hands jerking her shirt up.

"Get it off," he snarled, pushing her arms up, dragging the material over her head, then staring up at her breasts as her arms lowered. "Look how pretty."

His hands framed her breasts, his thumbs stroking her nipples as a whispered cry left her lips and she shuddered above him.

"Riordan . . ." The breathless moan was involuntary.

Her hands gripped his upper arms, fighting to hold on to a semblance of strength as his hips rolled, pressing the hard length of his erection tighter between her thighs. Creating a blistering friction as the heat of his flesh reached through denim and her cotton pj's to further heat her sex, her swollen clit.

"What, baby? Like that? Is it good?" With thumbs and fingers he exerted just enough pressure to her nipples to leave her senses reeling.

"Let's see if we can make it better, baby." He lifted one hand, stroking to her hip, moving her against his cock as his lips covered the tip of her breast and stole any objections she might have thought to have.

He sucked her nipple with firm, deep draws of his mouth. His tongue rasped over it, the heat of his mouth tightening it further.

Sensation whipped from her nipple to her clit, coursing through her body and burning through her vagina. She could feel her juices spilling, dampening her panties, slickening the delicate folds beyond. Slick and hot, they sensitized her clit further, made her thighs tighten on his hips as she ground herself closer.

She was riding him with desperate little movements now, unable to stop herself as he moved from one nipple to the next and feasted on the plump flesh. Firm nips, his tongue licking over each little love bite, then covering the tip, sucking it with those heady, rough draws of his mouth.

Sensation was tightening through her body, pulling whimpering cries from her lips that she knew would shock her later. When she could think again, when she could make sense of this insanity, she might be shocked.

For now, all she wanted was more. She was dying for more. If he didn't get rid of their clothes, then she was going to go insane. If he didn't take her, then she might not survive the blistering need burning inside her.

Each draw of his hot mouth, his tongue raking over her sensitized flesh was an agony of pleasure. And it wasn't enough. She wanted more. She ached for more with a violence she could barely contain.

Her hands were buried in his hair, holding him to her as she rode his hips with desperate movements. The stroke of his denim-covered cock through the material covering her pussy was killing her. She had to have more. She had to find a way to assuage the ache . . .

"Amara . . ." The bedroom light flared on.

Before the deep male voice processed in her senses, Riordan was moving. She was pushed from him to the seat of the couch, her body hidden as he faced the intruder, weapon drawn, finger on the trigger as Ilya stared at them in shock, and growing anger.

The dragon tattoo moved restlessly against the left

side of his face, angrily as his green eyes pierced Riordan with fury.

"She needs to dress. Quickly. And return her father's call before he ends up coming to this room and killing you," he snapped. "And perhaps you should try locking the door next door."

"Try knocking," Riordan growled, lowering his weapon. "Turn the light off when you close the door behind you. She'll get to her father's messages later. She does have a life outside him."

The door snapped closed, leaving a heavy, dangerous silence in its wake.

"The next time," Riordan mused as the light went off and the door snapped closed. "I may well kill him. Because I know that goddamned door was locked."

Just as she knew, because she had watched him lock it.

chapter six

Riordan was waiting for her the next morning.

After the interruption the night before, he'd pulled her to his room, told her to go to bed while he changed her locks, and promptly disappeared back to her room. And every attempt she'd made to watch him had resulted in this "look" that he'd sent her. One that assured her if she didn't return to the bed alone, he'd join her.

There was something about the hunger in his eyes then, the brooding sexuality and sheer lust that brightened them, that sent her scurrying back to his room. Not in fear. And even now, she wasn't exactly certain why she'd been wary of that look.

But it hadn't completely disappeared.

The moment he saw her his gaze moved from her black pumps to the tailored black wool skirt and cherry red snug sweater. He lingered at the hint of cleavage above the tiny black-pearl buttons then lifted his gaze to her eyes with a gleam of amused interest and deepening lust.

And why that look set her heart racing and made her breasts suddenly feel far too sensitive, she wasn't going to even try to understand.

"I didn't think I needed another bodyguard," she said as she strode away from him and headed for the stairs.

"Well, you never know," he suggested, following behind her. "And since your father's trying so hard to get rid of me, I thought it best to be diligent."

She rolled her eyes.

"Since when do cowboys use fifty-cent words? 'Diligent'? Really?" Turning, she shot him a mocking look only to narrow her eyes at the realization that he had been staring at her butt.

He'd done that before, she realized, as the memory suddenly just materialized. She'd caught him watching her butt as she walked more than once when he'd first come onto her security detail.

Unlike other agents he hadn't pretended he hadn't done so, nor had he been embarrassed or defensive. He'd lifted that arrogant brow over those intent blue eyes and all but laughed at her indignation.

"Really," he agreed, completely unapologetic that he was caught. "Though I rather doubt the word is worth fifty cents in this day and age. You'd be lucky to get a good penny for it. And if you don't want me to admire that cute little ass, don't display it so pretty. That's like telling a man he can't look at the sunrise, the sunset, or any other work of heavenly art. Not gonna happen."

He was going to be a problem, she could feel it. Hell, she already knew it.

"Find something to do rather than harassing me this morning," she demanded. "I'm tired of arguing with arrogant men. And try to look at something other than my ass. Unlike a sunrise, sunset, or other heavenly works of art, I'm more than just a cute butt."

She turned away and made her way to the stairs. As she entered the foyer, she met Elizaveta and Grisha, though she pretended to miss their questioning looks as they noticed Riordan behind her.

Five-six, slender and well-toned, her features austere and pretty, Elizaveta wore her thick blonde hair in a neat braid. She wasn't anyone's first thought of what a bodyguard looked like. Her twin, Grisha—nearly eight inches taller, with darker hair but the same gray eyes—suspicious watched Riordan. He had the look of a rough and ready Nordic sex god, one of her friends had sighed.

At six-two, with his short growth of beard and his slightly too long black hair falling around his sun-weathered features, he looked like one of the heroes in the action adventure movies she was so fond of. A look she much preferred, she thought in resignation as she realized she was comparing the two.

"The car is ready whenever you are, Amara," Grisha informed her, his accent, despite his perfect English, still layered his voice.

"I'll need my tablet from the office—"

"Excuse me, but I wasn't informed you were leaving the house this morning," Riordan cut in. His voice, despite its mockery, was dark with an undercurrent of warning.

Yeah, well, he could have been informed.

"You wouldn't listen when I tried to tell you last night." Shrugging, she headed past the stairs, through the hall to the other side of the house and the office her father had given her to work in.

She was all too aware of the fact that he was behind her, and Elizaveta and Grisha were not.

Nearing the door, she reached out to open it when she suddenly found him in front of her, all six-two, two hundred forty-five pounds of him. For a second, the warmth of him, the sheer power he radiated, wrapped around her.

Taking a deep breath, she stood back patiently she allowed him to open the door to the office and flip the lights on. Looking around the small room with its desk, sitting area, and shelves, he stepped inside and motioned for her to come in.

"That's just overkill." Shaking her head, she stepped to her desk, collected her tablet and the leather coat she'd left on the chair several days before.

"You wouldn't feel that way if someone had been in here waiting here for you." The amusement on his expression was beginning to irritate her.

"Sorry, Riordan, but I just don't see an attack coming from inside my office." At least, so far it hadn't. The last one had come through the front door of the New York penthouse.

Or so she'd been told.

It wasn't that she remembered the attack, but something just hadn't felt right when she'd been given those particular details.

As she started for the door he slid in front of her again, blocking the open doorway as he stared down at her, no longer amused or openly flirtatious. Pure arrogant command defined his expression.

"Where do you think you're going this morning?" he asked her, appearing about as immoveable as the wall next to him.

Why did men think it was okay to use their much larger bodies in such a way? That if they couldn't force women to do as they wanted by any other means, then they could use their bodies in some ways?

"I simply hate it when men think muscle is all that's needed to get their way," she pointed out calmly.

"Don't even try that argument," he quickly shot back as if her argument was one he was well familiar with. "I have a job to do, as do you. My job is to keep you alive, and yours is to live. Remember? I'm willing to work with you to a point, to make it as painless as possible—could you do the same?"

The strangest sense of déjà vu overcame her. As though she knew she had lived this moment, heard those words before, even though she couldn't explain how it felt so familiar.

"I tried to tell you about the meeting last night." The anger brewing inside her wasn't familiar. "I'm meeting with Poppa's lawyer in forty minutes, Once that's finished, Elizaveta and I have a spa appointment—and that, I refuse to miss. You're not supposed to be my bodyguard, Riordan, but my past lover. So, try acting less like a bodyguard if you don't mind."

His lips thinned marginally, irritation gleaming in his sapphire eyes.

"Let's go. We'll deal with this when we get back."

She rather doubted the coming confrontation could be considered "talk."

"I didn't invite you."

Before she knew what he intended, he had her back against the door, one hand at her hip, the other in her hair, pulling her head back, and he was kissing her.

It was a kiss of pure demand, of hunger, of lust at its most potent. Pure. Hot. Intoxicating. It reminded her of the interruption the night before, and reminded her that his patience was wearing thin. He'd join her in the bed, his or hers, soon.

"Fuck!" Jerking his head back, his breathing harsh, he stared down at her, his gaze going over her expression. "You look good enough to eat. For hours. And I'm a damned hungry man, Amara."

Lips parted, fighting to breathe, let alone think, it was all she could do not to beg him to force her to cancel that meeting for his bed.

"Let's go before my control is shot," he muttered, easing her back from the door and opening it with a quick, controlled move. "If we don't go now, we won't be going."

She left the room in a daze, leading the way to the foyer. She was off balance now, more aware of him than ever.

"Remember that whole 'working together' thing?" he reminded her. "Or do I need to give you lessons again?"

Working together? She had a feeling it wasn't so much working together as it was being dragged along in his wake.

Protesting wouldn't do her much good, and arguing

with him would be like talking to a brick wall. Pure stubborn arrogance was simply a part of him. She could see it in the set of his shoulders and in the hard gleam of determination in his gaze. Besides, her brain was still a bit scrambled from that kiss.

And she wasn't quite as certain of where this was going as she had been the week before. She wasn't quite certain how she felt about him. She wanted to say she didn't like him, but each time she tried that thought out for size, the discomfort in it made her a liar.

Resigning herself to being stuck with him for the day, she followed him to the limo and with Grisha and Tobias in a vehicle behind them, she counted herself lucky that Elizaveta remained in the vehicle with her. She was going to establish rules to this little joint effort between them it seemed.

Though she had a feeling it was fast passing the point where he could be controlled. If that point had even existed at any point. She doubted anyone had controlled that man since before he was a toddler.

And she knew that as far as he was concerned, he damn sure wasn't going to be controlled now.

The spa was just what she needed after meeting with the lawyer, Amara thought as she and Elizaveta relaxed after the masseuse had finished their massage. Hours of pampering, chocolate and champagne, manicures, pedicures, and waxing.

She remembered before when the trip took longer. When her long hair would have been trimmed, conditioned, and babied until it lay like a silken ribbon around her, the thick, heavy mass gleaming with a life of its own.

Before it had been chopped off.

Lying facedown on the massage table, she restrained a sigh of regret. She missed her long hair falling around her body now. Missed the sensual feel of Riordan's hands burrowing into it, clenching on the strands, and sending those exquisite little sparks of heated pleasure across her scalp and racing over her body.

"I was surprised to see Riordan return," Elizaveta murmured, dragging Amara from her thoughts. "Your poppa informed us this morning he is once again head of your security. That part did not surprise me perhaps."

The soft accent was tinged with a questioning tone.

"He didn't tell me." Amara turned her head and gazed back at her friend with narrowed eyes. "I'll have to ask why he didn't."

Elizaveta's expression was filled with concern.

"I did not know you were involved in such a way with him before the kidnapping," she said softly. "I would have told you . . . when you asked if you had a lover . . . I would have told you, Amara."

She would have, Amara knew that.

She and Elizaveta had been friends since childhood. She, Grisha, and Ilya were siblings, and such a part of Amara's life that she wasn't certain what she and her father would do if they were no longer there.

"It would seem no one knew." And she couldn't imagine why Riordan had allowed that, let alone why she had done it.

She could guess though. She knew how her poppa was, his little rules concerning any man she became involved with and his habit of firing them if it seemed she was interested in them.

Yeah, she would have tried to keep her relationship with him as secret as possible. But as she and her father had learned, Riordan wasn't going to be secret. And why did that cause a tingle of excitement to race through her?

Just knowing Riordan was there, waiting for her, watching her back, part of the worry had eased but it was replaced instead by a dark excitement she had no idea how to make sense of.

"Do you love him?" Amara asked, still watching her, her gray eyes intent, concerned.

Did she love him?

She did. As illogical as it seemed, she knew she loved him.

"That look on your face, it is all I need." The wistful sound of Elizaveta's voice reminded her there was a reason why her friend would have a reason to see another's emotions with such bittersweet envy.

At nearly five years older than she, Elizaveta with her tall, slender body, her training, and confidence in her abilities, loved a man who had forgotten how to love a woman a long time ago.

"I'm very happy for you, Amara," her cousin said softly. "I'm not jealous. Well, just perhaps just a bit." Amusement lit Elizaveta's gaze then. "Just a bit." She held her hands out to indicate a good two feet rather than mere inches.

"Be jealous if I don't kill him soon." Amara rolled her eyes. "I still can't believe I was able to deal with his arrogance long enough to let him in my bed."

The man had perfected that prickish attitude to a fine art. Even more than her poppa had. What was it about a strong, confident man that made him believe his word must be the end all, be all to any discussion? What was it about such a man that just made a woman want to tame him?

"He was different then." Elizaveta frowned at whatever she was remembering. "When you're around, he is different still. Not hard and cold as he was when your poppa hired him. Those eyes would freeze a person when he stared back at them when I first met him."

A flashing memory of those icy eyes, an unsmiling visage, no mockery, no lust or intent, filled her mind.

"That is what worried your poppa and why he sent him to England just before your abduction. I was with your mother when he told her of Riordan's reassignment. Aunt Talia went ballistic when she heard, you know," Elizaveta told her.

Yes, her mother probably had. She and Amara talked often, and it was her mada that Amara told her secrets where men were concerned. But even her mada hadn't known of the relationship with Riordan.

"What did she say to Poppa?" Amara propped her cheek on her hands as she lay on the narrow massage table.

"After she finished calling him names in several different languages?" Her cousin laughed. "That he had made a mistake. That was when mother sent Grisha and me home. She and Aunt Talia agreed that you would need us there if he was gone." Regret and pain twisted her expression. "We were too late. For that, I will always blame myself, Amara."

"They would have killed you." Sitting up, Amara held the sheet between her breasts and watched her cousin painfully. "You and Grisha both."

To that, Elizaveta nodded. "To take you, they would have had to."

And she would have grieved forever.

Rising from the massage table, she moved to the dressing room. She couldn't imagine losing Elizaveta and Grisha. They'd been a part of her life for as long as she could remember. Her mada and their mother, Tiana, were extremely close, almost inseparable after Talia had been born.

"You should have Riordan inform the others we'll be stopping at the coffee shop when we leave," she informed her cousin with a knowing grin as they met again in the main room. "Since he's once again head of my security, he should know these things, right?"

Elizaveta's eyes narrowed, then widened in playful amusement.

"You did not know he was reinstated with the agency, did you?" she asked with vein of laughter.

"He must have neglected to inform me." She let a mocking pout form at her lips. "Bad Riordan. I'll have to teach him better, yes?"

Their laughter, for the first time in months, was light-hearted, playful, like it had been before she'd had a year of her life stolen from her. Before she'd lost something, someone, she hadn't known she loved.

Because she might love Riordan, but she wasn't so certain that emotion was returned. She wasn't certain at all.

chapter seven

"This is ridiculous." Amara stalked into the family room before turning to face Riordan furiously. "You cannot hover over me like some shadow of retribution each time I leave this house. I simply won't have it."

From the moment they'd left the coffee shop, her anger had only grown. He'd made it impossible to actually talk to anyone, let alone attempt to continue to convince the waitress who worked there to talk to her. Which was her main reason for being there. There was something about the woman that bothered her, that caused the hidden memories to press against the wall holding them back. She'd been attempting to get that waitress to trust her for more than a month. Ever since the day Amara had noticed her lingering close to her and Elizaveta's table, a shadow of desperation darkening her pale green eyes.

There was no way that was going to happen with Riordan there. The woman hadn't even attempted to come close to her table. As a matter of fact, she'd completely disappeared. And Riordan had just kept sitting there, amusement filling his gaze.

"Of course I can," Riordan answered as she turned to face him, her hands settling on her hips as she fought to keep from slapping that superior look off his face. "It's actually part of my job description now. Remember?"

The vein of amusement in his tone raked across her already irritated nerves. The problem was, it wasn't just fury she was feeling. It was arousal. Her body was sensitized, her breasts felt heavier, her nipples were hard and aching, and the intimate flesh between her thighs was slick and wet.

She was actually going to have to change her panties at this rate.

Damn him. How was he doing this to her? Why? She couldn't remember ever reacting to another man like this. She didn't know if she wanted to smack his face or watch him bury it between her thighs. But she did know that the latter thought had those thigh muscles clenching in response.

"You and your job description can get fucked for all I care. Are you my bodyguard, Riordan, or my lover?" she snapped out, furious at herself, at her body, for the contradictory responses to him. "Keep this up, Mr. Malone, and I'll show you just how hard it can become to keep up with me. And just how much a lover I can, not, be."

He seemed to tense from the first sentence out of her mouth. His expression became darker, more sexual, those thick lashes lowered over his eyes with a hint of sensual promise as his gaze focused on her lips.

"Don't even think that's happening, Amara," he assured her, the roughened sound of his voice causing her sex to clench in greedy hunger. "And I'm never less than honest with you. Tell me what the hell those trips to the coffee shop are all about and I'll stop acting like a man who doesn't know what the hell is going on."

Her heart seemed to pause for a breathless moment before speeding up, pounding so hard she found her breath quickening in something approaching fear.

He couldn't possibly suspect anything other than the obvious. Not really. He had to be guessing, simply pushing her.

"The trips are all about a cup of coffee with friends," she forced the words past her lips, forced herself to hold back something she knew she could never tell him. "Friends you glared at the entire time like a jealous ass."

At the end of the day, he was a bodyguard, just like Elizaveta and Grisha. And at the end of the day, they all reported back to Ivan. And as much as she loved her poppa, she knew there were some things she simply couldn't trust him to know. And instinct warned her that he could never know about that waitress and the pure terror Amara had seen in her eyes the one time her poppa had joined her at the coffee shop.

Instinct. Perhaps knowledge. She wasn't certain what it was, but she knew it was a secret she had to keep to herself for now.

Riordan shook his head. "You're lying to me." Turning, he moved to the doors of the room, closed them, locked them carefully, then turned back to her.

"What was that for?" Wariness had her watching him carefully now.

"Your father believes those trips are a point of defiance. That you're merely acting out your need for your independence," he stated, moving closer, his voice nearly at a whisper of a sound. "Why don't you tell me what they're really about? . . . Let me help you."

Let him help her? He'd help her all right. He'd run straight to Poppa and tell him everything she said, just as every other bodyguard had done. She didn't dare trust him.

No matter how much she wanted to. He hadn't told her that her poppa had reinstated his position. He'd kept quiet about it and allowed someone else to inform her. That wasn't the action of a man who would help her.

But, she did want to trust him. Until Riordan, she hadn't even wanted anyone to confide in, hadn't ached for someone to tell her secrets to. And she knew from experience what awaited on the other side of that desire—nothing but disappointment.

"I oversee Poppa's committees, I take those bullshit meetings he's so determined I take care of, and play his dutiful hostess when required," she sneered. "I stay within this estate and I refuse to see people who swear they were friends before my abduction. I do all this for him and ask only for a few moments to have a cup of coffee with friends I actually do remember, and this is what I must deal with?" She threw one hand out to him in furious mockery. "Suspicion and questions?"

A knowing chuckle met her words and sent a shiver of pleasure up her spine. He didn't believe her, and he wasn't pretending otherwise.

"I saw your eyes," he told her as he moved behind her, his lips close to her ear, his warmth settling around her. "I saw the way you watched that room. You were looking for someone. Who was it Amara? A lover?" The final word was a rasp of danger.

She had a feeling that were it actually a lover, then it would be one she wouldn't keep for long. The playful, seductive warrior would become one who wasn't playing any longer.

"None of your business." she snapped.

"And that's where you're wrong." Oh yeah, he wasn't playing. "Trust me, Amara. If you had a lover, it would become my business really fast."

Her breath caught as the words seemed to echo through her mind. She couldn't have heard the complete possessiveness in his voice that she was certain she'd heard. It wasn't possible. Was it?

"Says who?" she demanded. "You waited six months to return, remember, Riordan? And still, I had to find you. You didn't come looking for me." And that was bothering her more than she wanted to admit.

"I say." He faced her once again, his expression brooding, shadowed with whatever memories he himself possessed. "And trust me, Amara, you were only a few days ahead of my arrival here. You were resting on borrowed time where I was concerned."

"Borrowed time, was it?" She stared back at him resentfully. "Six months, Riordan. That isn't borrowed time. That's a lover who didn't give a fuck to begin with."

Why hadn't he returned to her? Found a way to contact her despite whatever roadblocks her poppa put in his way. Why had he stayed away? His brow lifted mockingly.

"Why did you even return? Why did you stay away?" She hated this feeling. This knowledge that she cared more for him than he might care for her. He shrugged. "If you're so certain you're right, then remember it. Then you can answer all your own questions. You wouldn't need to keep asking everyone if you'd quit fighting those memories."

"You're a prick!" she threw out contemptuously.

"So I've been told, sweetheart." He shrugged easily, as though the insult didn't faze him in the least. "And it might very well be true. But if I have to be a prick to save your cute little ass from yourself, then that's exactly what I'll be. Whether you like it or not."

"I was never a danger to myself." Anger poured through her at the statement. How dare he speak to her as though she were a child. As though too incompetent to realize when she was in danger.

"Baby, I read the files your bodyguards kept for the year before, and again for the past few months." He actually had the nerve to laugh. "Your little jaunts to the coffee shop in the past months were child's play. Keeping up with you was like chasing the wind until the year you were abducted. You settled down for a minute then." He tilted his head and stared at her thoughtfully. "You found something more exciting in my damned bed than chasing the wind. When you remember that, maybe you'll remember the abduction and have all your answers." "I'm sure that isn't what happened." She clenched her teeth, feeling as though she would strangle over the denial she was so furious. "No one has the power to ground me. Especially you."

She was on the verge of shaking. The son of a bitch thought he was so superior, that he knew so much.

"Not even a lover?" He was closer, forcing her to tilt her head back to stare up at him. Her lips parted to throw every curse she knew at him when his hand lifted, his fingers brushing ever so gently against her cheek. "Could a lover ground you, Amara?"

For a moment—one fragile, too-short moment—she imagined him as her lover, their bodies entwined. His taller, stronger body sheltering hers, his darker flesh a contrast against her lighter one. His hands holding her, his lips covering hers as he moved over her, within her.

She stared up at him, lips parted, her breathing heavy as his head lowered, his gaze locked on her lips, and she knew, she knew he was going to kiss her. And all she could do was wait for it, long for it. Need it more with each caress he gave her.

Damn him, he was teaching her the meaning of addiction.

"What the hell is going on here!"

Amara jumped back at the sound of her poppa's voice. The whiplash of suspicion and anger filled it as he pushed the door open and stepped into the room.

"That door was locked, Resnova," Riordan reminded him, his gaze never leaving hers as she stared at him in surprise.

No one, but no one, spoke to Ivan Resnova in such a way.

"Fuck you, Malone," her poppa snorted. "And why the hell did my daughter feel the need to text me before she arrived home that you were threatening her?"

Riordan's eyes widened just slightly as Amara felt a flush stain her face. A chuckle vibrated in his chest as he lifted his hand and shook a finger at her chidingly.

"Shame on you," he murmured, a knowing glint in his eyes as amused mockery filled his expression. "We'll discuss that later."

"Amara?" her poppa snapped as Riordan moved away from her. "What the hell is going on? What kind of threats did he make?"

She should have never given into that childish little impulse. She'd been furious, but she should have known better, dammit.

"I threatened to spank her ass for playing games with her bodyguards and with me." Riordan was so obviously laughing at her before he turned to her father. "Your daughter's more like you Ivan than you like to admit to."

Eyes narrowed, his expression frighteningly calm, her poppa looked between them for long seconds.

"Amara, would you mind not driving these bodyguards crazy with your high jinks?" Ivan finally said, frustration flashing across his expression. "Just until we can ascertain whether or not your life is still in danger?"

Oh, Poppa, she thought mockingly, *what are you up to?*

The fact that he was definitely up to something wasn't in doubt. At any other time, with any other bodyguard, her poppa would have personally thrown him out the door on his ass. Instead, for once, he was placing the blame where it belonged.

On her.

And here she thought she could do no wrong in his eyes.

"Poppa, would I actually cause your bodyguards any problems?" she asked innocently, glancing between the two men suspiciously. "Riordan's imagining things. You know how men get when a woman doesn't bow and scrape at their overly large feet."

Did her father wince?

What the hell was up with him?

"Amara," he breathed out as though resigned to some inner thought. "Child, behave yourself."

Whoa! He had not just said that. She blinked back at her father.

"Let me remind you, Father," she stated clearly, with no small amount of offense. "I haven't been a child for a number of years now, and I damn sure won't be treated like one. Not by you, not by your bodyguards. Or my so-called lovers." She shot Riordan a scathing look. "Perhaps the two of you should discuss other ways to ensure I follow your asinine dictates. Because that one damn sure isn't going to work."

Rather than standing there and becoming embroiled in yet another screaming match with her father she swept past the two men, leaving them to figure things out on their own. Not that she actually expected either of them to make any headway where such a discussion was concerned. As far as she could see, one was just as stubborn as the other. And wasn't that just her damn luck?

She'd always sworn she'd only be attracted to nice, reasonable, logical men. Riordan was anything but nice, reasonable, or logical.

He and her father should get along wonderfully.

Riordan couldn't help but watch her grand exit with a grin. Damn, but she was pissed off. That little nose was lifted, those shoulders were straight, and the heels of her shoes made nice little clips against the floor. And that cute ass of hers beneath the wool skirt drew his gaze despite the fact that her father was watching.

"I'm going to end up killing you, Riordan," Ivan muttered as Amara moved quickly up the stairs outside the family room. "Painfully."

Riordan didn't think so. "She's playing you over that damn coffee house, Ivan," he reminded her father once again. "The last two trips there, Noah's agents identified the same two men following her. Her last trip there, they were actually waiting outside when the additional bodyguards you sent arrived. And today those same two men, using another vehicle, passed by the coffee house twice while she was inside. Explain that one as Amara just showing her need for a little independence." Crossing his arms over his chest he watched Ivan's eyes narrow as his expression drew savagely tight.

"Her bodyguards didn't report that." Ivan's jaw clenched as his pale blue eyes lit with anger.

"The two men who have been tracking her visits there were that good. But I also suspect someone here was alerting them to her trips from the estate. Noah's agents reported they were waiting on her wherever she was scheduled to be, then followed her to the coffee house. Today, they were rather late showing up." He smiled tightly. "Whoever's reporting her movements wasn't in a position to know she left until later."

Ivan shook his head. "I can't imagine anyone here betraying her." But the shadow of doubt that crossed his expression indicated he wasn't sure. "Goddammit, only my most trusted people are on the estate and in the house, Riordan. For the most part, they're family I brought out of Russia with us."

It was always harder to imagine family betraying a person, Riordan admitted. He'd been lucky, Grandpops and Noah had never betrayed him, but he knew others weren't that lucky. And he figured Ivan was in the latter group.

"Who else could get hold of her schedule?" he asked. "Who would have reason to know each time she left the estate?"

The look Ivan shot him was rife with fury. "I'll find out," he swore, and Riordan knew he'd just do that. The question was whether he could do it before the danger Riordan felt gathering around Amara struck.

"There's also a reason why she's stopping at the coffee house so often, despite your warnings that she could be in danger," Riordan continued. "Amara has no desire to tempt her own death, no matter what that psychologist believes. She's waiting on someone. Someone she believes will show up while she's there. And it's not those two men following her."

It wasn't a lover—he was sure of that. But he was just as certain there was someone. He'd seen her eyes, her expression when he accused her of it, before Ivan appeared. That had been guilt and fear he'd seen there. She was up to something and she was scared to damn death that someone would figure out what.

"What in the hell is that girl up to?" Ivan snarled, pushing his fingers through his hair in frustration. "Damn her. She has only to tell me what she wants, what she needs. I would make certain it was taken care of."

Riordan stared at the other man in surprise.

"She's not five, Ivan," he grunted. "I'd suspect she'd like to take care of a few things herself from time to time. Though, in this instance, I wish she'd tell one of us what she's up to."

The look Ivan threw him wasn't exactly agreeable. "Things such as choosing one of her bodyguards for a lover?" he questioned, his tone rather insulting.

Riordan grinned back at him. "I'd say that would top her list," he agreed. "At least she has good taste."

He had been her lover, and he would be again. No matter Ivan's objections. Hell, no matter Amara's objections. Because she could object until Hell froze over and it wouldn't matter. She wanted him. Just as damn bad as he wanted her.

She might not remember him, but the months he'd spent in her bed hadn't been entirely forgotten. Not deep in her soul.

"You have a rather high opinion of yourself," Ivan growled. "I'm not so certain it's not a character flaw, Riordan."

The brooding glare Ivan shot him was more amusing than anything else.

"Hmm. Grandpops can assure you otherwise." He shrugged. "Now if you'll excuse me, I need to go make certain that daughter of yours isn't tying sheets together to slip down from her balcony. The mood she's in, anything's possible."

"With any luck she's loading her gun and preparing to put a hole in your hide," Ivan muttered as he passed. "One could only hope."

He could keep hoping, Riordan thought without comment. Amara might threaten to shoot him, but he knew she wouldn't actually pull the trigger.

At least, he hoped she wouldn't.

chapter eight

The next evening Amara logged into the social media account of the coffee house and scanned the posts and various pictures, hoping to find the waitress she'd been trying to get the chance to talk to.

There were plenty of pictures of the owner and many of the employees, but there wasn't a single picture of the young woman she was looking for. And now, she could forget going back and attempting to talk to her. Riordan was way too suspicious, and she had no doubt he'd already alerted her father that she was up to something.

Bodyguards! She couldn't trust a single one her father hired. Even Elizaveta and Grisha weren't completely trustworthy. They could hold a few minor secrets, maybe convinced to make an unscheduled stop here and there, but that was about it.

Finally, after several hours of scanning the coffee house's page as well as that of employees listed as contacts of the establishment, she sighed, pushed her fingers through her hair, and held back the curse she wanted to spit out.

She'd spent six months completely in the dark concerning the memories she'd lost. In the past months she'd been surprised more than once by the knowledge that she'd forgotten important events. Her mother had gotten married to her longtime lover, her father had dumped the mistress he'd had for several years. Who else had she forgotten? What else had she forgotten besides her abduction? And her lover.

Shutting down the computer and rising from the comfortable desk chair, she glanced around her office before shaking her head wearily and leaving the room.

Locking the office door behind her, Amara retreated to the family room and the large fire Alexi had burning in the fireplace. He'd pulled the heavy curtains closed, darkening the room except for the firelight, and partially closed the double doors.

She hadn't slept well last night, which contributed to her headache and the irritation she felt building inside her.

Curling into the corner of the couch that faced the fire, she stared at the flickering flames, felt the warmth easing around her, and wished she could draw it inside her. There was no dispelling the chill that seemed deeper than before and had her pulling the cashmere throw on the back of the couch around her.

Kicking off her shoes, she drew her feet up beside her on the cushions beneath the long, dove gray skirt she wore and rested her head against the back of the couch.

The throb in her temple wouldn't relent throughout the day, and she knew it didn't bode well for the rest of the night.

Sometimes, she wanted nothing more than to slip into one of those deep, dreamless sleeps of years past. The ones where she woke feeling refreshed and ready to take on the world. Now, when she did sleep it was in a series of brief naps, or she awoke amid her own screams.

"Amara?" Elizaveta's soft voice, nearly a whisper, had Amara opening her eyes to see the other woman standing at the end of the couch watching her worriedly.

Shoulder-length dark blonde hair framed her cousin's kittenish features and emphasized her wide gray eyes. At five-six, she was slender and deceptively fragile, but amazingly resilient. Amara had seen Elizaveta and her brother sparring, and knew well the girl was no weakling.

"Are you well?" her cousin asked. "Can I get you dinner? You did not eat much during the meal." Her Russian accent was slightly stronger than Amara's father's, due most likely to Elizaveta's recent trips to Russia to visit her family.

"I'm fine," Amara assured her, then patted the couch next to her. "Sit with me for a few minutes."

She and Elizaveta hadn't had a chance to really talk in weeks. There was a time when they'd sit up long into the night, laughing, discussing her father's machinations and her mother's continual interference in his life.

"I am off duty for the night, I was going to have a drink," she said hesitantly. "Would you share one with me?"

The memory of fine Irish whiskey teased at her taste buds.

"Only if you can steal a shot of that Irish hooch, Malone . . ." she began, only to stop when Elizaveta turned on her heel and hurried from the room. No doubt she was going to ask Riordan for the whisky.

Amara dropped her head to the couch with a groan. Just what she needed, Riordan Malone harassing her further. After the day before, she was hoping to put a few days between another confrontation with him.

That didn't mean she didn't like looking at him, though, because she did. The way those snug-assed jeans fit him just right and paired with his scarred leather boots and button-down shirts with their sleeves rolled back to his forearms as he strutted around the estate like King Cock, attitude and all. He wore the tough-male persona like a cape. It wasn't even a conscious thing. It was an attitude born of winning more fights than he'd lost and refusing to bow down to anyone.

It wasn't a prick attitude, though she imagined he could easily act the prick when he felt a situation warranted it.

He was dominant. Sexually, personally, and every other way she could imagine.

He was the type of man who would dare a woman, challenge her, completely push her sexuality . . . And that was exactly what he was doing to her.

A sleepy smile tugged at her lips as the image played within her imagination. Him pulling her to him, his lips on hers, devouring her kiss. His tongue stroking, thrusting past her lips for a lick, a taste, before retreating then moving in again.

Her heart began to race, her body began to weaken, soften as she imagined what he'd do to her if he wanted her.

Her breasts swelled, nipples peaking beneath the loose sweater and lacy bra she wore. Between her thighs she could feel herself melting, growing slick and damp as a heavy daze of sensuality washed over her.

The image flashed to their naked bodies straining against each other in his bed. His muscular chest pressing against her breasts, the rasp of his chest hairs against her nipples, then the rasp of his tongue.

The image was so crisp, so clear.

Watching his kisses at her breast, then the sight of his lips opening, covering the hard, distended nipple awaiting him . . . sensation lashed from her nipple to her sex, causing her stomach to clench involuntarily and her breath to hitch in hungry need.

"Want more, pretty girl?" his voice whispered around her, causing her eyes to jerk open, her gaze to become locked with his blue sapphire one as imagination and reality clashed.

Fuck.

Riordan stared into the flushed, sensual features of Amara's face and he damn well knew where she'd been as she leaned in the corner of the couch, her head against the cushions, held within the embrace of cold leather but dreaming of an entirely different embrace.

Dreaming, or remembering.

Her lips were parted, her breathing rough and choppy as drowsy sensuality filled her expression.

And he was supposed to resist?

Hell.

He was barely aware of placing the glass and bottle he'd carried down with him on the table next to the couch. All he could think of was tasting her kiss, tasting whatever memory she was allowing herself to experience.

Her hand lifted and curled around his neck as he watched her soft gray eyes darkening with the deepening passion he knew was filling her.

Memory.

He saw it in her eyes, in her face as she drew his head down, met his lips with hers, and fucking seared his senses.

She wasn't asleep, she wasn't wholly awake, but lost instead in some memory she allowed free—and she was going to burn him alive with it.

Because he couldn't help but give her what he knew she wanted.

Sliding his fingers in the back of her hair, he clenched the shortened strands, gave her a brief taste of the burn, and took the kiss he'd been dying for.

He followed her as she slid down into the couch, her arms coming around his back, tugging at his shirt to reach bare skin. And he let her have what she wanted. Remaining just above her, letting her sink into whatever memory had her. He didn't push her.

God, he couldn't push her, couldn't let this slip away, not yet.

He'd been tortured by his own dreams of what they'd shared while recovering. Tortured by a hunger that ravaged him when he allowed himself to think about it while awake. This, the melding of lips, of tongues, of deep, desperate pleasure was like nothing he'd known in his life.

Her hands pushed beneath his shirt, found his back, and smoothed up to his shoulders. A whimpering little moan filled the air around them—her moan filled with hunger and need.

Breathing harsh, he pulled back, nipped at her lips, at her jaw. The smooth line of her neck drew him, the memory of its sensitivity causing his body to tighten as he fought to ensure she remained locked in whatever vision she was allowing herself to have.

"Please . . ." she whispered, arching to him, one hand smoothing along his side before sliding from beneath the shirt and reaching for his arm. "Touch me. Oh God, Riordan. Touch me again."

Touch her again.

He let her tug at his arm as he braced his knee between her thighs, and he let her pull his hand to her waist, beneath the soft material of the sweater, to the swollen curve of her breast.

Cupping it, he molded his hand to her flesh, his fingers stroking, caressing, releasing the front clasp of her bra and spreading the lace apart.

He was fucking dying.

She was going to come to herself any minute. But until she did, her hands were in his hair again, her neck arched as she tugged at him, pulling his head down until his lips were brushing the tight, hard peak of her nipple.

"Please . . ." she breathed out, arching, pushing the little bud between his lips.

He was a hungry man and he admitted it. Desperate. A son of a bitch for not pulling back and letting her know this wasn't some dream she was experiencing.

Instead, carefully, so carefully, he let his lips close around the bundle of nerves and drew it into his mouth. His tongue raked over it, the subtle taste of that edible dusting powder she used hit his taste buds and slammed into his senses.

How could he have forgotten that? The sweetness of it mixed with the elusive taste of feminine need made him drunk on her. Made him draw on the tight little peak harder, hungrier.

His dick was spike hard, pressing against the denim of his jeans, demanding release. Her hips were arching to him, pressing into his thigh as it slid between hers, grinding the soft pad of her pussy against him. Slowly rubbing against him, whispered little cries left her lips as her nails scoured his back.

He could feel a rivulet of sweat tracing down the side of his face as he burned for her. The effort of holding back, of keeping each touch, each draw of his mouth from pulling her out of her fantasy was killing him.

He had to touch her. God forgive him and pray she didn't shoot him, but he had to touch her.

His hand slid to her thigh, the silky flesh revealed from where her skirt pooled above was so damn soft. Softer than he remembered—warm, real. He wasn't dreaming anymore. He was touching her, dragging his lips from one nipple to the other as he stroked her thigh, moving with tortured stokes until his fingers brushed the damp silk of her panties.

And in that moment, he knew he was going to fucking burn in Hell, because he couldn't stop himself.

She was locked in the pleasure, the fantasy of every touch she'd dreamed of for months as well as the pleasure she'd found the night before. His body was covering hers again, heated and so strong, his lips drawing on her nipple, creating fingers of lightning-fast, incredible sensation, racing through her senses.

She forced her eyes open, knowing the fantasy would be gone—it always was when this desperate need to see him overwhelmed her . . .

The sight of his lips drawing on her, his fierce expression filled with hunger and naked need met her gaze. At the same moment, the feel of his fingers brushing the dampness at her panties, stroking over the swollen folds of her sex sent sharp, pulsing waves of heat straight to her womb.

Her clit throbbed, the building intensity growing in the little bundle of nerve endings was shocking . . .

And it was real.

It wasn't a fantasy. It was real. He was touching her, his hard, corded body warming her, braced over her, each touch, each caress making her needier.

It wasn't a dream.

It was Riordan . . .

His fingers were pushing beneath her panties, callused fingertips caressing her flesh. And they were in the sitting room.

Any second Elizaveta could return.

Oh God, her father could walk in . . . "Stop." The word tore past her lips, panic suddenly tearing through her. "No."

His hand paused. A final, lingering kiss to her nipple, and then he was pulling swiftly back, his expression savage with lust. His black hair was mussed, falling around his face, giving him the look of a dark sex god come to life. And he was aroused. Her eyes widened at the bulge in the front of his jeans as he jumped back from her, then to his feet. His eyes burned like molten sapphires in the flickering firelight, his gaze raking over her before he turned his back to her.

"Fix your clothes," the snarling demand had her looking down, eyes widening.

The dark gray sweater she wore was unbuttoned, her bra undone and spread to the sides. Her nipples were rock hard and glistening with moisture.

A cry escaped her and she pushed herself up, fighting to fix her clothes with trembling hands and failing miserably. No matter how hard she tried, the clasp of her bra slipped from her shaking fingers.

"Dammit," his curse had her jerking to him, flinching as he reached for her.

Those broad, callused fingers clasped her bra, then just as efficiently buttoned her sweater before pushing her skirt down her legs.

His hands paused at her knees. His head lowered, his jaw flexed furiously at the side of his face.

"I'm sorry," she whispered, unable to look at him as he released her and sat down on the couch, propped his elbows on his knees, and raked his fingers through his hair. "I was dreaming . . ."

He snorted at the attempt to explain and reached for the bottle of whiskey as he gave his head a hard shake. Uncapping it, he poured the shot glass half full then tipped it to his lips and finished it in one gulp.

"I didn't mean—" She tried to make sense of what happened.

"Save it," he growled, replacing the glass back on the table with a thud. "There's the whiskey you wanted. Keep it."

He refilled the glass but left it sitting as he slapped the bottle back in place and rose to his feet.

"I want to explain . . ." she tried again to make him understand whatever had happened.

"And I don't want to hear your lies, goddammit," he all but yelled, the furious words silencing her. "Lie to yourself if you have to, but do us both a favor and stop fucking lying to me. You're mine, Amara. You were mine before the abduction and nothing has changed. And by God, you better remember that much as least. Fast."

With that he turned on his heel and stomped from the room, anger vibrating around him like an invisible aura. And all she could do was stare after him, her heart racing, need burning through her as panic threatened to fill her senses.

Lie to herself? She wasn't lying to herself.

chapter nine

He'd known better. Riordan couldn't say he hadn't known what was going to happen, because he'd known *exactly* what was going to happen. From the moment he touched her until the second she'd called a stop to it, he'd known. And he wasn't angry with Amara as much as he was with himself.

He should have never allowed things to progress to that point. He should have pulled back long before he had . . . hell, he shouldn't have touched her to begin with.

But he'd seen the need, the aching desperation that went beyond anything sexual as she stared up at him with those drowsy eyes and he hadn't been able to resist.

No more than he'd been able to resist that first kiss. The memory of her teasing had the power to singe his senses, even now.

"You want to kiss me," she laughed softly, amused

by his distance. "I know you do. You act all hard and cold but I bet you think about it when you're in bed alone at night."

"Do you mean I jack off to the thought of kissing you?" he all but growled at he stared at the innocence in her face. "Baby, if I were thinking about you while I jacked off, it wouldn't be kissing I'd be doing."

He meant to shock her, to make her angry.

Amusement curled her lips despite her blush. "So, what do you think about, Mr. Malone, when you're thinking about me and jacking off?"

His dick went hard so damn fast it was painful.

"Paddling your ass," he bit out between clenched teeth as his hands itched to touch her.

Her lips pursed with an enchanting pout. "I've never been spanked. Should I cry 'uncle,' or do you get really kinky and insist on 'daddy'."

She was laughing at him.

Damn her, she was killing him with lust and she was laughing at him.

"No, I'd get kinkier," he assured her. "Because after I spanked that smart ass of yours, I'd end up fucking it . . ."

And then he'd kissed her.

A smile quirked his lips despite the anger pouring through him, at the memory. He'd shocked her. Her lips had parted and color had filled her cheeks as her eyes widened. And he'd been helpless against that need to taste her.

Jerking open the front door he stepped into the icy cold Colorado night, nodded to the two security guards who stood watch in the hidden, heated alcove to the side of the entrance, and strode quickly around the side of the house.

The cold air with its hint of snow did nothing to cool his arousal. Hell, there weren't enough cold showers to cool what she did to him. He'd learned that the hard way the year he'd spent in New York working on her security team.

Ivan had never taken Amara's safety for granted. Elizaveta and Grisha were with her daily, but at night, he had two guards outside the penthouse entrance and two more inside. Not that Elizaveta and Grisha weren't damn nuisances during those months he'd spent in Amara's bed. They roved the apartment at all hours of the night and made sure he didn't spend a full night with her.

Because he hadn't wanted her to have to deal with her father when he learned Riordan was sleeping with her. He'd known the first thing Ivan would do was fire his ass, and he wasn't certain she'd go with him.

Pausing by the back patio behind the gas fireplace, he slid into the shadows of a heavy pine and blew out a hard breath.

He'd spent six months healing, building his strength, and each night he was tortured by dreams of touching Amara, or her nightmares. It had taken him months to figure out what was going on. Months of waking in a sweat, her screams echoing in his head, or her moans of need torturing him. Months where nothing seemed to make sense until the day his grandfather looked at him and asked him if he'd found his way.

Found his way.

Had his Irish eyes seen into the gaze of the one whose

soul would hold his own? Was he seeing through her eyes, her nightmares, her dreams?

And he realized then what had happened.

Noah had told him once how his bond with his wife Sabella had saved him through months of torture while he'd been held by the head of a drug cartel. How she'd come to him, try to ease him, and beg him to come home to her, even though she'd been told he was dead.

And he'd remembered during those years Sabella and Noah had been apart, how she'd wake screaming for "Nathan" the man his brother had been. She'd sworn her husband was alive, no matter what she was told, no matter that she'd seen his casket lowered into the ground.

And when Nathan Malone had returned as Noah Blake, it had taken her no time at all to realize that although he wore a different face and answered to a different name, even though he had another eye color and a different voice, he was her husband.

Because they'd found their way to each other. They were two parts of a whole and only death could truly separate them.

Had Riordan found his way?

He hadn't even realized what had happened during those months he spent in Amara's bed. And when Ivan had sent him to England, he'd gone. Despite his misgivings, despite the fact that something had warned him not to go, he'd walked away from her.

And less than a week later, she'd been abducted.

The sudden sense that he wasn't alone had him waiting, still, silent until Ivan stepped next to the pine and extended a pack of those damn strong-assed Russian cigarettes toward him.

He hadn't smoked since he was eighteen, when his had brother threatened to make him eat the damn things—until the past six months. He'd broken down more than once in that time.

And he broke now.

Taking the pack, he shook one out, used the matches tucked in the back and struck one, lighting the end of the unfiltered cylinder.

"This shit will kill you, Ivan." It was all he could do to hold in a hacking cough at the strength of the smoke he inhaled.

Ivan's expression was thoughtful as he lit one himself, shook out the match and, like Riordan had done, tucked it in the plastic pack.

"No doubt," he said, after inhaling deeply. "But, better to die by these than by many other things that are almost a certainty."

Riordan inhaled again, more to have time to consider the words than for any other reason.

Ivan wasn't one to just pass time, and it was obvious he'd come looking for him.

Remaining silent, he enjoyed the smoke, finding a sense of calm in the fragrant smell of the tobacco.

"Has she told you the last thing she remembers before the abduction?" Ivan asked as Riordan finished the cigarette and disposed of the stub in the smoker's post closer to the gas fireplace.

"No. We haven't talked about it." He was too busy trying to get his hand in her panties to think about it.

Putting out his own cigarette, Ivan nodded.

"Her last memory is arriving at lunch with me, nearly a year before the abduction. She was to meet her new security agent"—he paused—"you."

Riordan stared back at him, frowning. "The lunch where she met me?"

Ivan nodded. "She remembers nothing from minutes before that meeting until she woke up in the hospital."

She'd forgotten every moment of the time he'd been in her life. The months she'd spent teaching him, that he'd spent telling himself he couldn't have her. The months he'd spent in her bed, trying every way he could imagine to ensure she couldn't forget him. And she'd done just that.

"You think it has something to do with me?" he asked, not certain how it could. "She was conscious when we got to her. She was still conscious when we pulled her out of that pit. She knew who we were and what had happened."

Hell had happened as he and Noah's team had pulled her out of that dark little hole in the ground. The team tasked with taking out anyone waiting, had taken out the first team. They'd been unaware of the second team though, and Noah still hadn't managed to figure out how that happened.

"So the others reported." Ivan nodded. "Still, it is the last thing she remembers." He lit another cigarette, inhaled. "Why didn't you tell me when I sent you to England that you were sleeping with her?"

He breathed out heavily. He knew Ivan had suspected the relationship—the man had sent him away from Amara every chance he could. But he hadn't expected Ivan to broach it quite this way.

"Yeah, that's the first thing you do when you start sleeping with a woman. Inform her father," he snorted. "Especially when you're aware of all the men he'd fired just for flirting with her. Besides, it wasn't any of your damn business."

Ivan's head jerked around, his eye blazing with anger. "She's my daughter . . ."

"She's not a child, your wife, or your possession," Riordan snapped. "She's a woman. And if she had wanted you to know, then she would have told you herself."

And she hadn't.

He'd waited for it, certain she'd tell him so she wouldn't have to fucking sneak around and run him out of her bed whenever they heard Elizaveta or Grisha moving around. It had been Amara who had insisted on keeping the relationship a secret, not Riordan.

He'd have fought for her if she'd been willing to face her father, but she hadn't been.

"You should have come to me," Ivan argued. "When I sent you to England and you argued to stay, you should have told me why."

Riordan pushed his fingers through his hair and shot the other man a furious look.

"You were always sending me somewhere, dammit. The job in England was only supposed to be for a few weeks," he snapped. "How did you find out, anyway?"

"Because it is your name she screams in her nightmares," Ivan ground out. "It is you she begs for, Riordan. And that is the only reason I allowed you back into her life."

Son of a bitch. Ivan hadn't 'allowed' anything. Nothing could have kept Riordan from returning to Amara.

"And I'll be staying." He stepped from the shelter of the pine, glaring back at Ivan as he silently dared him to try to send him away again. "Don't think you can get rid of me now."

"Get rid of you?" A harsh laugh left the Russian. "You damn clueless cowboy, why the hell do you think you ended up on her damn security team to begin with?"

Ivan turned and stomped away as Riordan stared at him in surprise, and no small amount of confusion.

There was no way Ivan could've meant that he'd brought him onto Amara's team in the hopes that a relationship would develop. Could he?

With that son of a bitch, anything was possible.

Still, he couldn't get what Amara's father had said out of his head. Amara screamed his name in her nightmares, just as he heard in his own nightmares. Amara screaming his name.

What was he going to do? Forcing Amara to remember whatever she'd forgotten wasn't going to be easy. If it was, then that damn therapist would have already managed it. One thing was for sure though, they'd never be certain she was safe until they learned who had abducted her. To learn that, they had to know what happened the night she was taken, and only Amara could help them with that.

So how did a man convince a woman who had forgotten him, to remember him again and to hopefully remember everything that happened after he left her?

chapter ten

The storm was moving closer.

The next afternoon Amara cast a wary eye toward the mountains, the clouds thickening and rolling closer, as she stepped from the building where her doctor was located. Riordan was at her side as two more security agents flanked her.

Moving quickly across the sidewalk to the SUV, she stepped into the back seat and was surprised to see Riordan join her. The other two agents hurried to the vehicle behind them, and within seconds they were all pulling out and beginning the drive back to the estate.

Pushing her cold hands inside the pockets of her leather jacket, she turned her head and stared out the window, her gaze on the gathering clouds rather than on the man she could feel watching her.

She could barely face him after their confrontation the day before in the family room.

"Doctor's appointment go well?" the lazy drawl in his voice had her head turned before she stop herself.

She shrugged uneasily, wondering why he was asking.

"It was a doctor's appointment, how else could it have gone? She just wanted to be certain I'm having no problems . . ." She inhaled, unable to continue.

Her gynecologist had far too many questions, and the exam itself had made her uncomfortable. Not in a creepy way—but still—she'd felt off balance, uncertain in a way she couldn't explain to herself.

"The fracture healed without a problem?" he asked as she flinched at the reminder. Her pelvis bone hadn't been fractured completely, but the crack it had sustained was serious enough that it had required several months of physical therapy.

"Without a problem," she assured him, her voice tight as she turned and stared out the window again. She huddled deeper in her jacket, wishing they'd turn the heater up. She'd been cold since forcing herself to shower and get dressed that morning.

"Drew?" Riordan spoke into his cell phone to the agent in the front passenger seat.

He could have just lowered the window, she thought in exasperation.

"Turn the heat up back here. Miss Resnova's cold," he told the other man before disconnecting.

"You didn't have to," she said without looking at him. "I'm sure the temperature was actually fine."

"Hmmm." The noncommittal sound had her glancing at his image in the window once again.

She didn't say anything further, didn't know what to say after last night.

"Are you on birth control?" He didn't seem to have a problem finding something to say.

Her head jerked around as she stared at him, outraged.

"How is that any of your business?" she burst out, feeling the flush that burned in her cheeks.

A single brow lifted mockingly.

"I am the one who nearly had his hand in your panties last night." He grinned. "And if I'm not mistaken, you were just as wet as I was hard."

Oh my God, he didn't say just that.

"You're crazy." She couldn't quite catch her breath now.

"That's beside the point." The bastard was all but laughing out loud. "I just thought I'd ask in case I got the chance to actually get your panties off."

She could only stare at him for long moments, amazed at the sheer nerve.

"Not going to happen." She forced the words out.

He nodded slowly as he pursed his lips.

"Remember that thing about lying." He grinned slowly. "I'm counting."

She jerked her head around to stare out the window once again. One should never engage with a crazy man, her mother had always advised her. There was no way to win and a thousand ways to lose.

"Did you think about me while you were masturbating last night?" he asked her just when she was certain he would remain silent the rest of the drive. "I thought about you while I jacked off."

She would have blasted him for that if the heavy sense of déjà vu that swept over her didn't have her pausing, searching for the reason why.

"Stop," she whispered instead. "I didn't realize . . ."

"Remember, I'm counting those lies," he reminded her.

She wasn't speaking to him again. He was crazy. It was that simple. God, he was going to make her as crazy as he was in a minute.

"We have a few minutes before we reach the estate. If you want to slide over here, I'll finish what you started last night."

She had to close her eyes and force herself to stay in place. Because for all her outrage and disbelief, she wanted nothing more than to let him finish what he started. And it infuriated her. The arrogant ass. He shouldn't have even mentioned last night.

She opened her eyes, and her lips parted to tell him what he could do with his offer when the sudden sound of an explosion shattered the air. Before she could think or react, she found herself on the floor below the seat, Riordan's hard, muscular body on top, holding her down.

"Grisha, what the fuck?"

"Hang on . . . hang on," Grisha's hard voice ordered. "Goddammit, hang on . . . "

"Dammit, Grisha, that's a cliff . . ." Drew yelled as the vehicle lurched again along the narrow shoulder.

The vehicle careened, the sounds of tires screaming and metal against asphalt overly loud as the vehicle bounced, causing her and Riordan to slam against the seats. Fighting for something to hold onto, Amara felt her arm slip beneath the cushioned seat and slam into metal as the SUV bounced again.

Terror crashing through her, she fought to keep from

slipping into hysteria. Reality and nightmare seemed to converge as she fought Riordan's hold on her.

"Move out! Move out!"

"I know what the hell it is," Grisha was yelling as the tires screamed and the vehicle seemed to tilt, then shudder before righting itself and coming to a hard, slamming stop.

The silence was terrifying, filling her head as her fingers curled into fists, waiting, waiting.

Just one sound broke through

"We're losing him . . . we're losing him . . ." For a second, she wasn't in the SUV, she was in the dark, a cacophony of sound echoing around her, unable to look around, unable to see.

Someone was dying. They were losing him. He was dying.

Riordan . . .

"Riordan!" Her own scream filled the silence, and she was fighting the weight on her, fighting the restraints as well as her own weakness and panic. "No. Riordan don't . . ."

She was sobbing, fighting, and couldn't get free, couldn't break the hold on her. Panic and terror consumed her, nightmare visions filled her head as fireflies erupted around her.

And she knew, just knew, that Riordan was dying.

"Amara. Amara. Baby . . ." She was jerked into strong arms, warmth surrounding her despite the chill wind she could feel racing around her. "Come on. We've got to get you out of here."

He was pushing her arms into something . . . a Kevlar vest her father kept in the vehicles. Oh God . . .

"No." She slapped at his hands, tried to push the vest off, struggled against his hold. "Take it off. Take it off . . ."

She couldn't wear it. He had to wear it. He had to put that vest on.

She couldn't lose him again . . .

She stilled, eyes wide as the nightmare receded and she found herself staring into his eyes, her nails digging into his arms as she fought against what had to be something other than memory.

"You wear it." Her voice felt hoarse as she fought to speak past the shudders tearing through her. "Don't die for me . . ."

Her voice broke on a sob, the sound of the words echoing in her mind until she felt as though she were going crazy.

"I have one. I'm safe." He strapped the vest on her, then he was jerking on another, slapping the straps in place, then retrieving the weapon he'd placed on the seat beside him. "Grisha. Ready," he snapped.

The door popped open, and she was pulled from the vehicle, then rushed to the second SUV. The driver was ordered out of the driver's seat, and Grisha slid in as Drew and Riordan pushed her into the back. The agent who had ridden in the passenger seat now sat in the seat across from her; the previous driver in the seat beside Grisha.

The SUV peeled out as Riordan snapped orders into his phone. "We have three vehicles on their way from the estate, ETA no more than two minutes," he reported to the others before turning his attention back to the phone. "Get off my ass, Ivan, we're moving as fast as we can. Just get someone on the Suburban. I want to know what happened to that tire."

He was hard. His voice was hard, his eyes were hard, and his expression was savage as he cursed her father. "Ivan, I'm going to fucking shoot you if you don't get off my back," he growled, his gaze always moving, tracking everything as the SUV raced for the estate. "I see them now. Have Tobias head to the Suburban. I want his report ASAP. The rest of them can follow us . . . fuck you. Give him the message or I'll stop this goddamn vehicle and tell him myself."

Riordan wasn't screaming, though she could hear her father yelling on the other end. Evidently, he'd listened though. One SUV raced past them as the others executed a middle-of-the-road turn, tires screaming before they raced in behind them.

"Amara, honey, ease up." Riordan's hand covered both of hers, and it was only then that she realized the hold she had on his wrist, her nails digging in as she fought to hold onto her self-control. "It's okay. We're almost home."

As she released him, his arm went around her, dragging her closer, holding her to him as her father continued screaming through the cell phone. For once, she was damn glad she couldn't hear what he was saying—she could hear the enraged sound of his voice, and that was more than enough.

As she sat there, cradled close to Riordan's body, the shadows in her mind were roiling. Glancing memories, the sharp retorts of gunfire, the sight of brilliant red weapon discharges clashed with the memories of her teasing laughter, asking someone if they jacked off thinking about her; of snow falling as she lay in her bed in New York, aware of someone holding her, kissing her shoulder.

Nothing was clear enough—she wasn't even certain if it was memory or dreams mixed with nightmares that filled her head. She was too frightened, too filled with panic that someone was going to be hurt, someone was going to die for her. And she couldn't help but feel that someone had already done that. Someone she had cared about.

All she could do was hold onto Riordan, hold onto his arm with all her strength until they reach the estate. And then he was lifting her, carrying her from the SUV and into the house.

"Riordan!" Her father's explosive order was ignored as Riordan strode through the foyer and up the stairs.

The sound of others following could be heard: her father's curses, Noah's shouted demands. The sounds were spinning in her head, clashing through her senses as she buried her head in Riordan's shoulder and tried to tell herself she was safe. Riordan was safe. No one was hurt.

No one was hurt.

So why did she have the overwhelming feeling that someone had been more than hurt. That she'd lost someone and that the loss was breaking her from the inside out.

Riordan pushed into Amara's room and strode

straight to her bed before placing her on it. After stripping the Kevlar vest from her, he carefully removed her jacket.

"I'm fine." Her voice was thin, ragged, as she tried to sit up, tried to brush his hands away.

"Stay still." He couldn't soften the snap in his voice. "And stop lying to me."

When he gripped her arm, she flinched before she could halt the action. His firm touch moved to her right forearm. That arm was already weak, not fully recovered from the break it suffered during her abduction.

"I just sprained it." She jerked her arm back.

Gripping it again, he pushed the loose sleeve of her sweater up her arm to see the deep, darkening bruise marring her skin.

"Doctor will be here within half an hour." Ivan was calmer now as he checked the bruise before lifting his gaze to his daughter. "You don't have to be so brave, little flower," he reminded her as he always did when she was hurt. "Tell Poppa how bad it is."

She shook her head and swallowed tightly. "It's not broken, Poppa," she promised him. "I was trying to get up and my arm went beneath the seat and hit the metal I believe. It's just a bruise."

He brushed her hair back as she returned his stare, unable to control the trembling of her lower lip for a second. It was just a second, but it was enough for her poppa's face to contort, and before she knew what he was doing, she was in his arms, her head held to his heart.

"You don't have to be so damn brave all the time. You can cry," he whispered hoarsely at her ear.

"It's okay, Poppa. I'm fine." She tried to comfort him, to reassure him. "I'm safe. I swear."

"Stubborn girl." He released her, glared at Riordan as he sat beside her on her bed, then turned back to his daughter. "I'll see where that damn doctor is. He should be here."

He stomped from the room, snapping the door behind him.

Silence filled his absence.

"He's upset," she whispered, glancing at Riordan.

Her father had always tried to protect her, to make her life carefree and happy, but perhaps she hadn't realized the lengths he had gone to, or how he'd seemed to have put his own life on hold to raise her.

She turned to Riordan and stared up at him, the memory of the nightmare that slammed into her head when the SUV went out of control causing her breathing to hitch.

He was there, so obviously he hadn't died.

"By God, he's not the only one who's upset." Her head was tipped back, her lips parting in surprise when Riordan suddenly covered them with his.

The kiss was brief. It wasn't exactly erotic. It was desperate, filled with some emotion she couldn't make sense of and yet somehow had stilled the panic that was rising within her.

When he pulled back, she stared into those bleak, dark sapphire eyes and knew to the bottom her soul that he'd give his life for hers.

And that she couldn't allow that.

She couldn't . . .

"Did he lie to me about my rescue?" The question seemed to ask itself before she could stop it. "Did someone die? Did someone I care about die?"

Why did she keep fearing it was him? He was there with her. He was alive, not dead, yet she couldn't shake the fear.

His jaw clenched. "All the men who were sent in to rescue you are alive. Why do you ask?"

Uncertainty, confusion, the emotions that filled her expression, tore at him, made him want to tell her what she couldn't remember despite his grandfather's warning.

"I remember someone dying," she whispered, as though almost afraid to say the words. "I hear it in my head. Someone screaming . . ."

She shook her head as she lowered it and stared at her hands.

"Is that all you remember?" Why hadn't she remembered him? Remembered what they had been to each other?

"Grief." She swallowed tightly, her hands linking together nervously. "I remember grief. That's all. After the nightmares, whenever I hear that voice screaming that they were losing someone. I just feel grief."

Grief.

Riordan stroked her cheek, let his touch linger against the soft warmth of her skin, and he knew it was the fear of his death that haunted her. And he couldn't tell her. He couldn't tell her that the nightmares were memories, and that for precious seconds his heart had stopped beating.

"Everyone lived," he promised her again. "No one died for you, baby."

But he would have, if it would have meant her safety. He would have walked into the abyss and stayed there if it would have assured she would live her life without further threat of harm.

But he knew better. He'd known better then.

"I'm scared," she whispered, staring into his eyes, fine tremors racing through her body. "I lost someone there, I know I did and Poppa's not telling me . . ."

"You didn't lose anyone there, baby. I promise." But he could see her fear, her certainty that she had. "Ivan couldn't hide that from me. If anyone had died on that mission I would know it. And I swear, I wouldn't lie to you about it."

Not about that. She was lost enough within her own battle between her memories and her determination to hide from them. He wouldn't let her be ambushed when those memories did return.

"Whoever tried to kill me the first time is back, aren't they Riordan?" Her lower lip trembled before she controlled it. "Someone wants me dead."

The tears in her eyes didn't fall, and she wasn't sobbing in fear and hysteria. God, she shouldn't have to be this strong. She shouldn't have to face so much at one time.

"I don't know. Not for sure," he finally answered, knowing he couldn't give her false assurances. "I just don't know yet. But if they are, I promise you this, Amara, they have a whole lot of men they'll have to go through to get to you. And if they get lucky enough to get past those men, then they'll have to deal with me and Noah. And that's something they don't want to do."

Her hand lifted and touched his jaw as a single tear fell.

"Don't die for me, Riordan. Please, don't die for me . . ."

chapter eleven

Noah stepped into the house, gazed around, and couldn't help the clenching of his heart.

It was always liked this. Never changed.

The living room was scattered with children's toys, the girls lying on their stomachs coloring while Noah Jr. sat sprawled in a chair with one of the comics he liked while still keeping an eye on his sisters.

The boy was growing up older than his years, Noah thought. But, he'd been born with wise eyes. Fey eyes, Grandpops had said. A man in a boy's body.

"Hey, Dad," his son greeted him as he watched him intently, somehow knowing that his father was worried about something.

Immediately, the girls were off the floor and flying to his arms. Kneeling, he caught them to his chest, buried his face against each tiny shoulder, and hugged them firmly as they smacked kisses to his cheeks.

When love, laughter, and kisses had been dispensed

by the delicate girls, Noah rose to his feet and strode to the kitchen where his Bella waited with the go-bag he'd asked her to pack.

For more than eight years he hadn't left her for anything but the safest missions. Over watch, planning, or to help one of the men he'd trained with in the Elite Ops, less than half a dozen times, and each time he'd promised he'd be nowhere near flying bullets or crazy drug lords.

He could see the fear in her eyes now though. In all this time, he'd never asked her to pack his bag, nor had he ever pulled the young women from Ops Two in as security as he had this time.

"It's Riordan," he told her softly as he bent to kiss her cheek, knowing he had to explain, had to let her know he wouldn't just go operational on her at the drop of a hat.

Pulling back and staring into her pretty eyes, his stomach tightened, his need for her never far from the surface.

Glancing back at the kids and seeing them distracted by their various interests, he pulled her deeper into the kitchen.

"He's in trouble?" she asked, uncertain.

Riordan never got into trouble anymore. His wild days as a brash, unruly youth were far, far behind him.

"He's with Resnova in Colorado. Someone attempted to take the SUV out an hour ago. We suspect it was an attempt against Amara again. Tobias suspects the tire was shot out. I can't leave him there alone. Grandpops is worried about the girl. He's worried, period."

Why Grandpops had insisted on going, neither Noah nor Riordan could understand.

Riordan had still been yelling at him to keep his ass at home when Noah hung up the phone on him. His brother was furious with him.

"Micah's meeting me at base and we'll fly out from there. I just want to keep an eye on him," he promised her.

That was his baby brother. The brother who had been born amid death and pain. The one who had lost friends, lost his faith in those around him at a time when he'd needed it most. Noah had already deserted his wife and brother once, he couldn't do it again. Not and live with it should the worst happen.

"Keep an eye on him." She nodded, but her expression was still too solemn. "Nightly calls, Noah," she reminded him firmly. "And you come home to me in working order. Understood?"

In working order.

A grin edged at his lips as he felt his cock tighten. Damn, what he wouldn't give to slip her up those stairs, have her before he left, but it was one of those unspoken rules now.

He'd taken her just before a mission that had nearly killed him. It had killed the man he had been, Nathan Malone, and brought Noah Blake back to her. A man who loved her deeper than before, but one who bore the scars of his battle to return to her.

"Understood," he whispered, lowering his lips for a kiss. "Nightly calls. Return in working order."

The kiss threatened to become more than the kids should see before he lifted his head and turned to check on them again.

Noah Jr. stood at the side of the living room window, turning even as Noah did.

"Why are the aunts here, Dad?" The aunts. The girls of Ops Two were a steady part of their lives, but still, agents.

"They'll be staying while I go help Uncle Riordan with a few things." Noah didn't lie to him. Not exactly. "You know I don't like leaving your mom and you kids alone."

His son wasn't exactly fooled, but he accepted the explanation.

"He's so grown up," Bella sighed. "I worry. Grand-pops says he's just like you at that age."

Maybe, Noah thought, but in other ways, maybe not. Noah Jr. had a father who would never neglect him, never turn from him. Those children and their mother were his life, but so was his brother.

"I'll keep you updated," he promised, turning back to her. "We're just going to keep Rory's ass out the fire. I promise."

"Keep your own out while you're at it," she demanded fiercely. "You know the rules."

"I know the rules." He grinned.

He'd had to sign them before she'd agree to marry him as Noah Blake. Those rules were law as far as he was concerned.

Demanding another kiss, another that went almost too deep, too hot again, he forced himself from her. He gave each of his girls another hug with a promise to call before bedtime, then turned to his son.

The boy might be too old for his years, but he was hugged as well. A fierce hug was returned and a soft, "Take care, Dad."

Damn, it was always Noah who got him in the gut.

The boy really was too damned much like himself at that age.

"Love you, son," Noah said, kissing the top of his son's head. "Watch after your sisters while I'm gone."

"Always." The wry, put-upon tone had the grin deepening at his lips. "Love you too, Dad."

The final promise was something Noah never took for granted.

When he returned, maybe he and Noah needed to have another of those talks about brothers being too protective. Not that the last one had done him much good.

With his wife at his side he went to the door, gave her one last kiss, and strode to his truck.

Driving away from the house, he promised himself, as he always did now, that he was coming back. If there was a breath left in his body, he'd return.

And if there wasn't?

Well, like Grandpops said about Grandma Erin, he'd still return.

chapter twelve

Riordan stared at Tobias's report broodingly hours later, aware of the other men's silence and their presence. Because, dammit, they shouldn't be there. Knowing he'd have done the same thing if his brother were in a similar situation didn't matter. Noah had Bella, and she'd already lost him once. And now, they had the kids and another on the way. It was crazy for him to be here.

But here he was, along with his commander of the Elite Ops One. And it was obvious there was no getting rid of him.

The pictures, the state police report, Tobias's own findings as well as Noah and Micah's were displayed on the tablet resting on the low table in front of him.

He'd had the other men come to his suite rather than to Ivan's office to allow him to go over everything and form his own opinion before meeting with Amara's father. The sitting area was more conductive to a private conversation than anywhere else in the estate and he didn't fully trust Ivan's staff. But then, he didn't fully trust some people that he'd known all his life.

But he did trust these three men, especially when it came to vehicles or to covering his back. When it came to Amara's life, they were the only people, besides himself and her father, that he'd ever trust.

And their report on the tire was inconclusive.

There were several nails along the side of the road where the SUV had finally come to a stop, but the damage to the tire wasn't typical for a blowout of that nature.

Not typical, but possible.

The vehicle could have run over the construction-grade nails, or one could have been shot into it. A bullet could have also taken it out, but no evidence of that had been found.

Every instinct he had was warning him that the blowout was deliberate, that someone had taken that tire out. He just couldn't prove it.

"Impressions?" He looked up, his gaze going first to Noah where he stood next to the fireplace; to Micah, who stood just behind him; and to Tobias, who sat in the chair next to the couch.

"Doesn't make sense to me." Tobias shrugged. "All we found were nails, no bullets. There was too much damage to the tire to tell for certain what took it out."

Riordan turned back to Noah and Micah.

Arms crossed, Noah leaned against the side of the fireplace, his gaze narrowed as he stared at the tablet on the table, his lips thinned as a muscle jumped in his jaw. "There's ways to take out a tire that way, but I can't say that's what happened. As Tobias said, there's too much damage to be sure. My gut though"—a grimace pulled at his lips—"my gut says to watch our backs. But hell, that's normal under any situation that I can't fully explain."

"Yeah, yours and mine both," Micah snorted. "And my neck itches too."

Sitting back in the couch, Riordan breathed out roughly.

"Look, Riordan, like Noah there"—Tobias nodded to the other man—this doesn't feel good to me. But I don't care much for the two agents in the backup vehicle either. Grisha's damned good at his job, but the other two . . ." He shook his head at the thought.

"Grisha had to call both of them down for leaving the vehicle at one point," Micah injected. "Several times he had to keep watch on both vehicles because it was obvious they weren't."

He needed Ivan's men off his team. He didn't trust them, he didn't know them.

"I'd be more comfortable if we pulled Sawyer and Max in on this," Tobias said, mirroring his thoughts. "Max is a hell of driver. Micah trained her himself and I trust her and Sawyer a hell of a lot more than those two Russians. They'd never wander away from their vehicle, and they'd have eyes on both just like Grisha does."

Tobias had been with Brute Force for a year, but he'd been proving himself not just capable but intuitive, just as he'd done as Sabella's office assistant at the garage before Noah showed up.

"I agree with him, Riordan," Noah stated quietly. "I was going to make the suggestion myself, he just beat me to it."

"It seems we're all on the same page." Riordan

nodded then turned back to Tobias. "I'll contact them within the hour and have them here by morning. We have a blizzard moving in within the next forty-eight hours, and I want everything ready."

"I want Jarvis here as well," Noah stated. "Crowe's already contacted me and offered to send him out. I'd like to accept the offer."

Jarvis was hell with electronic security and his partner, Sabra was damn near as good. They were the best—and a hell of a lot better than the two Ivan currently had overseeing electronic security.

The fact that Noah wanted their own team members rather than Ivan's working security was a bad sign though. That blowout might be inconclusive on paper, it might appear to be an accident, but like Riordan, something was warning Noah that there was more to it.

"I'll go down and let Ivan know what we're doing. Contact Crowe and while you're at it, make the call to Sawyer and Max for me," he told Noah. "I have a feeling I'm going to be dealing with her father for a while. He won't be happy with my report."

He was going to be pissed as hell, and Riordan couldn't blame him.

"Like the rest of us, 'inconclusive' doesn't sit well with Ivan. I don't blame him much. If it were Erin or Aislinn, I'd be raising hell," Noah admitted.

Getting to his feet, Riordan met his brother's eyes and saw the same worry and suspicions he felt.

"He was tearing Ilya's ass as I came up, and it was all I could do to keep him from locking Amara in the safe room until this was over," he said heavily.

"She's still in her room?" Noah straightened from the wall and glanced to the connecting door.

The last time he'd seen her she was too pale, her eyes haunted and filled with nightmares.

"Grandpops is with her." His grandfather had actually insisted, even over Amara's objections. "He promised to let me know when he left."

Noah's gaze reflected his sudden amusement, while Tobias nearly failed to smother a laugh as the three men stared back at him.

"Yeah, I know, I know. He's probably showing her every embarrassing picture of me he could pack on his tablet, and relating every youthful indiscretion I ever had. He's hell on a man's ego." Riordan had fought his grandfather over accompanying them, as had Noah and their uncle, Jordan.

At eighty-five, his grandpops didn't need to be in a situation that could easily turn dangerous. Grandpops had only snorted at that and told them the good Lord already knew where and when He'd be coming for him, so he'd just do what he felt was best.

And he felt it was best to haul his ass from the comfort of his son, Grant's, home and accompany them to Colorado.

Ivan, Grandpops said, was a friend, and Amara was now a Malone, whether she remembered it or not. A man always stood with friends and family, he'd declared. And there'd been no dissuading him.

"I'll check with Grandpops and see if he needs a break. I'll sit with her if he does." Noah's gaze met his, understanding filling the darker blue depths. "But you need to do something soon, Riordan. That, my gut is definitely telling me."

And he wasn't the only one who felt that warning rising inside.

With a sharp nod, Riordan picked up the tablet as they left the suite and headed out himself to talk to Amara's father to get everything they needed in place. When he'd first arrived, there had been no warning of trouble, no reason to suspect that whoever had targeted Amara six months ago would be back.

There was still no proof of it, but Riordan couldn't help but feel that something simply wasn't right where that blowout was concerned. Just as he'd felt that whoever was behind the abduction wasn't going to give up. But until Amara remembered what happened that night and who had taken her, they were working blind.

And he couldn't allow that to continue.

"Now, girl, let me tell ya, ma Erin was a gentle little thing," Grandpops remembered with a soft, so-loving smile that Amara couldn't help but marvel at his expression.

For a moment, it was like looking into the face of a young man filled with all the passion and dedication of his first love. "But now, she was pure Irish," he chuckled. "With a temper to match. Kept five boys and one hard-headed husband in line she did."

"No daughters then?" she asked quietly, only to regret the question a moment later.

Grief filled his eyes as a sigh whispered from him.

"A tiny little thing was our girl." Sadness filled his gaze, his expression. "She was thirteen when we lost her." He looked down at his gnarled hands and gave a shake of his head. "She was Irish. Born in Ireland, wouldna ya know." He cleared his throat and blinked, then looked up at her with a somber smile. "She was pushed inta a stream by some bullies that didna like her accent. The fever got her soon after."

Because of judgmental bigots, this kind old man and his wife had lost their only daughter.

"I'm very sorry," she whispered.

Grandpops nodded slowly. "She was a good girl, my Edan. Always smilin', tendin' to her brothers, and always eager to help others. She didn't even blame the boys that pushed her to the water. Said it wasn't their fault what their da's taught them." A mocking smile curved his lips. "One of their das, he was with the men that caused ma Erin to wreck her car that night." He tilted his head and stared at her curiously. "Shoulda I have not blamed him but his da instead, do ya think?"

The quietly voiced question was filled with a resignation that such bigotry was simply part of some people.

"He was old enough to know better." Anger lashed at her for this gentle man's losses. "I hope he's burning in Hell."

He didn't say either way, but Amara saw something hard in his gaze for just a second and she suspected, as gentle as he was, he knew the value of justice.

"I'd had Grant and the baby boy, Jordan, left at the time. We lost Riordan Jr. in one war, and lost Dannan in another. Roark we lost in a car accident the night afore he was to marry." He sighed heavily. "A man should never have ta bury a child. It just never seems right, does it?"

"No, it doesn't." She had to blink back her tears at the loss on his face. To lose four of his children as well as his wife and to still remain so kind was a miracle, she thought.

"I'd have joined ma Erin years ago." He suddenly smiled, his expression turning playful and filled with amusement. "But Jordan was still just a young'un. Then there was Nathan, Grant's boy, and ten years later Grant brought Riordan for me to raise. It's hard for a man to leave when his boys haven't found their way yet. But Erin, she understands these things."

She'd noticed he often talked about his deceased wife as though she still walked by his side.

"We lost Nathan, but we gained Noah," he said with a nod. "An' Riordan, now *he* keeps an old man young he does." He chuckled. "That boy always was more wild Irish I think than the boys that were born there."

There was no doubt his pride in Riordan was tremendous.

"I'll agree with the wild part." She grinned.

"He's a good boy he is. All ma boys are good boys, Amara. Fine Irish boys," he assured her.

For a second, just a second, the shadows in her mind shifted, like the briefest shift of a veil—there then gone. And with the shift came a voice, a husky Irish brogue. *Go síoraí.*

Just as quickly, the shadows blocked memory again, left her fighting against what she couldn't remember but what she sensed, and only a single sound to hold onto.

"Go síoraí," she whispered.

"Ya know the word?" Grandpops asked. "A Gaelic word it is. Ya surprise me."

She surprised herself.

"What does it mean?" She was almost scared to know.

He watched her closely. " 'Forever.' It's the vow all Malone men give when they find their way to that one true love. The one whose soul will cling to theirs."

And why would she know that word?

Before she could ask how she could have possibly heard that word, a quiet knock at the door forestalled her. A second later the door opened, revealing Noah Blake.

"Miss Resnova, is he telling you all the Malone family secrets?" he grinned, stepping a foot or so into the room.

Grandpops chuckled at the question.

"We're just getting' ta know each other a bit, boy. Go amuse yourself elsewhere," he demanded with a grin and a tone filled with fondness.

"Yes, Grandpops," Noah agreed, laughter tingeing his voice as he turned to Amara. "I'm going downstairs. Would you like me have anything sent up to you?"

"Hot chocolate," Grandpops answered, then winked back at Amara. "I think the girl could use a pot of hot chocolate. Soothes the soul it does."

Amara couldn't help the soft laugh that fell from her lips.

"Cook makes a delicious pot of chocolate; if you wouldn't mind to ask him to send some up," she requested. "It soothes the soul."

"I'll take care of it right now." Leaving the room, he closed the door behind him, once again leaving her with the old man's soothing presence.

With the warmth of the gas fireplace whispering over her, the comfort of the butter-soft leather cushioning her body, and Grandpops' quiet company, she was slowly relaxing. The tremors she felt shaking her insides earlier were gone, and as she rested in the corner of the couch she was in no hurry to see the old man leave.

How nice it would have been to have had him for her grandfather, she thought as he told her about living in Ireland. The peat fires, the smell of the sea and the fields of heather. He'd grown up in a family with six boys and three girls, and parents who taught them to laugh and to love.

He told her how he'd met his Erin and found his way, and followed his older brother to America.

When the chocolate came, she drank a cup with Grandpops, then set her cup aside and relaxed in the couch once again to another story.

This one was about Riordan.

As the words drifted around her, her eyes closed; and warmed by the chocolate, the fire, and an old man's memories, Amara drifted off into sleep.

Riordan met his grandfather coming from Amara's room. He closed the door quietly as Riordan stared back at him questioningly.

"She sleeps deep," Grandpops said quietly, his expression, and his gaze somber. "Stay with her. Tonight, keep the nightmares at bay for her."

He frowned, glancing toward her door then back to his grandfather.

"What aren't you telling me, Grandpops?" Sometimes, his grandfather knew the damnedest things.

Wise, knowing blue eyes were filled with compassion as his grandfather gripped his shoulder. "She faced her nightmares today. The possibility, no matter how slight, that whatever happened before could happen again." His expression grew heavier. "She's comin' to her memories soon enough—show her where peace lies, lad."

Lowering his head, his grandfather walked across the hall to his own suite, opened the door slowly, and disappeared inside his room.

Yeah, sometimes Grandpops just knew things. Things a man wasn't always comfortable knowing.

Moving into Amara's suite, he closed and carefully locked the door behind him, then strode to the connecting door to his own room and opened it. He'd hear if anyone knocked and ensure no one knew where he slept.

Then he stepped to the couch and stared down at the woman he'd died for.

Bending, he rested on his haunches and stared at the elegant lines of her face, the short, wild curls that covered her head and fell below her neck. She'd pulled the blanket closer to her as she huddled in the corner of the couch, her nose all but buried in the leather cushions.

She looked like a damn teenager. Too damn fragile and far too innocent for the world.

Beneath the blanket she wore another of those silk pajamas she liked so much.

He'd finally convinced her to sleep naked that last month he spent with her. He'd wanted nothing between them, nothing separating his skin from hers. She'd been so damn shy about leaving her clothes off that he'd laughed at her just before he'd taken her again. All that innocent shyness just made him harder than hell. And melted his heart, even now.

She was such a contradiction at times, even now. Fiery passion and cool feminine determination existed hand in hand, and kept a man guessing from one minute to the next. A wicked sense of humor when she turned it loose, and a gentle heart.

And she terrified him at times.

"Go síoraí," he whispered, a breath of sound as he felt that tug of emotion in his chest.

Rising, he stepped to her bed and turned the blankets down. To keep from terrifying her by sleeping naked beside her he went to his room and changed into a pair of thin cotton pants.

Turning out her lights and leaving only the fire burning, he lifted her gently into his arms and carried her to bed.

Sliding in beside her, he tucked her close against him and felt her settle naturally into the curve of his shoulder as she once had.

"I was cold," she mumbled, more asleep than awake as his arms went around her and he kissed the top of her head gently.

"I'll warm you," he promised her.

Her fingers trailed down his arm to his hand, then twined with his.

"I missed you," she sighed, her voice blurred with sleep, with dreams as his fingers tightened on her. "Don't stay away so long."

"I missed you." God, how he'd missed her.

He'd missed her every long, lonely night, every endless day.

Six months of hell and the only news he had of her was what Noah could get from Cook, their only contact within the house.

Six months of waking in a sweat as he lived her nightmares, her pain, and her fears and fought through each of them to bring her a little peace.

Grandpops had always said that the color of his eyes was a legacy. Irish eyes. Malone men, he claimed, loved with a heart outside their chest, saw with eyes not their own. That their souls became bound to only one woman, and once bound, they were never the same again.

And he'd never really believed.

Even after Noah and Sabella had recounted the hell they'd lived through during the years they were apart, he hadn't really believed. He'd been certain that even if Noah and Sabella had that kind of love, he'd never find it himself.

He hadn't believed until he'd regained consciousness in the hospital after Amara's rescue and saw into her nightmares the first time. A bleak, dark world filled with pain, betrayal, and overwhelming loss. And his Amara was lost in it when the nightmares came. Lost, scared, and alone.

And he'd be damned if she'd be alone any longer.

chapter thirteen

Oh, now that felt so good . . .

The sensations eased over her, stronger than most, hotter, more real than any of the sensual sleeping fantasies she'd had before.

It was these dreams she ached for, the ones she sought when her eyes closed. Here, she found everything that was missing when she was awake, everything she'd forgotten . . .

Though a part of her knew this was no more a dream than the others had been, she wasn't quite ready to admit to it.

Amara stretched beneath the slow, gliding caress along the bare skin of her back. Warm, work roughened, the broad male hand stroked over her flesh, sending sensations racing through her. Heated arcs of pleasure whipped from his touch and surrounded her in warmth and need.

She arched, her leg lifted against the pressure slowly

easing between her thighs, and she gripped warm, muscular shoulders as she lay against him on her side. She needed to be closer, needed the clothing that separated them gone. She needed to be skin to skin, nothing between them.

It had been so long.

So long since he touched her, since he'd taken her.

She couldn't still her moan at the feel of his lips against her sensitive neck. The rake of his teeth, his tongue taking little tastes of her skin. The slow sipping kisses along her neck alternated between sharp, heated tastes of her and lingering caresses that had her trying to get closer.

Delicate nerve endings rioted with sensation. Static pleasure weakened her senses, left her trembling, gasping for more as he rolled her to her back, his hands sliding beneath her shoulders and lifting her to his kisses.

Her head tipped to the side, her lips finding his shoulder as one of those heated, rougher kisses sent arrows of sensations to tighten on her nipples, causing her sex to clench demandingly. Her nails flexed at his shoulders as the incredible pleasure built, increased with each kiss, each lick until the need was clawing her.

"Riordan." She buried her fingers in his hair, clenched them in his thick strands.

Then those incredible, too-knowing lips were on hers, parting them, his tongue owning her mouth, his kisses suddenly greedy, deep, ravenous.

Flames erupted over her body, burning beneath her flesh as the most delicious heat sizzled through her senses. She lived for these dreams, she thought distantly.

Lived for the moments he held her again, touched her again.

Arching beneath him, her thighs parted as he moved between them, his hips settling between hers, the hard length of his shaft pressing against the silk that separated her from him.

Why had she worn anything to bed? She knew if he joined her after she went to sleep he'd torture her with pleasure before he ever removed them.

The torture was so good though.

She ached for it, longed for it. For the kisses that dragged her into that place of complete sensual abandon and pure sensory delight.

His lips moved to her neck again, hungrier, hotter. Hard, heated caresses had a cry spilling from her lips, her hips writhing beneath his. The friction against her clit stole her breath. The rising desperation for more of his touch, for deeper kisses, wild hunger, was growing by the second.

"Yes," she whispered, her head pressing deeper into the pillow, arching closer as she felt his teeth rake her skin, felt the hot, suckling kisses he placed along her neck. "It's so good . . ."

It was incredible.

It had been so long since he'd touched her, so long since she'd felt this fiery lash of arousal tearing through her system.

A low moan left her lips as he pushed one hand beneath the camisole top of her pajamas, pushing it up, his fingers curling around the mound of a breast, cupping it, as his lips covered the sensitive peak.

"Riordan," she cried out, twisting, writhing beneath each sensation.

Spikes of shattering pleasure tore through her senses, raced from her nipple to her womb as he sucked on the peak with firm draws of his mouth. His tongue licked, his teeth scraped against sensitive flesh as he pushed the hunger inside her higher.

Oh God she needed him. If he would just stop with the torture and take her like he used to. He could tease her to death later. Instead, his lips moved to her other breast, drew that nipple in his mouth and treated it to the same intense pleasure.

She couldn't bear it. She needed more. Wanted more.

She'd waited too long . . .

The thought was hazy in her mind. There was something she should know, something she should remember.

"Amara." The sound of her name on his lips as his lips pressed to the curve of her breast had a shaft of denial tearing through her. "Are you awake, baby?"

She didn't want to wake up, ever.

She didn't want to face the fuzzy memories that still whispered through her mind. She didn't want to face the fact that she'd lost so much.

"I don't want to wake up." She couldn't still the hitch of her breath, the sob that threatened to make itself known.

If only she could force whatever she was remembering into focus, make the blurring images within her mind make sense.

Her hands dropped from his head as he pulled back,

his hands gently pulling the material of her top over her breasts before he lifted himself off her.

She wanted to tell him she was dreaming, that she was unaware it wasn't a fantasy as she turned to him, but she knew it wasn't just the dreams that had her turning to him in the dark.

Since she'd come home from the hospital, she'd awakened to the sense that her bed was empty, that something within her was also empty. Until tonight. Until she'd felt him holding her. Until she'd awakened to the knowledge that it wasn't just a dream, but he was really there, touching her, warming her.

And her bed didn't feel empty.

Damn him.

She watched him as he lay on his back, one hand against his chest, staring up at the ceiling, his expression unreadable in the shadowed light of the room. That hard, golden bronze body was sheened with firelight; his erection straining beneath the cotton material of his pants was easy to make out, even in the low light.

She liked to think she wasn't a stupid person. A little naive sometimes, far too innocent other times, but she wasn't stupid. This man was far too comfortable in her bed, and she was far too comfortable with him being there than she would be with a stranger.

Those barely there memories weren't drifting away as they had each time she awoke from one of the erotic dreams in the past. They were there, not exactly clear, not enough to be certain, but enough to suspect that the truths being held from her were far more important than she'd imagined.

She sat up in the bed, turning to him as she crossed her legs and tilted her head to watch him curiously.

Was that suspicion she saw flicker across his expression? Perhaps a bit of wariness?

"Why are you in my bed?" she asked him curiously.

His brow arched slowly, mockingly.

"Are you going to tell your father?" he asked, making no effort to leave her bed. "I hear Resnova has any guard that so much as flirts with you fired."

She smiled sweetly. "Oh, he does. You should see what he does to those bold enough to actually touch me. It would no doubt be interesting to see what he does to one who's found to be in my bed."

Was that a hint of amusement at the edge of his lips as he settled more comfortably against the pillows? One hand lay against the center of his chest while the other curved under his pillow as he stared at her.

"It *would* be interesting," he agreed with far too much arrogance. "Are you going to tell? Or should I?"

Oh yes, that *was* amusement tipping his lips. And that arrogance, the sheer confidence wrapped around him, wasn't as misplaced as it should have been under the circumstances.

"Do you take advantage of your clients' weaknesses often then?" Somehow, she knew better though.

"Want to try again?" the suggestion was made with an undercurrent of a warning.

"So, I was just lucky that way?" she asked him, enjoying the byplay perhaps more than she should.

Oh, he and her father were in so much trouble if what she suspected to be true was actually true.

"You could say that," he drawled, his sapphire gaze definitely amused. "I can be rather picky which clients I take advantage of."

This one was definitely in trouble.

She narrowed her gaze on him before staring around the bedroom for a moment, taking in the darkness outside the French doors, the flickering gas logs, and the air of intimacy that lay over the room.

When she turned back to him, she saw he was watching her closely, his gaze far too familiar.

"You can go back to your own room," she informed him, rather put out with him at the moment now. "As we've established, it's only sleeping clients you take advantage of and I no longer fit that description. Good night, Mr. Malone."

Perhaps if he left, she could at least masturbate and ease the aching need a little herself.

"You like to live on the edge, don't you?" Dark sexuality edged at his voice as he watched her. "You could get more than you bargained for there, sweetheart."

There was something about that look that had her body more sensitive than ever. Something that warned her that pushing him could come with unexpected results.

"My bed, Riordan, my rules." She shrugged as though the warning didn't mean much. "And I think I'm ready to go back to sleep now."

She was uncurling her legs and preparing to do just that when he suddenly moved. Faster than she would have expected, he was on his knees, one hand gripping her hair, holding her in place as he knelt in front of her.

"Your rules?" His voice was rough, far too sexy. "Not this time, baby. This time, we play by my rules."

Would they now?

She allowed a knowing little smile to tip her lips before she leaned forward and pressed them to the hard, flat plane of his abdomen. The muscles clenched then flexed, and a hard breath hissed between his lips.

"You're playing a damn dangerous game," he warned her a second later as her tongue licked over his flesh. "Sure you wanna go there?"

"Do I want to go there?" she mused. "Let me try and find out."

Let her? Let her make him crazy? Let her drive him insane with her touch?

Gripping the hair at the back of her head, Riordan watched as her lips pressed to his lower stomach again, her heated little tongue licking over the area, and felt every muscle in his body clench in anticipation as her lips and tongue delivered heated, hungry caresses.

"God, Amara . . ." The groan tore from his chest as her lips moved along his flesh to the elastic band of the cotton pants he wore.

She'd kill him.

There wasn't a chance in hell that he could maintain control if she got his dick in that hot little mouth of hers. He knew from experience just exactly what her innocent wonder and desperate hunger would do to him.

He'd fuck her. He'd lay her back on that bed like he'd done so many times before and lose himself in her. In her sweet cries, in the tight clasp of her pussy gripping his cock, her arms holding him.

He knew this, but still, he couldn't stop her. She was like a drug he'd never stopped withdrawing from, one he craved every breathing moment since his last taste.

Her teeth raked over the hard planes of his abs as her fingers moved to the band of his pants, instinct and unconscious knowledge converging as he watched her expression become dazed and so filled with arousal that his balls drew up tight to the base of his shaft in reaction. That look on her face had always mesmerized him. The flushed features, her lashes lying against her cheeks.

"Look at me." His fingers clenched in her hair, pulling at the shortened strands just enough to pull her head back as her eyes opened, the cloudy depths meeting his gaze. "If you're going to do it, then watch me. Know who you're doing it to, by God."

Silky, slender fingers tucked beneath the elastic.

"The head jackass," she whispered, some vein of amusement creeping into her voice as she eased the material lower. A breath later she eased it lower, revealing the painfully erect stalk of flesh awaiting her touch.

"Don't close your eyes," he ordered as they began to drift closed again. "I said you'll watch me."

Her gaze on his, sensuality and arousal filled her expression as she gripped the shaft. Her head lowered, her tongue licking slow and easy around the throbbing, mushroomed crest.

Sweet Jesus have mercy on him.

His hips jerked at the heated caress, the need to fill her mouth almost overcoming what little control he had left.

Oh, he knew the brazen little sensualist kneeling between his thighs, even if she didn't remember. And he knew exactly what she liked, what she longed for. How she loved that harder edge, the dominance and sheer force he could take her with. How she'd tease and taunt until he made her take what he knew she wanted.

His eyes narrowed on her as her fingers trailed down the shaft, the uncertainty, instinct vying with lack of memory and driven by the same hungers that tormented him night after night.

Curling her fingers at the base, unable to completely circle the wide flesh, she held the throbbing shaft steady, licked her lips, and stared up at him with a silent plea.

Lack of memory versus subconscious knowledge—which would win? he wondered.

"You've come this far." He had to force himself to speak, force himself not to push the throbbing crest past her parted lips. "Finish it, or stop torturing the hell out of me."

Finish it.

Oh God, she wanted to finish it. She wanted to close her eyes and sink into that place where hunger overrode everything, even the confusion and fear.

"Don't you dare close your eyes," he demanded as her lashes lowered once again. "If you're going to drive me fucking crazy, then you can watch me while you do it."

Demanding and forceful, he wasn't going to let up, wasn't going to allow her to hide from the knowledge that somehow she knew she'd done this before. She'd done him before.

Keeping her eyes on his, she did as he demanded. She watched him. Kept her gaze on the sapphire depths, parted her lips, and surrounded the thick, heated crest she was so hungry for.

As his hips jerked, burying the full length of the mushroomed head in her mouth, taste exploded on her tongue. Earthy, tinged with a hint of a hot summer night, and all male. The hardened flesh clenched, throbbed, and another taste—subtle with a hint of male saltiness—touched her tongue. And she wanted more. She wanted that taste filling her senses and locking her inside the sensuality of it.

"That's it," he groaned as her mouth tightened on it. "Suck it inside. Suck me, Amara. See how crazy you can make me."

Could she make him crazy? She was certainly going to try her damnedest.

Stroking the heavily veined shaft, she drew the blunt width as deep as possible, stroked it with her tongue, sucked at it, and found she could become as lost in his gaze as she could in the darkness if her eyes were closed.

Teeth clenched, his expression stricken with lust, his fingers clenched in her hair, sending tiny darts of pinching heat through her scalp as she sucked him and tugged at the hold each time her head lowered to take him deeper. It eased as she lifted, her tongue swiping, licking, and tasting, only to burn again as she took his iron flesh deeper.

She loved this. Loved watching the flush that mounted his cheekbones, the way his nostrils flared, the way the muscles at his jaw clenched.

"Fuck yeah," he whispered as her mouth tightened on him, her tongue rubbing beneath the crest as the moist sounds of her sucking pleasure filled her ears. "Oh baby, that's it. Sweet God . . ."

His hips jerked as she took him marginally deeper and a breathless moan vibrated in her throat. The cords at his throat tightened, a rivulet of sweat drifted down the side of his face.

His gaze narrowed, something too knowing, too hungry flashed in his eyes as his fingers clenched her hair tighter and began pulling, releasing, forcing her head back, then pushing it down.

"Deeper," he demanded as another moan left her throat. "Let me feel that hungry little sound on my dick. Swallow me baby, and when you get done . . ." A throttled growl rumbled from his own throat as she did just that.

She took him deeper and moaned, felt the warning clench of his cock and knew it wouldn't take much more to push him over the edge.

"I swear to God, when I get between those pretty legs, I'm going to shove my tongue so deep up that tight little pussy you won't have a choice but to come from it."

The vision ripped through her senses. The thought of him holding her to him, his tongue pushing inside her was too much. Her body tightened, the heated slide of her response between the swollen folds of her pussy a caress, a torturous touch of hungry need.

Her mouth moved on him, sucked him as deep as possible as another moan tore from her. She wanted it. Wanted the taste of his release. Wanted to find her own as he pushed his tongue inside her. Consumed her with his lust.

He was moving her against him faster, the tug and release of her hair making her crazy with the burning pinch of sensation to her scalp, over and over again.

Would he be as forceful as he took her?

Would he give her what she dreamed of? A hard hand delivering firm taps to her ass, to the wet folds between her thighs? Would he . . .

"Damn you. Fuck . . ." He tightened, the curse a hoarse groan as she suckled him harder, taking him as deep as her mouth allowed, her moans rising, her hunger for him growing as her tongue lashed beneath the head.

"Amara . . ." His voice was almost strangled, desperate, as she loved the taste, the feel of him in her mouth.

It was like a drug, potent and overwhelming, the power she felt as she pleasured him. The male taste of him, each throb of his cock and shallow thrust of his hips, pushing the crest inside her mouth, sent her senses spiraling deeper into the hunger building inside her.

She didn't know the woman kneeling in front Riordan, working her mouth over the male flesh and loving every harsh groan that left his throat. She didn't know the body burning for him, slick with her own wet heat and dying for his touch.

And amid the desperate breaths and his hard growl came a strident, eerie sound . . .

"Fuck no!" Riordan snarled.

One moment he filled her mouth, the next he was off the bed and jerking his phone from the table next to the bed. Features that were tight with lust were now savage with fury.

"Riordan . . . ?"

"Come on." In a single move, the pants were at his hips and he had ahold of her wrist, dragging her from the bed. "That's the alarm. Someone's managed to get past the main wall."

chapter fourteen

Someone was playing with them, Riordan could feel it. The alarm had been set off by a tree limb that had apparently snapped the day before. It just so happened to have landed on the one section of the wall they hadn't finished the upgraded electronics or cameras for yet.

From all appearances, it had just broken off and fallen. The break was jagged enough to support that theory. Under any other circumstances, Riordan could have given it the benefit of doubt.

Under any other *normal* circumstances, that is, but this wasn't exactly normal. The same night that they'd also had problems with their SUV? He simply wasn't buying it.

Riordan could feel the icy rage beginning to build an hour later as he met with Noah, Micah, and Ivan in Ivan's office.

The other man wore jeans for a change, shirt and leather coat, with a weapon strapped to his thigh.

He could see the steel will and pure icy control that took Ivan out of the Russian crime family he'd once been a part of and into a fortune in legitimate business enterprises. The determination to do whatever it took, to push any limits he had to push, was there in his hard, savage expression, in his stubborn will.

Ivan had always said that for Amara, he'd changed the course of his life and tried to become the man she could find some pride in. A man an intelligent daughter could love. For the most part, he'd succeeded, but Riordan could also see the man who had already been honed by deceit, blood, and lies. A man willing to use every criminal lesson he'd ever been taught to save his daughter.

"They're testing my security," he growled as he strode to the bar and uncapped the whiskey Grandpops had brought him a supply of.

After tossing back the first shot, he poured five more as Ilya collected them and handed them out. Riordan let the first sip of the homemade liquor burn its way down, the fiery wash stilling only a small amount of his rage.

"You have a spy in the house, Ivan," Riordan warned him. "That's the only area we didn't have completely finished. If we hadn't put the alarms in place and tied them to our phones instead of waiting to tie them into the electronics, they would have gotten in."

And no one knew they'd manually programmed the alarms in such a way. Even Ivan.

"The wind could have actually brought that tree limb down in just the right place," Noah pointed out, though Riordan could tell by the tone of his voice that he didn't actually support his own theory.

They just couldn't ignore it.

Shooting his brother a brooding look, Riordan finished his drink before taking the glass to the bar and placing it next to Ivan's. But not for a refill. Dawn would make its appearance within the hour, and that section of the security system was going to be finished before that blizzard struck. There would be no getting out of the estate for days afterward, and hopefully, no getting in.

"I have to leave in the morning." Ivan grimaced, worry reflecting in his gaze as he glanced to his assistant, Ilya. "I'll no doubt be stuck at the hotel in Boulder for the duration of the storm. Amara would be far safer here."

"That will leave us short of security personnel," Noah pointed out.

He gave his head a slight shake. "The agents you requested will be here later this morning. I'll take two of the house security with me."

"It'll be good to have them back." Riordan nodded before looking out the window and gauging the cloud cover thickening in the predawn sky. "We'll have snow by tomorrow evening if not sooner."

Ivan nodded at that though he said nothing in reply.

"I'll oversee the work on the remaining security installation this morning," Micah offered. "That way we'll keep our schedule. Noah will take second watch, and once Max and Sawyer show up, Noah can settle the rest of the day with them."

Riordan glanced briefly at his brother before turning back to Ivan. "I want Amara's medical file as well the therapist's notes. I want to know why those memories are blocked, and I'm not getting anywhere with her."

Ivan simply stared back at him for long moments, his expression considering, thoughtful. Riordan couldn't help but wonder at that moment, what he was hiding, though. He knew Ivan. He'd worked for him for the past several years in Brute Force as well as a few jobs he'd done for the Elite Ops that Noah oversaw.

The fact that the Elite Operations division had been pulled in on this didn't surprise him, but the lack of information where Amara's medical records were concerned did.

Reaching up, Ivan rubbed at his forehead, his hand shading the side of his left eye as he stared back at Riordan. He was hiding something. Something he wasn't comfortable about, and if the tense set of his lips was any indication, it pissed him the hell off. Was it what he was hiding, or the fact that he was hiding it, that pissed him off?

"How will her medical records answer that question? You're no doctor, Riordan." The scorn in his voice was telling.

He'd studied people long enough—and Ivan in particular, for years. As implacable as the man could be, he still had his tells, those tiny ways his expression gave him away.

"Let *me* determine whether or not those records will help me," he countered. "I want them and I want them today."

If he didn't get them from Ivan, there were other ways to acquire them. Flicking a look to Noah, he noticed his brother was watching the other man closely as well, though he was being far subtler about it.

And if he wasn't mistaken, Ivan would do whatever it took to keep those records from him.

"No." Ivan rose to his feet. His expression, as icy and arrogant as it became, also held an edge of grief. "The medical records will have to wait."

They would have to wait?

Riordan narrowed his gaze on the other man, watching him carefully, noting the slightest edge of grief not only in his eyes but in the flicker of emotion tightening his lips.

Not that Riordan could blame him for his grief. God no. The grief and guilt rested on his shoulders as well. He should have never taken that assignment in England. He shouldn't have left her. He'd known that at the time. He'd felt it clear to his soul, and he'd left anyway. That was on him, and he'd never allow it to happen again.

"Don't, Riordan," Ivan said as he stared at him. "Not right now. It's not in her best interests, and I don't believe the reason she lost her memory is in those medical records. I think the reason she lost her memory is because she knew you died in that helicopter. I think she lost her memory because of you."

Because he'd died. Because in those first moments that he'd been lifted into the evac chopper his heart had stopped beating. Noah and Micah had told him of the fight they'd waged to keep him alive as the pilot raced for the nearest hospital equipped to perform the surgery he required.

They'd lost him twice, then twice more during surgery. He didn't remember the struggle or his fight to live, though the doctors were amazed he'd actually done so.

Don't die for me, she'd cried out to him as they lifted her out of that hole.

He remembered her crying out his name when that first bullet struck him and again when the second slammed into his back. He didn't remember a lot after that but he did remember her crying out, begging him not to leave her.

She hadn't lost her memory before that chopper lifted off, she'd lost consciousness. When she'd regained it, she'd lost a year of her life.

From the day she'd met him, to the moment she lost consciousness.

Because of him.

A woman who had done everything possible to hide a relationship with a man lost her memory because she thought she'd lost that man?

"I want those records," he repeated. "Today."

Turning on his heel, Riordan stalked to the door, jerked it open, and left the office. He didn't slam the door behind him, but God knew he wanted to. He wanted to rip the damn thing off the hinges.

As bad as he wanted to disbelieve Ivan's reasons for Amara's loss of memory, he couldn't. Something had been off with her for the entire three months he'd been sleeping with her. Even before then. She'd been holding back, and he'd thought it was shame. Shame wasn't a reason to forget a year of a person's life.

And he'd been playing fucking patty-cake with that stubborn-assed woman when he should have been playing hardball right from the start. Whatever the hell had caused her to shut out a year of her life, Ivan had been right, the time coincided with the time he'd met her, to the second she'd lost consciousness on the chopper.

Why?

He wouldn't be able to answer that question until she remembered, just as he knew she wouldn't be safe until she remembered.

She was holding back, just as she'd held back before she'd lost her memories.

For some reason, Amara was determined not to remember.

chapter fifteen

The storm was on them.

Already, fat fluffy flakes of snow were drifting on the air outside the estate, falling around the heated solarium with lazy abandon. Clouds were lying thick and heavy, obliterating the sight of the mountaintops and giving the landscape a pre-dusk look despite the early hour.

According to the weather report, the snow would soon be flying thick and heavy, making the land around the estate treacherous to be out in. Even the gardens outside the heated glass room attached to her father's office would be dangerous. But then, that was why he'd had the room built, because Amara loved to watch it snow.

Poppa wasn't there to share that first snowfall with her though, as he had been in years past.

Business, he'd said.

Business.

She was never certain exactly what his business was

when he said that. Was he the mafia lord his father had been grooming him to be when she was born, or just the slightly shady businessman, as he always assured her?

Or was he in league with a slightly shady government agency, as she'd once suspected?

Not that it mattered in the scheme of things, she guessed.

He was her poppa and she had to trust that he wasn't the criminal that journalists and rival businessmen accused him of being. She had to trust that he was the man who taught her to be independent, to think for herself. He hadn't raised her to blindly and obediently follow him as his father had tried to raise his children.

He loved her and he'd taught her to love. And he'd taught her to be honest, not just with others, but with herself. And if she had to be honest with herself, she had to admit something wasn't right where Riordan was concerned. Especially her reaction to him.

She'd never wanted a man the moment she'd laid eyes on him. She'd never felt as though she knew him intimately when she hadn't. And she'd never, to her knowledge, gone down on a man. What made it worse was the fact that she'd known how to please him, how make him moan for her, how to pull those harsh, male groans from his chest.

Rubbing at her upper arms, she turned from the view long enough to check the fireplace and replenish the wood before curling in the corner of the leather sofa to view the flames as well as the blizzard blowing in. Pulling the imitation fur blanket around her legs, she let her fingers linger on the exquisite quality of the beautiful fake wolf's fur.

As her fingers stroked the soft material, her eyes drifted closed, but not in drowsiness.

It was one of those barely there, wispy memories of lying before the fire, her naked back cushioned by the thick comfort of several heavy blankets beneath her. Above her, the bronzed perfection of Riordan's body.

Her sex clenched at the ghostly sensations of a caress and within the fog that hid so much from her, she saw images so sexy they stole her breath. So erotic, so dark and filled with lust that a flush heated her flesh to think that she had actually done such things.

Swallowing deeply, she forced her eyes open as she felt her breasts swelling, her nipples beading with sexual need. Between her thighs, she was slick and damp and aching for touch. For his touch.

Her fingers clenched in the blanket, her eyes narrowed on the scene outside.

It had been snowing then as well. An early spring snow, one of those end-of-the-season storms that blew in and held the land captive for several days, making skiers ecstatic. She'd found a far different ecstasy in this room, before this fire.

For a moment, the sound of her moans drifted through her head as he whispered at her ear. Wicked, naughty phrases, demands that had acted like a drug to her senses. The feel of her own hands touching herself as he watched, watching him as those long, powerful fingers stroked the heavy width of his shaft.

"Show me," he demanded, his voice dark, commanding. "Let me see how you stroke yourself when I'm not here . . ."

She covered her face with her hands, a deep sense of disbelief sweeping over her as the memory materialized slowly. It wouldn't be kind enough to flash across her mind. Hell no. She had to relive it in slow motion, the fog parted enough to remember how she'd used an intimate toy on herself as he watched. Driving it inside her, lost in his gaze, desperate for release.

Just as she'd dreamed of him last night. Disjointed, sex-driven dreams that were so explicit, so erotic, she could barely believe she'd done such things. Or allowed them to be done to her.

She'd tried for days to convince herself that it was just fantasy, her mind playing tricks on her, her intense arousal for Riordan, but after the night before, there was no denying it.

"Remembering how we used this room, baby?" Riordan's low, deep voice vibrated from behind her, causing her to jerk her head to the side.

A blush suffused her entire body as he walked slowly around the couch, his gaze watching her closely in the dim light of the solarium. Her head turned as she followed him, watching him carefully as he walked in front of the couch and stared down at her. His expression was in shadow now, but the gleam of his gaze held her, just as the hunger on his face did.

"Oh, sure I am," she declared mockingly. "Too bad you weren't here to remind me."

His lips tightened, but she could see the grin that wanted to escape. The bastard. He was laughing at her. Amused by her anger and her uncertainty.

Amused by her.

"I have some damn good memories from this solarium," he said, looking around before returning his gaze to hers. "Damn good ones."

"Stop." Her fingers clenched in the fur, digging into it as she fought against too many emotions she simply didn't know to process.

They didn't make sense. There were no memories to give them definition, or depth. They lashed at her, undefined and lost and so filled with a sense of grief that they made no sense. She didn't want to deal with them. She didn't want to try to make sense of barely there whispers and shadowed suspicions any longer.

"I can't deal with you tonight." Throwing the blanket, she surged to her feet, intent on escaping, running from him and everything she didn't know how to feel.

"Well, too fucking bad, stubborn-ass," he snapped, his arm snagging her waist before she made it two steps and dragging her against his chest.

"Did you think I wasn't coming for you? That after this morning, there wouldn't be a reckoning, Amara?" His fingers gripped her jaw, holding her head in place, forcing her to stare up at him. "Did you think I was going to let you continue to hide from me?"

Savage and imposing, his expression seemed carved from stone and inset with sapphires as his gaze held hers. There was hunger, lust, and anger and something remorseful that shadowed his gaze.

"Why, if we were lovers, would I hide from you?" She jerked against his grip, glaring up at him, so angry— at him, at herself, at things she couldn't remember, and at events she was too terrified to relive. "Maybe it was all wishful thinking on my part."

She was lying to him and she knew it. Her body remembered, and the shadowed images slowly making themselves known within that abyss of lost knowledge assured her she knew. For six months she'd waited for him, and she could deny it to him until Hell froze over, but truth was truth.

His eyes narrowed, his thick, black lashes shielding whatever thoughts his gaze could help her decipher. "Liar," he growled. "I always knew when you were lying to me, and you're no better at it now than you were then. And I'll tolerate it even less now."

Amara couldn't help but be surprised, shocked by his claim. She'd never dated men like him, and she'd had offers. Strong, proud men, arrogant and imposing and so damn certain of themselves. They treated her like a child, like a possession, and her father hadn't raised her to be any man's possession. He'd raised her to be just as strong, just as arrogant, until the day she stared into sapphire eyes across a restaurant table and felt her femininity in a way she'd never imagined she could.

That memory was suddenly there. Hazy, uncertain, and shadowed. The way he stared at her when her father introduced them, the deep pitch of his voice as he greeted her, the touch of his hand against hers, and she'd known this was the man she'd tried so hard to avoid. The man who would replace so many life plans . . .

"Let me go!" She jerked against the hold he had on her even as she realized how weak her demand was.

The arm around her back tightened, and if his expression could become harder, could become more stubborn, than she couldn't imagine it.

"So you can keep lying to yourself?" His head

lowered until they were almost nose to nose. "So you can keep hiding from yourself and whatever happened during that fucking abduction?" Fury flashed in his eyes.

"You left me." The cry tore from her when she hadn't even realized the accusation was in her mind. "You weren't there."

He would have been in the bed with her. He and his team would have been in place, not those men who worked for money alone.

Even as she said the words, the unfairness of it slapped her with a lash of sorrow.

"I didn't mean that," she whispered, her hands suddenly clenching his shoulders, desperate that he realize she didn't blame him. "Please. God. Riordan, I didn't mean that. I don't blame you . . ."

Because she could have kept him from leaving. How she knew that, she didn't understand. But the certainty that it was the truth filled her, causing regret to tear at her.

"You don't have to blame me." His hold tightened on her, the hand on her jaw moved, cupping her cheek instead. "You don't have to blame me, Amara, because I know you wouldn't have been there if I'd stayed. I blame myself."

His thumb brushed against her lower lip softly, his gaze softening a bit, a very little bit. She wanted to sob at the look on his face. The hunger that filled it was like a drug in her system, filling her, washing through her, and weakening with needs she had no idea how to decipher.

"Riordan . . ."

"I was going to take you to Texas that week, do you remember? Grandpops wanted to meet you. I wanted to show you my home." There was something in his voice, something that hinted that he had wanted her to see more than just his home.

"It wouldn't have changed anything," she tried to protest.

"It would have, Amara," he promised her. "It would have, because I would have never taken your safety for granted. I might have been sleeping in your bed, but there wasn't a night I didn't take precautions to make certain the hours I spent listening to you cry out in plea-sure didn't endanger you."

For one precious second, she lost her breath.

Hours spent pleasuring her? Had he really spent hours? She had plenty of friends who had lovers and they never mentioned "hours spent" being pleased.

"I can't . . ." She tried to tell him she couldn't remem-ber, couldn't talk about this.

"The night we spent here, in this room, in front of this fire, I spent hours taking you, touching you. Do you remember?" he asked, his voice lowering as he pulled her tighter against him. "It was snowing then too."

The snow falling around the glass-enclosed room, the fire burning as she lay on the thick, cushioned rug. His body over her, his expression savage.

"No . . ."

"Liar," he whispered, his head lowering again to brush against her lips as his gaze held hers captive as he held her body. "We rode each other to exhaustion that night. There's no way you don't remember it."

There wasn't a single ounce of uncertainty in his voice.

"You don't . . ." She tried to protest that he didn't know what he was talking about, again.

"I dreamed about it last night, Amara," he growled. "Did you dream with me? Did you dream of me going down on you as you watched? Watched my lips, my tongue, tasting all that silken, pretty flesh between your thighs?"

A harsh, involuntary inhalation of air gave her away. Because she had dreamed. And the memory of those dreams had a flush washing through her again, heating her face, her body, as anticipation increased the need only building through her senses.

"And no one told me I didn't just forget my life, but my lover," she whispered painfully, staring into his eyes as he came to one knee in front of her, keeping her in place when she would have risen, would have run from him. "Someone had to have known."

A mocking smile tilted his lips. "No one knew about us, Amara. Just you and me."

There was something about the way he said it, an edge of anger in his voice. He stared back at her.

"You could have told me." Her fists clenched as shards of broken dreams and nightmares pierced her head.

He'd been her lover. She wouldn't have let him anywhere near her bed if she didn't love him. She knew that much about herself.

"What happened?" she demanded when he wouldn't speak. "Why didn't you come back? Why did you make me find you?"

Had he left her? She would have loved him, a part of

her evidently still remembered too many emotions where he was concerned because her response to him was too strong. Her need for him was too strong.

"That's something *you* have to remember." His voice deepened, became darker. "I just thought I'd help you with it."

Before she could do more than gasp, he gripped her forearms and tugged, bringing her off the couch and into his arms. Turning, he had her back on the thick rug as he rose over her, locking her firmly in place.

"You left me, didn't you?" She could feel it in the heavy pain that tightened her chest and the regret as she stared up at him. She knew he'd left her.

"Remember, Amara." A vein throbbed at his temple as some unknown emotion flashed in his eyes. "You forgot *me*, not the other way around." His expression was brooding, turning savage as firelight shadowed his features.

Her hands tightened at his shoulders as she struggled to remember and tried to fight the languorous weakness invading her. There was something she needed to find in the fog that tumbled and swirled through her. Something she'd lost . . .

Before she could remember anything, his lips covered hers, his tongue parted them, and he stole any resistance she might have managed. It was hunger and anger, greedy lust with something dark and wild.

And it was impossible to resist.

Was that her whimper she heard? That mewling little sound of pleasure . . . that and hunger, like a woman too long denied.

She had been too long denied. She had to have been,

because her arms refused to push him away. Her fingers pushed into his overly long black hair, clenched and luxuriated in the feel of the strands caressing them.

Her lips parted for him, accepted him, and in less than a second she was caught up in the sudden whirlwind of sensations whipping through her body.

Oh, her body remembered him. Her lips remembered his kiss, her tongue remembered his taste, and it was intoxicating. Drugging. It was better than any dream or fantasy she could have conjured up.

As his kiss deepened, his tongue licking against hers, tasting her, letting her taste him, she felt consumed by the needs rising inside her, overwhelmed by them.

"Riordan," she gasped when he eased back, just enough to give her air as she felt the material of her robe part and fall away. As the material eased across the bodice of her gown, his hand was there, cupping, molding the flesh as his thumb found the hard point of her nipple.

Forcing her eyes open and staring up at him, she watched as the blue of his eyes deepened, became more sapphire as his pupils dilated with lust. The savage planes and angles of his face were harsh with need, the brooding expression made more so by the shadows cast by the firelight.

She had to touch him, touch his face, ease the stark look of pain about his eyes. But as her fingers touched his face, it became about something more. Watching her fingers touch him, she became mesmerized by the feelings that overtook her. And she knew she'd done this before. She'd laid beneath him, just touching his face, just . . .

Her breath caught. So close. She had been so close to remembering something. Before she could make sense of it his lips were covering hers again, his tongue sweeping across them, parting them and then pushing inside in a dominant thrust of pure male hunger.

So long . . .

The feel of him settling against her, his lips on hers, his thumb stroking her nipple and sending clashing sensations racing through her—it was more than she wanted to fight—more than she could fight. This wasn't another dream. She couldn't excuse her inability to resist it, to resist him, on a fantasy or an illusion she'd slipped into. And it was far better than any illusion she'd ever built in her mind.

"Beautiful," he whispered, his lips drifting from hers to her jaw, her neck. "So beautiful."

He didn't just drop a few kisses along her neck on his path lower, he stole her senses with his lips, with the rake of his teeth, with the licking strokes of his tongue.

Oh God, she loved it.

The feel of his lips, just a little rough, caressing the sensitive skin of her neck was incredible. Her head tipped back, nails biting into the material of his shirt as she felt him pull aside the elastic bodice of her vintage gown.

"Damn," he whispered, his head drawing back, his broad, callused palms stroking not just her nipples, but caressing her breasts, cupping them, stroking them. "How I love your pretty breasts, Amara. Those pretty, hard little nipples."

His lips covered one tight peak in an inferno of searing

sensations, lashing pleasure, and firm draws of his mouth.

Amara heard the cry that escaped her lips and knew she'd be shocked later. Just as she'd be shocked by her hand sliding into his hair to hold him to her, to feel the incredible pleasure as long as possible.

"Sweet baby," he groaned, his head lifting a second before her other nipple was treated as well.

Oh God, she could barely breathe for the pleasure. It was incredible. The feel of his thighs against hers, his erection pressing against her between his jeans and her gown, rubbing against the mound of her sex.

His lips, his mouth sucking at her nipple, his hand caressing her other breast. And it wasn't enough. She wanted more. She needed to feel him closer, skin to skin. So much so that before she knew it she was tugging at his shirt, desperate to feel his flesh against hers.

"Take it off," she panted, pulling at the material again, her breathing ragged as desperate need began to build inside her. "Now. Take it off."

Levering himself, he did just that, grabbed the bottom of his shirt and all but tore it off.

Muscle rippled beneath his chest and abdomen, in his biceps and forearms. Then he was releasing his belt, tearing at the snap and zipper of his jeans before his lips came down on hers once again.

Deep, drugging kisses, wild with desperate hunger and overwhelming pleasure filled her senses. She was only distantly aware of the fact that he'd quickly shed his clothes. All that mattered was he was naked and hot against her, the warmth of his flesh sinking into her and easing the aching chill she'd felt for so many long months.

When he released her senses again and drew back, there was no regaining sanity. In a matter of seconds her robe and gown were removed, leaving her naked and aching before him.

There was no shame, no hesitancy in her. When his kisses began easing down her body, gentle sips of her flesh and heated nips, there was only anticipation. She'd dreamed of this for so long. So many nights she'd spent suspended in a pleasure that only built her desperation for more.

Pushing her legs apart, he settled between them, his broad shoulders holding them open; and between, his head lowered as her eyes opened, watching, desperate. It was a kiss that destroyed her.

Amara's neck arched as pleasure sliced through her senses.

Riordan's tongue slid through the narrow slit of her pussy in a slow, gliding stroke, found her clit, circled it, and destroyed her mind.

His hands slid beneath her rear to lift her closer, making her intimate flesh more accessible to his hungry kiss. Her hands buried in his hair once again, her hips lifting to him, her senses exploding with so many sensations they overwhelmed her.

As his lips and tongue toyed with her clit, she felt his fingers at the entrance of her sex, easing inside her, slowly filling her. Riotous arcs of pleasure lashed at her, pulling a low, desperate cry from her lips as he stroked her inside and out.

Oh God, nothing should feel this good, this powerful. It was like being pulled into a storm of too many emotions, too many sensations, all refusing to relent.

Each lash of pleasure only built, grew in intensity until she was arching against him, begging for more.

She'd make sense of it tomorrow, she assured herself. She'd make sense of all the emotions, the flashes of memory and the desperation some other time. Nothing mattered now but each lick, each kiss, each thrust of his fingers inside her, filling her, pushing her closer to the brink of a release.

As his lips surrounded the sensitivity of her clit, and the pressure of his fingers inside her increased, she knew she'd never survive the explosion coming.

It built inside her until she was crying his name, begging him.

"Please . . . please . . ." The words were falling from her lips, gasping cries she couldn't hold in as the thrusts of his fingers increased, penetrating her, stroking inside her in cadence with the suckling heat of his mouth at the straining bud he held captive.

"Riordan . . ." she gasped as she felt herself closer, teetering on the edge of chaos.

Her skin was damp with sweat, her hands desperate as she held his head to her. Her hips writhed, arched. There was no escaping nor getting closer to the unrelenting lash of rapture stealing her mind.

Just when she was certain she couldn't survive it, knew she'd die from the buildup of tension inside her body, every breath, each sensation and jagged lash of pleasure exploded inside her.

She felt herself trying to draw in enough air to scream, but she couldn't make a sound. Her body tightened, became nothing but a mass of exploding ecstasy, and

Riordan was the catalyst who refused to allow her to escape the diabolical pleasure tearing through her.

Just when she felt that final detonation of rapture easing away, he was rising between her thighs, the broad head of his cock pushing against the entrance his fingers had filled and pushing inside her.

Already clenched, spasms of release attacking it, her pussy began parting for the penetration, stretching to accommodate the heavy width of his erection as the additional sensations, the fiery lash of the invasion, threw her into another storm. This one more violent than the last, and destroying the last of her sanity.

Her hands gripped his back as he came over her with a groan, hips pressing between hers, his cock burrowing deeper. Each thrust and retreat took him deeper, stretched her tighter around him and stroked against nerve endings so violently sensitive that each impalement only intensified the edge of pleasure and pain she was poised on. All she knew was that she needed more.

"Sweet baby," Riordan groaned as he nipped her ear. "That's it sweetheart. Take me. Suck me in . . ."

Her hips jerked, burying him deeper.

"Fuck yeah. Take me, Amara. All of me, baby. Every fucking . . . inch . . ." He powered inside her, drove the thick wedge of flesh fully inside her as her wail of pleasure echoed around her.

"Riordan . . ." She writhed beneath him. Her inner flesh flexed and rippled repeatedly, involuntarily, as she fought to accommodate the intrusion even as her body, greedy for every touch, every sensation, sang its pleasure.

"God, Amara . . ." he gasped at her neck, his body

straining as he possessed her, each muscle tight, bunching against her as his cock throbbed inside her. "That's it . . . ah hell, that's it baby, let that sweet pussy suck my dick."

Her womb spasmed, the flesh surrounding him flexed in a deep, clenching caress that nearly drove the breath from her lungs.

"Fuck!" He jerked against her, his hips drawing back then suddenly pushing forward again and driving deep.

The shock of the thrust had her nails biting into his back in reaction and gasping cries falling from her lips.

Her knees bent, hips lifting him, silently begging for more, desperate for more.

And he gave it to her.

His groan echoed in her ears as he began moving, fucking her in deep, rhythmic thrusts, pushing inside her, filling her, retreating and impaling her again until their bodies writhed together, frantically reaching for and finally throwing her into a fiery explosion that overtook all her senses.

As the cataclysm raced through her, she felt his thrusts increase, become harder, stronger, until he drove inside her in a final thrust that had him stiffening against her, her name falling from his lips as she felt his cock pulse inside her as he found his own release.

Collapsing beneath him, exhaustion drawing her into a black velvet embrace, Amara gave herself to it. Just for a moment, she promised herself. Not long enough to dream, just long enough to relish the overpowering contentment beginning to fill her.

Just long enough to let herself regroup before she faced the man she had forced herself to forget . . .

chapter sixteen

Riordan bit back a groan as he eased his cock from the grip her body had on it. Sweet, silken flesh still flexed around the semi-hard erection as he retreated, as though trying to hold him inside her.

Collapsing beside her, he forced himself to slide the condom that covered his cock free before disposing of it in the fire that blazed across from them.

Then, sitting next to her, one arm propped on his upraised knee, he pushed his fingers through his hair and stared at the woman who drew him to her, even past death.

He felt his chest clench at the sight of her lying against the thick rug, her black hair framing her stubborn features, her lips parted as she breathed, those expressive eyes closed as she slept.

He'd never forget the sight of her when he'd found her in that damn dark little hole, bones broken, bloody, so weak. And so desperate to stay there and die rather than face the risk she knew might await him as they pulled her free.

Riordan hadn't gone in with just the men from his Brute Force rescue team. Hell no. He'd called Noah, and his brother had come with the highly advanced shadow team he commanded with the covert private Elite Ops warriors. Dead men. Men who trained like no other group. And still, the enemy had almost taken away his chance to claim her.

Whoever had kidnapped her had known her father would send in the best, and they'd been waiting. The first group waiting for them had been taken out easily enough, but Riordan had known that somewhere, somehow, there would be more.

He couldn't risk Amara or his brother. Noah had lived through hell, just as his wife Sabella had, during the years they'd believed he was dead. When he'd returned with a new face and a new name, he'd been given a second chance with the woman who hadn't been able to let him go.

Just as Riordan hadn't been able to let Amara go and as Amara hadn't been able to let him go.

Why had she forced herself to forget?

The psychiatrist Noah had brought in had made that determination within weeks as she recuperated in the hospital. But why she'd forced herself to forget, the doctor couldn't say. That wasn't to say he didn't know. His exact words were that he "couldn't say." Psycho gibberish for the fact that Ivan probably threatened to rip his nuts off if he told. Because there was no doubt in Riordan's mind that Ivan knew why.

So what had made Amara forget a year of her life, including the identity of the men who kidnapped her, and nearly killed not just her, but him as well?

Turning, he dragged the thick throw blanket free of the couch and covered Amara carefully. The fire was warm, but the delicate shiver he'd seen wash over her couldn't be allowed to continue.

She was often cold from what he saw, and Ivan had made certain there were thick throws and small, warm blankets in the sitting areas she was known to rest in. Fires were kept burning in the fireplaces and every attempt was made to make certain she didn't chill.

Why?

Ivan was like a bear with a sore paw, even more so than normal, where Amara was concerned. Before, he'd been bad enough, but now there was an edge of grief about him when he looked at his daughter.

"What happened to you, pretty girl?" Riordan sighed heavily, staring at her features, amazed that the bastards who had struck her hadn't broken the fragile bones of her face.

But they'd broken other bones. Two ribs, her leg, and her wrist, and they'd kicked her hard enough to put a hairline fracture in her pelvis.

There was no way she could have pulled herself out that hole, despite the ladder they'd left in place to tempt her. They were going to let her die as she stared at her only means of escape, unable to use it.

And still, they didn't know why.

All they knew was that her nightmares were growing worse. And as they did, the attempts to breach the security of the estate were increasing in number. Someone was testing them, searching for a weak spot. Someone who was damn good at it.

And as much as her father hated it, even he had to acknowledge that someone on the inside had to be helping whoever was so determined to get to her.

The original abduction had all the earmarks of an inside job as well, though the bodyguards on duty at the time had passed even Noah's stringent vetting. They'd had the code into the penthouse, they'd breached the apartment, and within minutes they were exiting with Amara. Tracking them had taken all of Noah's resources, which were far superior to Ivan's.

Easing beside her once again and pulling her against him, he tucked her head against his chest and shared his warmth as she shivered again.

The nightmares, according to Ivan, were frantic, her screams terrified as she cried out for him. Not for her father, or for her bodyguards, but for Riordan.

Don't leave me . . . Riordan, please don't leave me . . .

The cries he'd heard on the recordings Ivan made from the audio device in her bedroom before he arrived had sent chills down his spine. The ones where she begged him to save her had ripped his soul from his body.

It had taken half a bottle of the whiskey his cousin had sent before he'd been able to function again.

Lochlan, surprisingly enough, was a redheaded Irishman of Viking descent. At six-four, he was a powerhouse, and his brothers were no weaker. They were now in place, two in the house, the others only God knew where.

Noah and Micah needed to return to their homes, out of the line of danger. Having them there was wearing on his conscience. They'd risked themselves enough in the past, and Loch's men were eager for the challenge.

Their training wasn't as fine-tuned as Noah's and Micah's, but sometimes, fine-tuning wasn't needed. He needed men who were unknown and able to infiltrate. Loch and his twin, Lorcan, were as Irish as they came. If anyone could learn who within Ivan's estate was a threat to Amara, it was those two.

Until the enemy showed their hand though—he tightened his hold on Amara, his eyes closing for a brief, tortured second—until he knew who the enemy was, he couldn't afford to allow Amara to come to her memories in her own time, when she'd be able to handle them. Whatever it was that had forced her to hide from a year of her life, Riordan had no choice but to drag it from her, whatever it took.

It could be the only way to save her life.

"Riordan"—she burrowed closer before sighing at the feel of his arms tightening around her—"missed you."

It was no more than a breath of sound, a sigh of longing dragged from whatever dream drifted around her sleeping mind. But it held him, just as she did—heart, body, and soul of a man who hadn't believed he'd find a love this deep.

"*Go síoraí,*" he whispered, pressing a kiss to her brow. "I'll love you forever."

Amara stood still and silent in front of the bank of windows in her father's penthouse. A blizzard raged beyond, obliterating the view but for the heavy fall of snow. The white fluff whipped and fell through the air, battering at the window as though seeking the warmth inside.

It surrounded the view, insulating the apartment and isolating her inside. Leaving her alone with only one other person there.

It was the first time they'd been truly alone.

The other bodyguards were stuck at the main office several blocks away. Only Riordan and the two outside the penthouse doors remained. But only Riordan mattered as far as she was concerned.

She stared at the glass and watched him enter the room.

Tall, black hair falling around his rough-hewn features, dressed in jeans and a T-shirt that emphasized all the hard muscles and power. And cowboy boots. God, he looked good. It should seriously be illegal for a man to look that damn good in boots.

"Amara, would you come away from the window?" he asked, not for the first time in the months he'd been assigned to her security detail. His tone reflected the repetitive nature of the request.

Turning slowly, she shot him a look from beneath her lashes.

"And what do I get for denying myself the view?" she asked, staring back at him with flirtatious innocence. "It's not as though there's much else to do right now. Is there?"

His arms went across that broad chest, and despite the frown on his face, she saw his gaze grow darker, his expression harden just that little bit as a grin teased at the corners of his lips.

"What do you want?" He sounded so business-like.

That was okay, she knew how to negotiate. At least, she knew how to negotiate with him. He'd taught her how.

Biting her lip as though considering her wants, she then let an innocent smile shape her lips.

She was gonna go to hell for this one for sure.

"A lollipop," she answered, then let her tongue peak out to touch her lips for the briefest second.

Was he holding his breath?

"A lollipop?" he asked carefully, but she saw the way his gaze touched her lips and his hands tightened where he had his arms crossed. "What kind of lollipop?"

She pursed her lips. "A really big one. One that lasts a while."

Did she really say that as though she were serious? It sounded serious. And for a moment, he simply stared at her.

"Like your lollipops, do you?" His brow arched, his gaze grew darker, and his lashes lowered just enough for him to pretend to hide his interest.

"I do." She sounded far too breathless now, but he was walking toward her. That cocky stride of his just made her hot.

"So how many licks does it take you?" he murmured, reaching her, his arms lowering.

"Hmm, I don't know. I like to savor my treats, you know? So it takes a lot of licks."

He inhaled slowly, lust filling his expression, male hunger reflecting in his gaze.

"*Sounds good.*" Still, he just stood there, watching her.

"*Do you like lollipops too?*" Her eyes widened and she swore she was going to start laughing over that one.

The smile that curled his lips was pure, lazy sex.

"*Oh no, but come away from that window and I'll watch you enjoy your lollipop. . . . Hell, I'll love every lick . . .*"

chapter seventeen

Amara opened her eyes, the dream dissolving; but unlike in the past, the memory of it was not. And it *was* a memory. They'd been lovers, just as they were again. And she'd loved him. She still loved him. But she was no more certain of *his* feelings than she had been during that first snowstorm in New York.

All those feelings, those emotions, were rushing through her again, swamping her, overwhelming her.

The feel of him behind her now, heated and warm against her back, her head on his shoulder, his arms encasing her, wasn't unfamiliar, even if she didn't remember more than that one snippet of time and the emotions that went with it.

Staring into the barely lit expanse of her bedroom, the gas flames of the fireplace casting playful shadows about the room, she felt a flush heating her cheeks. She'd definitely enjoyed him that night.

Just as she'd enjoyed what he'd done to her earlier.

So why had she forgotten both him and the abduction? The psychiatrist's suggestion that she'd forgotten because the abduction was too traumatizing to remember, didn't explain why she'd forgotten everything from the moment she'd seen Riordan walk into her favorite restaurant . . .

She remembered that meeting, she realized in shock.

The way her heart had picked up and raced when their eyes met and the awareness that even though he was trying to hide it—determined to hide it—he hadn't been unaffected. Powerful and hardened, the man who moved toward the table she and her father sat at, was not unaffected when their eyes met.

Over the years she moved within her father's world, she learned certain tricks to help determine the character of those she met. She was able to size some men up immediately, though that was rare. But never had she reacted to one as she had to Riordan at that first glance.

She'd found it nearly impossible to pull her gaze from his. Those sapphire depths had mesmerized her, and with each heartbeat he'd held her gaze, she swore he'd seen further into her soul.

And she imagined she'd felt him in hers. Strong. Complicated. A man who had learned that his arrogance and strength were his greatest defenses. One shadowed and alone in ways that merely having others around him would never ease.

Whether that inner man was a good one, a bad one, or one with qualities of both—as she often thought of her father—she didn't know. But she knew in those seconds before he reached the table and sat down with her and her father that it would never really matter. She knew she'd never be completely free of him.

"Why did I forget you?" she asked softly, sensing he was awake, waiting. "Why did I forget us?"

How could she have forgotten someone she had given her heart to?

His hand gently stroked down her arm before lying against her hip, a warm weight against her skin.

"I don't know." Drawing her closer, he kissed her shoulder before settling against her again. "You were aware, and knew everyone on the team when we arrived. You were in pain, but there were no head wounds and you sustained no further injuries in the rescue. You lost consciousness though as you were being loaded in the evac chopper. When you came to in the hospital, the memories were gone."

She stared into the darkened room, frowning.

What was it about that description that bothered her, that caused her heart to ache?

"Do you remember anything else?" His lips brushed against her ear, fracturing her thoughts.

"I remember the day we met at the restaurant. I remember when we were snowed in at the penthouse. Bits and pieces of things, but not about the abduction itself."

She also remembered that she had loved him. That brief moment in time as her eyes met his in the window's reflection. She had loved him. But had he loved her?

"How much do you remember of the time we were snowed in?" Behind her, the heated length of his cock pressed thick and hard against the seam of her rear.

"Just a minute or two," she admitted, fighting back a

grin. "I believe you were giving me a treat for coming away from the window during the storm."

Her heart began racing, pounding with excitement as he lifted behind her, rolled her onto her back, and stared down at her. Brooding and intense, his expression was also heavy with dark sexuality.

"And how much do you remember of *that*?" The rough rasp of his voice stroked over her senses, filling her with heat. The suggestive sexual tone was both playful and filled with pure sexual intent.

"It's a little fuzzy," she whispered breathlessly. "Maybe you could do something to help me with that."

He wasn't the least bit fuzzy about that particular memory. It was a memory that got him through months of recuperation, of painful healing. Of her nightmares, fears, and needs that came to him in the dreams she shared with him.

"Oh, I can definitely do something to help you with that." He had to tighten every muscle in his body to keep from coming right there. His erection was spike hard, throbbing and damp with pre-cum as the visions of that memory drove him crazy.

As he moved between her thighs, his lips lowered to hers, her soft, silky hand slid down his abdomen, heating his flesh, striking at his balls with bands of pleasure as a finger slid over the head of his cock.

Then damn her—and God help him—she lifted that finger, slowly, with sensual promise, to her lips and curled that hot little tongue right around it. Her lashes fluttered, then lifted, drowsy sensuality burning him straight to his fucking heels.

Gripping her wrists, he pushed them to the bed, his head lowering, his lips taking hers, tasting them. She was killing him, but then, hadn't she been doing that since he first met her? Since the second his gaze touched hers?

And as she was doing now. With her hungry lips beneath his, she was making him wilder, hotter by the second as her little mewling cries reached his ears. She wasn't a loud lover. The deeper her pleasure, the more breathless she became, her cries more gasps than screams.

Moving his hands to the swollen curves of her breasts, he groaned as he felt her breath hitch. Gripping one hardened nipple between his thumb and forefinger, he tugged at the tight tip and felt her shudder.

Her hands were at his shoulders, nails digging in, claiming him. She always left her mark on him, in one way or another, just as he made certain he left his. He'd never been able to make himself delve into the implications of that one.

He pulled his head back from the kiss, because God knew, if he kept losing himself in her, he'd never get beyond the driving need to sink inside the sweet heat between her thighs. Dragging his lips down her neck to her breasts, he paused to pay homage to their tight, hard tips before jerking to his knees.

He wasn't going to make it much longer. Damn her, he'd never had enough willpower where she was concerned. Self-control became nonexistent once he touched her. And that self-control nearly exploded as she sat up and reached for him, her slender fingers curling around his erection like living silk. Her lips parted as she stared up at him, her gaze slumberous, filled with sensual hunger.

His teeth clenched as she licked over the head, a slow, sliding caress as he pushed the fingers of one hand through the shortened curls of her hair. He gripped her jaw with his other hand exerting just enough pressure to force her mouth open. Excitement flared in her gaze, her face flushing with it as one of those mewling little moans vibrated in her throat.

He clenched his teeth in his fight to hold back, to give her just the head of his dick, no more. Not to sink into the wet heat of her mouth.

Her tongue curled over the violently sensitive flesh, as her mouth closed around its thickness. Her heated suction, the lash of each playful lick and stroke, had his shaft clenching, blood pounding through it as his release threatened to slip the hold he had on it.

Innocent, hungry, her mouth did things on the head of his dick that made him want to growl like an animal. Damn her. Innocent, sultry seductress.

"Like that, do you?" he demanded, watching as he gave her more, sliding deeper, his thighs bunching with the effort to hold back. "I know I sure as hell do."

She sucked him like she loved his cock, and he damn sure knew he loved her mouth. There was nothing practiced or experienced in her touch, and it was all the more sensual in the enjoyment she displayed.

With each draw of her mouth, each stroke of her tongue, she kept him on the razor's edge of release, fighting to hang on, just one more minute. Just a little longer, because it felt so fucking good. Because the sight of her, lips stretched around his erection, eyes drowsy, dazed with her pleasure, was more intoxicating than the finest Irish whiskey.

"Beautiful," he whispered, his voice hoarse, grating even to his own ears as she worked her mouth over the head of his cock, drew on the engorged head, and rubbed that wicked little tongue along the underside.

Hot, rich pleasure seared his senses. His balls tightened warningly, causing him to tense with the raging need to spill his release into the suckling depths of her mouth.

"Enough." He was nearly panting with the effort to hold back. He could feel the sweat easing along the side of his face, the heat traveling up his spine, threatening to explode at the base of his skull.

Tightening his fingers in her hair, he forced her head back, ignoring her protesting little moan as he dragged his tortured flesh from her mouth. Amara's breath caught as Riordan pushed her to the bed, spread her thighs further with his knees, moving until the broad head of his cock met the swollen, wet folds of her sex. There were no further preliminaries, and she didn't need any. She didn't want any. She wanted him inside her, wanted the feel of him, the pleasure of him, overwhelming her senses again.

"Sweet baby," he groaned as the broad crest of his erection parted the slick, intimate folds between her thighs.

Sensation shuddered through her as he began pushing inside the heated, slick depths of her pussy. Stretching her, sending rapid-fire pulses of exquisite ecstasy. This went beyond pleasure, beyond any description of pleasure she could come up with. It was pleasure amplified.

Eyes closed, hands gripping his biceps, Amara began to feel the physical pleasure mixing with an inner pain she didn't know how to process. How had she forgotten him? How had she forgotten *this*?

As he slid deeper inside her, she forced her eyes opened. She wanted to see him—his gaze snared hers instead, trapped her in their gem-bright depths as his hands framed her face, a grimace tightening his expression.

"I missed you baby," he whispered. "God help me, I missed you."

His hips flexed, pressing his cock deeper as pleasure tore through her. "So sweet, Amara. Touching you, feeling you wrapped around me, it's like a damn drug I can't escape."

Her breath broke as his hips jerked against hers, driving his cock deeper, harder, filling her completely. Stretching the inner tissue, stroking over the violently sensitive nerve endings, he buried inside her fully as a ragged groan escaped his chest.

"I dreamed of you even when dreams shouldn't have reached me," he whispered, his gaze still holding hers, his expression fierce, hard with lust and something more.

"I dreamed"—her breathing hitched as he moved against her, his cock stroking slow and easy inside her—"I'd awaken and looked for you beside me . . ."

For him. She'd known he should be in the bed beside her, holding her, warming her—oh God, pleasuring her.

Lowering his hand, Riordan gripped her thigh and lifted it, until she was moving both legs, knees bending, her hips lifting as she gripped his, allowing him to sink deeper inside her. A whimpering moan left her lips as burning pleasure tore through her, despite the slow, rhythmic thrusts that he refused to speed up.

Lowering his head, his lips covered hers again, kissing her slow and deep as he worked his cock inside her, his breathing harsh, ragged. With each stroke, with each thrust, the sensations became stronger, whipping through her harder. And still, he took her cries with his kisses, held her to him, and destroyed her with pleasure.

Just when she was certain she couldn't bear it another second, when her pussy was tightening, involuntary spasms rippling through it as the need to orgasm rose desperately, he began to move harder, faster.

Penetrating her with increasingly hard strokes as his lips moved from hers to press against the bend of her neck, he drove them both to the edge of such crazy pleasure, she lost her ability to even cry out at the sensations. Then, he pushed both of them over, hurtling them into such a storm of pure ecstasy, she was certain she'd become lost with it.

Riordan held her to him, their combined releases shaking their bodies, her soul. His arms held her tight, the warmth of his body sheltered her, covered her, possessed her.

Claimed her.

He claimed her.

Dawn was peeking over the horizon when Riordan slipped silently from the room and headed to his brother's. The vibration of his phone on the table beside the bed had brought him from a deep sleep and had him dressing immediately. Making his way down the hall and rounding the corner, he gave a brief knock to the door before stepping inside. Noah stood on the other side of the room, his expression somber, worry showing in the crease of a frown at his forehead and in the look of bleak sorrow that shadowed his gaze.

"What's happened? Sabella and the kids okay?" That look was one Riordan had rarely seen on his brother's face.

"They're fine." Noah cleared his throat before his shoulders shifted in apparent discomfort and he stepped to the desk at the side of the room.

It was obvious that whatever his brother had to say wasn't something he wanted to say.

"Then what's going on?" He closed the door carefully and stepped farther into the room.

A primal warning tightened his gut as a chill raced up his spine. He'd trained with his brother, fought with him often enough to know what that feeling meant.

Noah looked away for a second, swallowing as a grimace tightened his face before he turned back to face him.

"What the hell's going on, Noah—"

"I know why Ivan's refusing to allow you to see Amara's hospital records," Noah spoke over him. "I sent Frankie in to question the surgeon who operated on her."

Riordan knew this was going to be bad. He knew his brother, knew his expressions, his body language. And he knew that what was coming couldn't be good. The fact that his brother had sent Frankie, a former Israeli Mossad agent, was even more telling.

"Riordan." Noah's jaw clenched as he seemed to consider his words. "Goddamn." He pushed his fingers through his hair, anger resonating in his voice. "I'm sorry. What Ivan had no intention of telling you was that Amara was pregnant. About eight weeks. She lost the baby due to her injuries . . . the blow that fractured her pelvis"

Riordan stood still as ice seemed to wash through him.

Never had he felt the chill that was tearing through him in that moment. Beneath the ice, he could feel himself shattering. A ragged wound unlike anything he'd ever known was ripping through his soul, gouging its way through with jagged bites.

He was only distantly aware of Noah pouring him a drink then pouring another for himself. He took the glass, swallowed the fiery liquid, then stepped to the bar to snag the bottle before he stopped himself.

He stared at it as the heat of that first shot spilled through his chest, into his belly. He knew he could numb the pain for a minute, but doing so would be another injustice to the child he hadn't even known existed. The child stolen from him and Amara.

His hand dropped to his side and he forced himself to turn away.

There was a time when he'd tried to hide in whatever bottle of liquor he could find. He'd learned then that it didn't help. Nothing could help this agony tearing through him. This was all he could give the baby he hadn't known Amara carried.

"No wonder she forced herself to forget." His voice was so ragged he barely recognized it.

And Ivan had hid it from Amara. He'd hidden it from everyone.

"The surgeon told Frankie that Ivan threatened to kill him with his bare hands if he didn't lose Amara's records. He didn't destroy them, but we haven't managed to locate them yet either."

Riordan couldn't speak. He had to breathe. He had to make sense of this. God help him, if Ivan was on the estate, he wasn't sure he could keep from trying to kill him. Amara's father should have never kept this from him. He should have told him the second Riordan showed up, demanding to resume his place as head of Amara's security.

Funny, he'd been confused over Ivan's lack of argument over that demand. He had simply nodded and given Riordan instant control. He hadn't argued over a single decision or demand that Riordan had made.

He should have known, he should have demanded those medical records then.

The day she'd had the gynecologist's appointment, she'd been so quiet, almost confused afterward, and intensely somber. If the memories were close to returning, then it made sense.

She'd known she was pregnant when he left for England.

She'd known, but she hadn't told him.

But then, he hadn't exactly been given a chance to tell her he was leaving. Ivan had put him on a helicopter and flown him directly to the airport to meet up with his team within an hour of informing him of the job.

Riordan's arguments concerning Amara's safety had been waved aside. Her father had been so certain he could protect her, so certain that the men he would use in Riordan's stead would be able to protect her.

And God help him, he couldn't blame Ivan for believing in them. In the end, Riordan had ignored his misgivings because he knew those men as well. But even more, he'd thought Elizaveta and Grisha would also be with her. He'd had no idea they hadn't returned from Russia on time that morning.

"I'm sorry, *brathair*," Noah said softly, the pure Irish in the last word a hint of the man he had been, the brother he had been, so many years ago.

God, he felt as though he were dying inside. That rending pain tearing at his heart wouldn't stop. It refused to stop.

She hadn't told him she was pregnant.

Why? Why hadn't she told him? Was it the same reason she had refused to allow her father to know she was sleeping with her bodyguard?

Whatever *that* fucking reason was.

"Riordan." Worry, and grief, filled Noah's voice.

Riordan shook his head as he turned away from his brother and forced himself to breathe in deep, to control the rage tearing through him. The bastards who abducted her, tortured and beat her, had stolen not just her memories, but their child.

When she did remember, would she grieve that lost life or would she consider it a lucky escape from the lover she'd been determined to hide from her father? She would grieve—he couldn't imagine otherwise. The woman he knew would, of course, grieve her lost child. But would she grieve the loss of the man who had fathered her baby? Without that child, there would be no way that he could hold on to her, no reason to inform her father that she had lain with one of the men hired to protect her. The very type of man her father had ordered his young daughter to avoid.

"Chatter was picked up concerning that blowout the other day," Noah said softly behind him. "It wasn't an accident according to what we've picked up. But someone wanted it to *look* like an accident. I have two of my agents on it."

Riordan cleared his throat. "Ops has other missions, I'm sure."

"Ops command has covered Ivan's back for years, Riordan," Noah told him. "He's one of their assets. They won't turn their back on him with this."

Yeah, he was one of their best assets, one of their greatest manipulators in that shadow world between legitimate business interests and criminal design.

"Is there any chatter concerning why she's a target?" Focus. He had to fucking focus.

"Not yet, but we have a place to look now. We didn't have that before," Noah assured him. "She's beginning to remember though, isn't she?"

Yeah, she was beginning to remember and when she remembered what would it do to her? He turned back to his brother. "Small things. Mostly pieces of our relationship before the abduction. The day we met. She knows we were lovers. But she hasn't remembered anything about the abduction yet."

But she would. She was stubborn and she was stronger than even Ivan realized. She knew the memories would hurt, but she'd still face them.

"Let's hope those memories return soon." Noah breathed out heavily. "It could be what helps us save her life."

Because whoever had targeted her was not going to stop.

"What are you going to do, Riordan?" Noah asked. "What are you going to tell Amara?"

What was he going to tell Amara? The Ops psychologist and the one Riordan had hired agreed that telling Amara what had happened in the months missing from her memory was not in her best interests. She needed to find her own memories, not hear someone else's views of them.

"Nothing. I'm not going to tell her any more than I would've before I learned about the baby," he said, hearing the harshness in his own voice. "I'm not going to tell her a damn thing."

"Is that really how you want to handle it?" Noah asked immediately. "Think about it first, Riordan. Think about what you would want her to do if it were you."

He faced his brother fully then, anger surging inside him. "If she thought I was dead, I sure as hell wouldn't let her live with it for three years before I returned with no intention of telling her who I am as *you* did to Sabella," he snapped furiously at the judgmental look he saw in his brother's face.

Son of a bitch, he wasn't a dumb kid or an untrained young man any longer. There were decisions he knew how to make without his brother's help.

"No, but what you're getting ready to do—I've been told—is no different. Sabella asked me to remind you that I wasn't able to hide from her. Not who I was, or what I had been. Remember that, Riordan. Because hiding from Amara will have the same results, but without the bonds Sabella and I had in the first years of our marriage. Think about it first, that's all I'm saying. Be certain the direction you're going to take before you make the turn."

Without replying, Riordan turned away from his brother, jerked the door open, and stalked from the room before returning to his own. Amara still slept in his bed, blankets still wrapped around her, her slight body relaxed as she seemed to sleep dreamlessly.

Watching her, his emotions were in turmoil, his fists clenched as he fought the need to hold her. If he had known about the baby, he would have never gone to England—hell, he should have never gone to England, period.

He should have never left her.

chapter eighteen

It wasn't a dream that washed over her, because she wasn't asleep. She'd awakened the moment Riordan left the bed. Silently, she'd listened to him dress and quietly leave the room. But minutes later, the fog that normally covered her memories parted and allowed a fragment to slip free.

She stood in the living area of the penthouse as she faced her father, feeling sick to her stomach and fighting to hold back a ragged cry of denial.

Because he was gone. Riordan was gone.

"What do you mean 'he left'?" She stared back at her poppa as he faced her from the bank of windows that looked out over Central Park.

The spring blue of the sky was a brilliant backdrop as the warming sunlight spilled into the room. A warmth that couldn't hope to touch the sudden cold chill that washed over her.

Her poppa stood, shoulders straight and head high,

his dark blue eyes and hardened expression giving away little.

"I mean, he is gone." He shrugged. "The new team will be here in about an hour—"

"Where did he go?" Her nails bit into the back of the chair she stood behind, unable to believe he'd left her.

He wouldn't leave her. Surely, he wouldn't leave her. He hadn't even said goodbye.

"Does it matter?" He tilted his head to the side and watched her thoughtfully. "You've never cared when I've changed your security before. Why now?"

He knew.

Staring back at him, Amara could see the knowledge lurking in the flat line of his mouth, in the faint gleam of anger in his eyes that he couldn't hide. He knew she'd been sleeping with Riordan, and he'd fired him.

But it really didn't matter what her poppa had done. What mattered was that Riordan had left.

"Did you hurt him, Poppa?" she asked faintly, praying she wasn't wrong about the man who had raised her, the man she had loved more than any other until Riordan.

"No. No bruises, broken bones, or gunshot wounds. Is that what you're asking?" The muscle at his jaw jerked as the question snapped out at her. "Did I have a reason to hurt him, Amara?"

She wanted desperately to lay her hand against her stomach . . .

Why? Why had she not placed her hand over her abdomen, even though the need to do it had been almost more than she could resist?

"No," she answered softly, her gaze dropping to her

hands as she forced herself to release the cushioned back of the chair. "There was no reason, Poppa."

Except her shattered heart. No matter what her father ordered, if Riordan wasn't hurt, then he would have come for her—if he loved her. Nothing her father could have done would have held him back. Riordan was too strong, too arrogant to ever walk away from a woman he considered his.

As she had considered him hers.

"I'll leave you with Ilya and my own team until the new security agents arrive," he stated. "They're the best I have in the agency."

No, they weren't, she thought. Riordan was the best. Twice he'd protected her from seemingly random violence. Violence he'd been certain wasn't random at all.

"I'm certain they are," she answered. "Excuse me, Poppa, I'm still rather tired this morning. I believe I'll return to bed."

She was breaking apart inside. Her heart was breaking in a way she had never imagined it could be broken.

She'd been so certain she'd kept her affair with Riordan secret from her father. They'd been so very careful. And yet, still, somehow, her father had learned her bodyguard was sleeping with her.

That was the only type of man her poppa had warned her he would never accept. Should one of his security personnel become her lover, he would ensure that man never worked for him again. Perhaps he'd never walk again, because that would be a blatant breach of trust. A man who was sleeping with her could not effectively protect her, he'd warned.

"Amara?" he stopped her as she reached the short hall that led to her room.

"Yes, Poppa?" She didn't turn back to him—she couldn't. There was no way she could hide the tears if she did.

"All he had to do was face me," he said gently. "I would never take someone from you who you loved. But you're no man's secret. And I won't allow one of your bodyguards to make you one."

The tears fell then. She couldn't hold them back.

"He did it for me."

"No, Amara." His voice hardened. "No matter a woman's wishes, a man who truly loves her would not allow it. But even more, he'd never walk away."

She couldn't argue with him, because he was right. If Riordan had loved her, he wouldn't have left her. He wouldn't have walked away.

"I know," she whispered. But it didn't help, it didn't stop the pain. "I know, Poppa."

She moved slowly, every bone, every muscle in her body hurting, aching for a man who hadn't really wanted her. Stepping into her bedroom, she closed the door, locked it, then moved into her bathroom.

Stopping in front of the sink, she stared at the small, plastic stick lying on the counter. The pink stripe mocked her, reminded her that Riordan had left far more behind than he realized.

He hadn't just left the woman who loved him. He'd left their child . . .

Her eyes opened moments after Riordan had returned from the bathroom. Lying still and silent in the bed, she let her hand move to her abdomen.

She'd been pregnant when she'd been abducted! She'd been carrying his child. A child she had obviously lost.

She fought her ragged breathing, fought the tears and the cries that would have slipped free. Pushing the blankets from her, she forced herself from his bed, from his room and entered her own. Locking the door behind her, she fought to stay upright, to keep from collapsing as rage and pain swept through her.

Whoever abducted her caused her to lose Riordan's baby.

A ragged sound of pain escaped her, slashed at her. Oh God, it hurt. It hurt so bad. She'd wanted her child. It hadn't mattered that Riordan hadn't wanted her, she had loved the baby he'd left her. And now, that baby was gone.

Breathing in, she forced back her cries, forced back the ragged fury, and moved toward the shower. She needed to move, needed to find a sense of balance. Not that a shower would do that, but it *would* wash Riordan's scent from her body. It would take the scent of him out of her head, the feel of him out of her body.

Grief lanced her as she stepped beneath the water and let it spill over her head, let it wash away the tears. She wished she could wash away the sorrow and the feelings of betrayal as easily.

She let the driving pain have its way. She knew from experience that the only way to control it later was to give into it when she was alone. When she could let the tears fall without anyone knowing any better.

She wouldn't cry in front of him. She wouldn't let him see what his leaving had done to her. She couldn't bear to let him know he had nearly broken her.

And her poppa was not innocent in this, not by any means. When she'd protested Riordan's appearance at his arrival this time, he'd told her that Riordan had been recovering from some injury for the past six months and had been unable to join her security team.

What was the truth and what was another of his subtle play on words? He never lied to her, but when he was determined that she not know the truth of something, he was a master verbal manipulator.

As she stepped from the shower and began drying off, she wondered why her father had allowed him back into her life. She knew her poppa, knew he didn't just change his mind so drastically. What had happened to make him bring back the man he had removed from her life six months ago?

Oh, when he returned, there was going to be hell to pay.

While Riordan had headed her security team, her poppa had been largely absent from the penthouse, staying in the apartment at the Brute Force Security headquarters instead. Something he had rarely done before that. If she didn't know him as well as she did, she would have sworn he was waiting for her and Riordan to become lovers.

For a moment, the seamless access to another memory shocked her.

Could it be that easy? Could the return of her memories come so easily after six months of struggling to pull them free?

Why now? Why was she remembering now, when even the nightmares that had plagued her before Riordan's return couldn't free them?

Was it the fact that Riordan had returned?

Wrapping her towel around her body, she ignored the fierce pounding of her heart and the panic that threatened to surge past her control. One part of her was eager to remember; the other was tight with fear. She hadn't lost her memories because she had lost Riordan's baby. As painful and shattering as that realization was, she knew it wasn't the reason she'd been hiding from the months she'd forgotten.

There was more waiting on her. She could feel those memories now, though. Swirling just beyond the fog, amassing, struggling to push free.

Why they had begun now, she didn't know, but as she stepped into her bedroom and came to a stop just beyond the door, she knew Riordan had much to do with it.

He stood in the sitting area, his expression carved in stone, though his eyes burned like sapphire fire. His black hair was still damp, his powerful body dressed, and she couldn't stop a sharp tinge of regret that all that bronze flesh overlaying powerful muscle was covered. Jeans, a white shirt, sleeves rolled up to his strong forearms and the tail tucked in. A belt cinched his hips, and he wore those scarred boots on his big feet.

And she was still dressed in a towel.

"I need to dress." Her voice shook and she hated it.

Compressing her lips she skirted around him to her dresser and pulled a pair of panties and a bra free. When he didn't speak, she threw a glare at the broad expanse of his back before entering the walk-in closet and quickly dressing.

The ankle-length steel blue cashmere skirt and dove gray sweater with its tiny pearl buttons was comfortable and warm. She had a feeling she'd need that sense of comfort this morning. Rather than pushing her feet into shoes, she pulled on a pair of thick soft white socks instead.

She rarely wore shoes in the house when her poppa wasn't there. There was no danger of his business associates arriving, or acquaintances dropping by. The only person she had to worry about was Riordan.

Exiting the closet, she kept him in her peripheral vision, stalked across the room, and before he could stop her, jerked her bedroom door open and walked out.

"Amara." She ignored the sharp, demanding tone of his voice as she hurried down the hall to the stairs.

She couldn't deal with him.

Not right now.

If she had to confront him, there was no way she would be able to hide the anger and pain that was still far too close to the surface.

As she moved quickly down the stairs, she could hear the thud of his boots behind her.

Uh-oh, he was pissed. He only stomped when he was pissed. And she knew if she looked back, she'd see an arrogant, determined—and far too sexy—expression on his face. And why the sexy part should be one of her first thoughts just struck her as wrong on too many levels.

"The hell you'll run from me like this." Catching her arm just before she reached the dining room, he swung her around to face him, and sure enough, too sexy for words.

"Like you ran from me?" she cried out, jerking her arm out of his grip as his gaze narrowed on her.

"What have you remembered? How much have you

remembered?" he demanded without so much as a single doubt that she'd remembered something.

"Does it matter?" she sneered before turning and heading to her office.

She'd be damned if she was going to yell at him in the foyer where everyone would hear, and she sure as hell wasn't going back to her bedroom.

Riordan ended every argument they'd ever had in her bedroom, in her bed.

He was incredibly sexual. Intense and hungry, seductive and wild.

Another memory, another piece of the puzzle. Bits and pieces were just there, where before they hadn't been.

"You're damn right it matters." He followed her into her office, slapping the door closed behind him. "And what the hell do you mean I ran from you? Like hell I did."

Turning to him, Amara was taken aback by the expression on his face. Arrogance, yes, but also anger, hunger, and all the other wild emotions she'd always glimpsed just a shadow of before. Those emotions filled his gaze now, his expression, hardening his features and giving them a stark, hungry look.

"You damn sure did," she informed him, furiously pointing a finger at him accusingly. "You couldn't even tell me goodbye, damn you."

"And why the fuck would I tell you goodbye?" He stalked to her, bending his head until they were nearly nose to nose. "It wasn't fucking goodbye. It was another of those damn half-assed missions your father was always sending my ass out on."

She stared back at him in confusion.

That wasn't what her father had told her, but she knew how he got when he felt she didn't trust him, or when he was angry. He didn't lie, he just didn't tell the whole truth.

"Let me guess. He didn't tell you about the mission he sent me on to England?" He drew back, censure flashing across his expression. "Manipulative bastard. The entire time I commanded your security, he tried to play his damn games with me."

Her poppa was good at his games, she admitted that.

"It doesn't matter," she said, her voice hollow even to her own ears. "You left, Riordan, when you could have stayed. But you left me."

Had he loved her, he would have stayed, wouldn't he?

His gaze seemed to flatten, harden. "You're right, Amara. I should have stayed," he stated, the harsh rasp of his voice shocking her. "I should have ignored your tears and pleas to keep our relationship from him and I should have by God never left you. But I did. Now both of us will just have to deal with it."

They would just have to deal with it?

She stared back at him in shock.

"I don't just have to deal with it. I don't just have to deal with a damn thing," she cried out, furious that he'd even think she would have to. "What I can do is make sure it never happens again. You can sleep in your own bed. Alone."

For a second, the office was so silent, so still within the wave of tension that swept through it, that Amara found herself holding her breath.

Then he laughed. A low, harsh sound as his lips curled with mocking amusement.

"Oh Amara, you really haven't remembered enough about the man you're dealing with," he told her softly. "Or you would have never considered such a dare."

Before she could avoid him, he gripped the hair at the back of her head, holding her in place as one arm went around her back and jerked her to him. Pulling her head back, his lips captured hers as a gasp escaped her and he stilled any protest she could consider with a kiss that shocked her to her core.

If he had kissed her in such a way before, surely she couldn't have forgotten it.

This was nothing so tame as a kiss.

This was a carnal claiming.

It was lips and tongue, nips and greedy male lust. It was dominant, hot, and impossible to deny. He held her head immobile and kissed her with such carnal male lust it was intoxicating. He claimed her with his kiss until she didn't know anything beyond the riotous sensations surging through her.

She was only barely, distantly aware—and didn't give a damn—that the buttons of her sweater were loosening, spreading apart. The clip of her bra released and broad palms cupped her breasts, molded them as callused thumbs rasped their tender peaks. The demanding nature of the kiss combined with the possessive caresses overwhelmed her senses with something that went far beyond pleasure.

As his lips continued to move over hers in long, drugging kisses, his hands slid to her thighs, cupped them through her skirt, and lifted her until her rear was sliding over the top of the desk. His lips nipped at hers, took a series of hard, hungry kisses before they moved to her jaw, her neck.

Whimpering moans were falling from her lips as those burning caresses moved to her neck and her skirt moved up her thighs. He pushed the material to her hips, his fingers cupping the aching mound between her thighs.

"Riordan!" The sharp cry shocked her.

She'd always managed to remain quiet, to stifle her moans. To keep from being heard. But she couldn't control it now. Couldn't fight the pleasure, or the moans falling from her lips.

"There you go," he groaned as he spread her thighs farther and moved between them. "Let me hear all those wild cries, baby."

His lips moved against her neck in a heated kiss. The caress sent waves of intoxicating sensations racing through her, drawing another cry despite her attempts to hold it back.

And once wasn't enough for him. As her head fell back, exposing her neck, he explored, tasted, and teased, tormented the sensitive flesh and rocked her with the pleasure of it.

There were no more than a few heartbeats between one exquisite, shocking sensation and the next. When he finished claiming her neck, his lips moved to her breasts. He first kissed one nipple then the other as his hands smoothed up her inner thighs. Then, he captured one straining tip in his mouth with a suddenness that had her arching, crying out, as her sex clenched with a sudden wave of need.

Her hands were in his hair, her thighs spread wide, hips lifting as she braced her feet on the edge of the desk. As his mouth surrounded her nipple and began drawing on it, the fragile silk that covered her pussy was ripped aside and his fingers were parting the slick folds, his thumb glancing over her clit, his fingers stroking the narrow slit that led inside.

There was no time to prepare herself. No time to accustom herself to the arcs of heat and sharp sensation already striking at her nerve endings when he added one that tore free that last fragile hold on any control.

The sudden penetration of his cock inches inside her sent a pleasure-pain strike of pure ecstasy tearing through her.

The cry that spilled from her was lost in the overwhelming heat and steel-hard impalement. Pulling back, he thrust again, and again, finally burying his cock to the hilt as she arched and tried to scream his name.

He was so large, so hard. Her inner muscles clenched, rippled, and struggled to accommodate the flesh filling her. Not that he gave her time for that either.

"Like that, baby?" he groaned, lifting his head to her neck once again. "Let's see if I can make you love it. Come on, give me all those sweet, wild cries."

He began thrusting inside her, pulling nearly free before thrusting inside her hard and fast again and creating a rhythm she couldn't resist, and a savage pleasure she couldn't fight any more than she could fight the cries that spilled from her lips.

"Damn you! You're mine, Amara." Driving harder inside her, he held her to him, bent over her, his hips pistoning between her thighs as she felt herself unraveling.

She was coming apart. Too quickly. The ecstasy rose inside her so fast, so hot, she couldn't escape it, couldn't fight it. Until it erupted inside her with such force, with such incredible pleasure, she lost herself in an ecstasy she knew she'd never be free of. A man she'd never want to be free of.

chapter nineteen

He'd marked her.

Amara stared at the love bite at the base of her neck and the one closer to her shoulder and lowered her head as she braced her hands on the sink that evening.

A break in the snow had resulted in a message from her father that he would be back at the estate before the next wave began. It was just her damn luck that her poppa hadn't forgotten how to travel dangerous snow-packed roads.

He'd spent his youth learning how to navigate Russia's roadways during the worst parts of winter. It was a skill he hadn't forgotten, no matter her wishes.

So much for keeping her private life private. That simply wasn't possible now.

"Don't worry, he can't ground you," Riordan assured her, his tone mocking as he stepped to the open doorway and watched her.

"He can shoot you," she muttered. "If I don't first."

He snorted.

"I let you convince me to keep our relationship hidden once. I won't allow it again," he informed her, his tone tight and hard as she turned her head and stared at him.

"Poppa never let me know when he had a mistress," she said faintly. "I never had to deal with jealous lovers, or catty remarks. Perhaps I only wanted to give him the same respect he afforded me."

It seemed it was something neither Riordan, nor her father, understood.

Straightening, she stared at the marks again and sighed heavily. "You're a caveman, Riordan."

And she had loved it, that was the part she didn't understand. When he went caveman, she melted

"I told you, I'm not going to hide the fact that you belong to me again," he informed her, the determined expression on his face assuring her there were no arguments she could use to sway him.

"I don't belong to you—"

"Want me to prove it again, Amara?" The sudden rasp to his voice had her staring back at him warily.

He leaned against the doorframe, arms across his chest, his gaze narrowed on her as she felt the tenderness of her body as well as the sudden sensitivity between her thighs. She felt pathetic. Pathetic wasn't even a good word for how weak she was when it came to him.

"Your ability to make me respond to you sexually does not mean I belong to you," she told him, proud of the firmness in her voice. "It takes a hell of a lot more than that."

His lips quirked at the words.

"You love me. You loved me before I left and you damn well know it. Just as you know you still love me." The pure arrogant confidence in his voice was enough to cause her to clench her teeth in anger.

"You left me—"

"I was coming back." Graveled and intense, his tone deepened as his arms dropped from his chest and he shifted, straightening as he stared at her broodingly. "Ask that manipulating bastard you call a father what happened that day, sweetheart. Ask him why I left, because it's evident you didn't ask a damn thing when he informed you I was gone."

No, she hadn't. She'd felt too broken, too betrayed to ask her poppa why Riordan had left. She'd accepted that he had just left, and she should have known better.

But her poppa had been right about one thing.

"If you had cared as much for me, Riordan, as you're certain I care for you, then you would have told him to kiss your ass. You wouldn't have left." She struggled to keep her voice calm, to hold back the pain, the bitterness. "And you damn sure wouldn't have left without finding a way to tell me goodbye."

He nodded sharply. "And any other time, I'd accept that—if waiting wouldn't have meant a man's life. We flew straight to England and were loaded into a transport on the airfield before flying to the evacuation zone. The second I returned to the temporary base in London I called, only to learn you'd been abducted."

For a second, he appeared haggard and filled with regret, but just as quickly it was gone.

"You were wounded then?" she asked, remembering her father's statement that he hadn't been on her team in the first six months after her rescue because he'd been wounded.

The tension increased in his large body for long seconds as he stared back at her.

"No. I wasn't wounded then. I was wounded rescuing you, Amara. I spent four months working to regain my strength to return to you. Now, how's that for someone who supposedly doesn't give a damn." Turning on his heel, he stalked from the bathroom as she stared back at him in shock, her lips parting on a soundless cry.

Before she could move to catch up with him, the sound of her bedroom door slamming echoed through the room, the crack of wood against wood causing her to flinch.

Why hadn't her father told her that Riordan was part of the rescue mission? That he'd been wounded rescuing her?

A chill raced over her despite the sweater she wore, an icy breath that had her heart racing as she tried to find that memory, tried to remember her rescue. The fog in her mind was more like a cement wall when it came to her abduction and rescue—as well as everything in between.

Slowly, memories before the abduction were falling into place. Too slowly, but at least they were making themselves known again. She couldn't forget the child she'd lost though, and the thought of that baby was killing her. Pressing her hand to her stomach, she closed her eyes, her breath hitching as she fought the pain of it.

She'd held the secret of her pregnancy even from her father, wanting to tell Riordan first. Why had she been so certain he'd want to know? She'd been excited, waiting for him. Why?

There were still too many gaps left in her many memories, and she could sense the fact that she needed to remember things quickly. Day by day she could feel an edge of panic growing inside her. There was something she needed to remember. Something she *had* to remember if she was going to survive this winter. And she had a feeling that that was the reason she knew she wasn't safe—whatever had happened during her abduction. The certainty of that was growing by the day. She could feel the knowledge, almost touch it, but it still hung just out of reach.

Turning back to the mirror, she stared at the mark Riordan had placed high on her neck. It wasn't as clear as the lower one, the one near her shoulder, but there was no hiding it either. He'd made certain everyone who saw her would know she was claimed. And she had a feeling he'd make certain everyone knew that *he* was the one who claimed her.

He was going to make her crazy.

Turning away, she undressed quickly, showered, and dressed in a pair of cranberry red slacks and a cream-colored sweater that hid the darker mark. There was no help for the higher one, though. She didn't own a turtleneck, and there was no way a scarf alone would hide it. She'd just have to own that one.

She couldn't imagine how her father was going to react. One thing about it though, she'd find out if Riordan was indeed prick enough to deal with her often too-strong, too-manipulative father. She'd worried about that . . .

She paused for a second before leaving the room. She'd worried about that when she and Riordan had been together before. Worried that if her father knew about their relationship, he would not have hurt her by forcing Riordan from her life, he would have played his stupid male games instead by forcing Riordan to marry her.

She hadn't wanted that. She'd wanted it to come naturally, but for some reason she'd been certain it would happen.

Why had she been so certain?

Rubbing at her still tender arm, she gave a quick shake of her head and continued down the hall. Bit by bit, piece by piece, she told herself, she'd remember.

She only prayed she would survive the return of those memories.

As she reached the staircase, she stared down at the foyer in shock and the thought that she'd have to survive the night first raced through her mind.

Riordan stepped from Amara's room, the door slamming behind him as he bit back a curse. She was going to make him crazy—and if she didn't, then his own emotions would. Damn her, he wanted nothing more than to haul her into his arms, hold her there, and ensure nothing or no one would ever cause her a moment of fear again.

The knowledge that he couldn't do that was ripping him apart on the inside.

"Riordan. In the foyer." The dark undertone of warning in his brother's voice had him pushing back his emotions—his fear for Amara and his anger over Ivan's machinations—as he reached up to activate the audio on his communications earbud and hurried down the hall.

"Get the main gates opened!" Micah was yelling in the link. "Now! Move. Move."

The sound of gunfire was impossible to miss, as were Micah's curses. Riordan raced for the stairs as he jerked his weapon from his hip holster.

Downstairs, Noah, Tobias, and Elizaveta were racing in the foyer, now fully armed with the compact automatic weapons they'd retrieved from the hidden armory.

Reaching the bottom of the stairs, Riordan caught the automatic Noah tossed him. "What the hell—?"

"Ivan's coming in hot," Noah snapped. "Micah and Grisha are at the gates to provide support. Ivan just called in as the sound of gunfire reached the guard at the gatehouse."

Tobias was pulling the front doors open, the sound of gunfire unmistakable as headlights raced for the gates. Micah, and Grisha were at the gates providing backup when vehicles swerved into view.

Immediately, Micah's team were firing on the vehicle racing behind Ivan's SUV, lying in cover as the Suburban tore past the gates and the truck running behind it slid in a perfectly executed turn, the wheels fighting for traction, biting in past the snow and tearing away in the wake of the gunfire being leveled on it.

"Ivan's hit," Ilya was then shouting into the link.

"Alexi," Riordan shouted to the butler/medic. "Get ready."

Ivan was shouting something, fury straining his voice

as the SUV rocked to a stop in front of the side steps leading to the house. Immediately the door was thrown open and Ivan jumped out.

Blood stained the shoulder of his white shirt and rage tightened his face. As Ilya jumped out behind him, Ivan turned and threw his fist into Ilya's face so fast and with such force his assistant went flying back, almost catching himself on the side of the truck before sprawling out in the snow.

Ivan reached into the SUV and, before Riordan's stunned gaze, dragged a young woman out of it, jerking her upright when she slid in the snow, his hold on her arm tight.

"Get her fucking ass inside," he shouted, pushing her to Elizaveta. "And don't take your goddamn eyes off her."

Elizaveta caught the young woman as she stumbled, her expression stoic as the bodyguard caught the woman's arm and hustled her inside.

"Follow them," Riordan told Noah, sparing only a second's glance to his brother as he turned and moved behind Elizaveta.

"Dammit, Ivan," Ilya cursed, pulling himself to his feet, his face flushed and angry, causing the tattoo at the side of his face to stand out in stark relief.

"Get away from me Ilya before I kill your ass," Ivan commanded, stabbing a finger in his assistant's direction. "Get far away from me, damn you." He turned on Riordan then. "Stay the fuck out of my way, cowboy."

He stalked past Riordan as Micah and the others jumped from the truck they'd taken from the guard-house, their expressions hard, though Riordan could see the question in the older man's eyes.

Turning, Riordan entered the foyer in time to see the redhead Ivan had jerked from the SUV tear away from Elizaveta and put her own fist squarely on Ivan's jaw.

The hall erupted in commotion then as Riordan jumped for the girl. The rage that filled Ivan's face was unlike any he'd seen in any man's. For one heartbeat, he was certain Amara's father would erupt in violence.

In the shock that surrounded her, the girl managed another blow. This one, straight into Ivan's lips. While blood, and a roar of fury, erupted from Ivan, the girl went for a third blow when Elizaveta tackled her.

"Noah!" Riordan shouted as everyone seemed to stand in shock as the two women went to the floor.

The woman was smaller, and obviously untrained, but neither mattered when the smaller, untrained one was fighting for her life. And there was no doubt the other woman thought she was fighting for her life.

She kicked, her nails went for Elizaveta's eyes, and she kept Elizaveta off balance just long enough to reach with her other hand for the weapon at the bodyguard's side. And she would have gotten it if Riordan hadn't managed to drag Elizaveta off her as Noah caught her hands and hauled her to her feet.

"Enough!" Riordan shouted as Ivan moved for the redhead.

Pushing Elizaveta aside, Riordan stood between Noah, who held the redhead, and Ivan. "What the fuck is going on here?"

He could see that Ivan was going to have a hell of a

black eye, that his lips were busted with the blood marring his face, and that murder gleamed in his dark blue eyes.

"Out of my way." Ivan snarled.

"Let me go!" Fear and anger filled the voice of Noah's captive. "I'll kill the bastard. . . . You son of a bitch, you don't know what you've done."

"What *I've* done?" Ivan tried to push past Riordan. "You little bitch, I thought I was trying to help you."

"That's the problem with you, Resnova," she accused him with furious sarcasm. "You're under the impression you know how to think. You can't do anything but cause chaos!"

"I'll make you eat those goddamn words." Ivan tried to get to her again.

"Dammit, Ivan, stay away from her." Riordan blocked him again.

When Ivan's fist flew at his face, Riordan barely managed to avoid it before Micah and Grisha grabbed Ivan's arms and hauled him back.

"Stay there!" Riordan shouted at him, furious now. "What the fuck is going on here?" He turned to Ilya, catching an almost calculated look on the assistant's face. "What the hell is their problem?"

The dragon tattoo flexed and rippled as Ivan clenched his jaw, his gray eyes steel hard as Ilya glanced at his employer.

Ilya crossed his arms over his broad chest but didn't speak as Ivan growled something that sounded more like an animal's snarl than a man's voice.

"I'll tell you what his problem is, he's crazy!" the woman behind Riordan cried out. "He's insane and can't take no for an answer. Just has to take everything over."

"They would have killed you!" Ivan shouted.

"They wouldn't have found me if it hadn't been for you, you damn prick!" The accusation was strangled with anger and what sounded like tears. "At least Amara had the good sense to sit and wait for me to get a chance to talk. You're a fucking bastard!"

Riordan turned to the woman slowly, his gaze going over her quickly.

He realized that she was the young woman from the coffee house. The waitress who had disappeared when Amara had shown up for coffee a few days before.

She was dressed in jeans and a long-sleeved gray T-shirt marred with what was probably Ivan's blood, dirt, and several tears in the sleeves; scuffed boots; and pure feminine fury as she glared at Ivan.

"What do you have to do with Amara?" he asked her. His voice was soft, but by the narrowing of Noah's eyes he knew he hadn't completely hidden the warning danger brewing beneath the surface of his control.

The girl's lips lifted with no small amount of disgust. "Yeah, cowboy, it's going to be that easy." She sneered.

Riordan was becoming rather tired of that particular nickname. But he'd address that later. First, he'd find out what kind of threat this woman presented to Amara.

"I won't ask you again," he warned her softly. "I'll have the man behind you hold your ass still while I fingerprint and photograph you, then I'll start with law enforcement. If I don't get anything there, I'll start pulling in contacts from the other side of the law. I'll get the answers I want, lady, one way or the other."

"Get fucked!" she cried, her thickly lashed eyes narrowed but didn't hide the deep, dark green that gleamed in fury as she struggled against Noah's hold.

"Get the damn fingerprinting kit, Ilya," Ivan snarled.

From the corner of his eye Riordan caught the disgusted look Ivan's assistant shot him. Ilya didn't move though.

"Girl, whatever you have chasing you appears to be a hell of a lot more dangerous to your welfare than we are." It was Noah's calm voice, without a threatening undertone, that had her pausing in her struggles. "No one's going to hurt you here. I give you my word on that, but we don't have a choice but find out what you have to do with whatever the hell's going on."

A shudder raced through her as her gaze moved quickly around the foyer, staring at the men facing her. The panic hadn't abated, but she was trying to think, to consider her options. The men who dragged her to the estate, or Noah's calm promise of safety.

"Why were you trying to talk to Amara?" Riordan fought to ask the question without the hint of danger his voice had held moments before. "If you need help, that man behind you will make damn sure you have it. But nothing will change the fact that we need answers."

Noah had sensed what he hadn't. That fear was the reason for her fury. Adrenaline flushed her features and had her eyes fever bright. Trembling lips and small, almost imperceptible shudders were barely controlled as she watched him carefully now.

"Syn!" Amara cried out, rushing down the stairs as Riordan turned slowly, watching her, knowing in that second that if she hadn't known who the woman was at the coffee shop, she damn sure did now.

"Syn?" Ivan snickered behind him as the young woman shot him a narrowed look of dislike. "Now by God doesn't that just beat all."

Riordan wanted to curse at the expression on Amara's face, at the scathing look of contempt that she shot her father. The one she gave him wasn't much better.

If those looks were any indication, she was not happy with either of them.

"Let her go!" Amara slapped at Noah's hand, causing him to release Syn's upper arms, slowly allowing Amara to drag her into a tight hug. "I'm so sorry," she whispered as Syn seemed to sag against her. "I'm so sorry."

Syn held onto Amara for long moments before drawing in a deep breath and swallowing tightly. "I'm okay. I am. But I think I busted your dad's mouth."

Amara drew back, her gaze going quickly over the other woman before she turned slowly to her father.

Ivan spat blood to the foyer floor as his gaze met his daughter's, the action causing her to narrow her eyes back at him in disapproval . . . until they landed on his shoulder.

"You're shot?" she whispered, fear suddenly flickering across her expression.

"Flesh wound." He shrugged, though the action was obviously less than comfortable.

"Alexi, take care of Poppa," she snapped at the butler as he hovered near the staircase with his medic's bag. "I want to know the moment you're finished no matter Poppa's demands. Are we clear?"

Riordan stared at her in surprise at the demanding tone in her voice.

"Yes, Miss Amara. Immediately," Alexi answered quickly.

"My staff seems to have forgotten who signs their paychecks," Ivan snarled, less than pleased at the butler's instant response.

"Excuse me, sir, you sign the checks, but Miss Amara actually makes certain they're printed out when you and Mr. Ilya are attending other things," Alexi murmured. "Of which the staff is most grateful."

Riordan could have sworn Ilya muttered something along the line of "Traitors every damn one."

"Ilya, what happened to your face?" Amara demanded then.

"I hit the bloody bastard!" her father snarled, his earlier fury reflected in his voice.

"Did he fire you again, Ilya?" she asked as though unconcerned.

"Twice," Ilya growled, that tattoo on his face rippling with almost lifelike movement as his jaw clenched furiously. "He hits me again and I swear to God, I'm hitting back."

"I swear to God, the two of you are worse than children," she informed them both with such a tone of feminine ire that Riordan was hard pressed to keep his surprise to himself. "Get yourselves cleaned up while I make certain you haven't traumatized Syn and get her settled into a room—"

"She's a prisoner." Her father made a step closer to Amara, his expression hardening, when Riordan saw the most amazing transformation in Amara's body language.

Hell, his own balls nearly shrank in fear as she lifted her head, put her shoulders back, and gave her father a look Riordan was certain he'd seen on his sister-in-law Bella's face several times. Times his tough brother had tucked his tail between his legs and became a lap puppy rather than the war dog he thought himself to be.

"Amara, don't you dare—" Ivan began

"Get your wounds looked at, father. I'll deal with you later," she said softly.

Ivan didn't tuck his tail, but his lips thinned—as much as possible considering the fact they were rapidly swelling—and his nostrils flared in displeasure. But he didn't say another damn word.

"Ilya, unless you need Alexi's care as well, please have Cook send dinner to my room. I know I smelled chicken stew earlier and there should be fresh hot rolls by now. And hot tea. Ask him for the peach blend I had him buy last week." She turned to Syn again. "Come on, we'll go upstairs and let Poppa get himself together before he and I speak."

As Amara led the way, Syn shot Ivan a look of pure spite and mocking triumph. Riordan rubbed at the back of his neck, grimacing, but he followed the two women. There wasn't a chance in hell he was letting an unknown alone with Amara.

"Keep your damn teeth off my daughter's neck, you little bitch," Ivan muttered as Riordan passed. "You're a disgrace."

Riordan merely grunted at the insult. He wasn't about

to get into a pissing match with Ivan. He was damned if he wanted Amara shooting him that look of disappointed disgust she'd shot her father. If Ivan wanted to risk his daughter's wrath, he could go for it. But Riordan was damned if he was risking his place beside her in bed.

And that look . . .

Yeah, it didn't bode well at all.

chapter twenty

Crimsyn Delaney.

Amara remembered her the moment she saw her. With her flame red hair, deep green eyes, and gently rounded features, she was as unique and fiery as her hair. Temperamental, deeply loyal, and normally quick to smile, Crimsyn could just as quickly become embroiled in a debate or protest. As evidenced by the brawl she'd evidently just been involved in.

Amara still couldn't believe her poppa had dragged Syn into the estate, followed by a barrage of gunfire. And what the hell was she doing here anyway? The last time she'd seen Crimsyn was in the New York County District Attorney's office where they'd both worked. Crimsyn was several years older, twenty-six or twenty-seven. They hadn't been fast friends; "friendly acquaintances" would be more accurate.

Pacing her bedroom as she waited for the other woman to eat and shower, she bit at her thumbnail and tried to remember as much as possible about Crimsyn Delaney.

While Amara had worked as an intern at the DA's office, Crimsyn had been an administrative assistant, working mainly in research. Crimsyn was more often to be found in the file storage rooms than in the offices.

They'd gone out for lunch occasionally with some of the other assistants and interns. They hadn't socialized outside the job, and Crimsyn, though aware of who Amara's father was, did not know him or hadn't ever met him, as far as Amara knew.

What the hell was she doing working in that café in Boulder?

And why hadn't she actually spoken to Amara rather than waiting for Amara to speak to her?

What could Crimsyn possibly have to do with anything that was going on now?

"You okay?" Riordan spoke from the connecting door, causing her to turn quickly to face him.

"Okay?" she asked him mockingly. "I don't think I'll ever be okay again. I still haven't remembered my own abduction, I don't know who wanted to hurt me or why, and I have no idea why Syn is here."

There were still too many blanks in her mind, too many things she couldn't remember. But she knew the memories were coming. She could feel it.

"Ivan recognized her when he went out to the coffee shop with Ilya earlier. He said she wasn't on the employee list when he checked it before," he told her, moving farther into the room as his lips quirked into a smile and his eyes gleamed with sapphire amusement.

"She packs a punch though. She laid into your father so fast he didn't know what hit him for a second."

She would have been amused, at any other time, and would be laughing in her father's face.

"How's Poppa's arm?" She'd checked on him just after seeing Syn to a suite, but like always, he was tough. "Just a scratch—nothing to worry about," he'd said. His declarations tended to piss her off when she knew he was hurt but he pretended he wasn't.

"A flesh wound, just as he said. Last I saw he was half drunk and on the phone with *associates*," he grunted. "He was screaming in Russian when I left him with Ilya and Noah. Noah was muttering something about babysitting."

Reaching for her, he pulled her into his arms, his hands moving over her back, stroking, caressing as her eyes drifted closed and she fought to keep from holding on desperately to him.

"You okay?" His head bent over hers, his lips brushing against her ear as he spoke.

"I'm okay," she promised him.

God, she could be such a liar. She was anything but "okay." She'd been anything but okay since she'd opened her eyes in that damn hospital room six months ago.

"Hmm." The murmured response was filled with doubt, but he let her go as she moved away from him. "So who's your friend in the other room?"

Blowing out a hard breath and glancing toward her door, she pushed her fingers through her short hair and felt the curls that clung to her fingers as well as the edges of panic building in her chest.

"We worked at the DA's office when I was interning there. We weren't best friends. We were work friends I guess." She frowned, probing at her memory of Syn to be certain she was right. "I don't understand why she's here or what's going on, Riordan. It doesn't make sense."

Nothing made sense anymore.

Swinging away from him, she stalked to the balcony doors, staring out to watch as the snow swirled outside. It had begun snowing heavily once again, the curtain of white insulating and icy.

Through the window she watched his reflection move toward her, his expression somber, his gaze holding hers, and she wanted to scream out at the pain tearing through her.

She couldn't forget the knowledge that lay in her soul like a heavy weight.

She hadn't been able to forget or to cry for the child she'd lost and the knowledge she was holding back from him. Why was she so certain he would even care?

"Say it." He had stopped just behind her, and the demand in his voice caused her to flinch.

"What do you want me to say?" Clenching her fists at her sides, she fought the need to scream, to release all the fury and pain trapped inside.

"Whatever I can see burning in your eyes," he answered her, his voice harsh. "Whatever I can feel tearing you apart. It's lying between us like an invisible sword just waiting to slice us both open. What aren't you telling me?"

She lowered her head, her eyes closing briefly. She fought the tears building behind her lashes as hard as she fought to hold herself back and deny the need to beg him to hold her.

There were so many emotions tearing at her, but uppermost was the love she felt for him. The love she knew he felt for her.

He'd loved her.

He'd loved her then and he loved her now.

As her lips parted, the words hovering on her tongue, a sharp knock at her bedroom door had her swallowing them and swinging around.

Riordan strode quickly to the door.

"Who is it?" The low, graveled tone of his voice indicated his displeasure at the interruption.

"Elizaveta," came the answer quickly.

Riordan opened the door and allowed her inside.

"Miss Delaney has showered and finished her meal," she told them, her voice tight. "Ivan has asked that he speak to Riordan before you speak with her. And I will tell you now"—she flashed Riordan an uncertain look—"he's going to demand you allow him to listen in on your meeting."

Amara was surprised her cousin revealed that information in Riordan's presence. That small sign of trust she gave him hinted that perhaps she and her brother hadn't heard of Riordan telling her father things he shouldn't know. Things he didn't need to know.

"He won't be alone." He turned to Amara. "You'll need to wear one of the earbuds to allow the others to hear what she's saying and for Noah to communicate with you as you talk to her. He'll be checking her information as she gives it, and if anything comes up, he'll be able to let you know."

It made sense. Agreeing to being bugged, as her father called it, Amara listened as Riordan explained the small device that tucked inside her ear. It was programmed to link her only to him, to her father, and to the team that worked specifically with Riordan, rather than to the general security team.

Amara's hair was just long enough to curl over and around her ears, allowing the device to be hidden but not interfere with reception.

Finally, after ensuring the others were receiving the link clearly, Riordan nodded and stepped to the door. "Ready?" he asked her.

Amara nodded her answer when she really wanted nothing more than to hide in her room.

"Ready."

She wasn't going to hide any longer. By God, enough was enough. She'd let the missing memories, the fear and uncertainties steal six months of her life, and she wasn't going to let it steal any more. And if Crimsyn was involved in the abduction somehow, involved in the loss of her and Riordan's baby, then God help her. Because Amara didn't think she'd be able to forgive her.

"Let's go then." Riordan held his hand out to her, broad, and strong.

Taking it, she watched his fingers clasp hers and swore she felt him wrap around her soul as well.

"Everything's going to be okay," he whispered, lowering his head to the opposite ear of the communications bud, so the words reached only her. "I'll be right there with you."

Yes, he would.

As she stepped into the hallway and paused, waiting for Elizaveta to follow her and then for Riordan to secure the room, those darkened, misty memories parted. She remembered the hole they threw her into, the agony of her broken bones and her broken dreams as she felt the blood that stained her thighs.

And she'd cried out for Riordan. Huddled in the dark silence, she'd reached for him, certain she could reach him, certain she wouldn't have to die alone if she just tried hard enough.

She'd convinced herself she felt him. Lying on the dirt, her body wracked by pain, she'd felt his horror, felt his arms surrounding her, his voice calling to her . . .

"Amara?" The touch at her arm had her jerking her head to the side and staring up at him, her heart racing, her breathing heavy at the abrupt shift from memory to reality.

What had happened in that pit her father had said they'd found her in? Where had she gone to escape the pain, the loss, and the certainty that she was dying?

"I'm fine," she whispered, answering the question she could sense in the heaviness of his expression. "Let's see what the hell she's doing in Boulder, why the hell Poppa got shot, and how the hell Ilya got fired twice in one night. It's bound to be a hell of a story."

It was bound to make her crazy was what it was bound to do.

Her father and Ilya had been best friends since they were boys. They often fought—her father was always firing Ilya—and they wound up hitting each other a few times a year. They loved each other like brothers, but they disagreed often. And sometimes, they disagreed violently.

Hopefully they could keep their tempers intact for as long as it took her to talk to Syn. She'd liked the other woman when they worked together, but she couldn't imagine why she was in Denver and obviously trying to find a way to talk to her without anyone knowing.

Stepping into the guest room with Riordan following closely, Amara caught Elizaveta's eye and motioned her from the room. She stayed silent while waiting for her cousin to leave, and when the door closed she met Syn's eyes purposefully.

Syn had showered, her hair was still damp. Amara had sent a pair of soft gray lounging pants and a T-shirt for her to wear.

"I'm sorry about the way Poppa seems to have handled this. Sometimes, he can be a little intense." Especially where his only child's safety was concerned.

Syn glared at her at the mention of Ivan. "Your father's deranged," she snapped. "And a pervert. He propositioned me, Amara." Pure outrage filled her voice. "He can say what he wants about trying to help me, but he actually asked me to spend the night with him."

Amara stared at her in surprise. Strangely, her father wasn't protesting that fact through the communications link. Though she heard the strangled little sound Riordan made behind her.

"Be that as it may," Amara said firmly, facing her, "the moment I saw you, tonight, Syn, I remembered you. We were friends, but that doesn't explain why you were in Boulder waiting for me to speak to you, rather than approaching me and explaining why you're here."

Syn watched her for long moments before giving her head a brief shake. "Hell, I had no idea you'd lost your memory until I overheard two of the guards who work here talking about it last week. If I had known, I would have shown up on your doorstep."

Amara frowned at the response. "Why wait though?"

Syn grimaced. "I thought you were deliberately ignoring me until you could get a chance to talk. I've become a little paranoid over the past six months, Amara. Maybe more than a little."

Amara watched as she pushed her fingers through her hair, her expression twisting with fear and uncertainty.

"Syn." None of this made sense. "Why? If you needed my help—"

"Your help?" Syn burst out incredulously. "God, Amara, I was certain your father would have already taken care of this. Instead, those bastards followed me from New York and nearly killed me tonight. When is he going to put their murdering asses six feet under so I can live in a small amount of peace and get my life back? You'd think a Russian mobster would know how to take care of these little things without help. Ya know?"

Muttered curses and a rush of sound could be heard through the link at her ear as Amara stared at Syn in shock. She could hear her poppa demanding to know how Ilya missed questioning Syn and his snapped reply that she wasn't on the staff of the DA's office when he questioned them.

All the while, her heart was racing as panic began to surge through her system, but the memories weren't there yet. Close. But they weren't there yet.

"Miss Delaney, do you know who kidnapped Amara?"

Riordan asked. His voice was low, but Amara could hear the harsh rasp just beneath the softness of the tone.

The look Syn shot Riordan was scathing. "If I knew, I'd kill him myself," she snapped. "All I know is who it had to do with. The first woman they kidnapped showed up dead three days after Amara was kidnapped. And just after Amara disappeared, I was nearly kidnapped. They just didn't expect the fight they got, and I managed to get away."

Amara listened, feeling the strange numbness that seemed to fill her and, underlying that, the panic that threatened to slip free. She felt cornered, as though something, someone dangerous was getting far too close.

"Syn, I have to call the others up here," Riordan said then. "This is something we all need to hear, and you need to tell us everything you know. You want the bastards six feet under, right?" he questioned, his voice harsh as she seemed ready to protest. "Then help us make that happen. Work with us."

And all Amara could do was stare at Syn and feel the shadows in her mind shifting, coiling like vipers preparing to strike. It was happening too fast. Too much information, too many revelations. The memory of the lover Riordan had been, the child she'd lost before she could tell him, and now this.

She wanted to run from whatever was coming. She wanted to make it stop, just for a little while, just long enough to prepare herself for what she could sense was coming. She wasn't ready to deal with more, and yet she didn't have a choice.

She could hear her father and Ilya on the link as her father snapped out orders and Ilya replied with calm determination. Noah was talking to someone, demanding a full background on Syn and some kind of communication link to an unknown "base." And all of it was distant, as though happening somewhere else, to someone else.

As Syn plopped down on the couch and covered her face with her hands, Amara moved to the chair across from her and sat down as well.

"I need a drink," Syn muttered.

"Irish hooch," Amara suggested. "I could use a few shots myself."

Syn stared back, regret shimmering in her eyes, filling her expression as she rested her arms across her knees then dropped her head. "I'm so sorry, Amara," she whispered, shaking her head before lifting it to stare back again.

She was so sorry? Yeah, well she wasn't the only one. Amara couldn't imagine being on the run for six months, always looking over her shoulder, wondering when a friend was going to reach out to her while too terrified to reach out herself.

Syn was thinner than she'd been six months ago, her face pale and drawn. There was no doubt of her fear and the toll that fear had taken on her. Amara remembered a laughing, always joking Syn. She'd never seen such stress on her face in the year they'd worked together.

"I'm sorry," Syn whispered again. "I really didn't know about the memory loss. I thought you were just being careful. I knew your father was searching for your abductor, that he was questioning the staff at the office. I thought you knew."

Amara blew out a hard breath as she rubbed at her arms.

Knew? She didn't know a damn thing, but she had a feeling it was all there, behind that curtain over her mind, just waiting to strike. And when it blew open, would she be able to handle it?

Knowing what had resulted from the beating she'd taken and actually facing the memories was another thing entirely, she feared. Just the knowing was breaking her heart. She'd wanted Riordan's baby so much. Not to hold on to the father or to tie him to her, but because it was precious. Innocent.

Her father had once told her that he'd faced pure innocence the day she was born, and that it changed something inside him. The boy who was so filled with anger became a man determined to protect what he'd seen in his daughter's eyes. The sound of his voice, the look on his face when he'd said those words, had given her a glimpse into the magic she'd find with her own child. A child given to her by a man unlike any other she knew. A man she had given her heart to.

"He's very protective of you," Syn said softly, drawing Amara from her thoughts and forcing her back to reality.

"Your bodyguard." The other woman nodded at Riordan as she spoke, her voice low.

His back was to them, his leanly muscled body tense as he kept an eye on them through the mirror on the door.

Her gaze met his, the somber sapphire shielded by thick black lashes and far too sexy for a woman's peace of mind. But in his gaze she saw something she knew no other woman had seen. Even more, she felt something each time his gaze touched hers. She swore she felt him, wrapping around her spirit, grounding her where she hadn't been grounded before.

"He is," she agreed softly, turning back to Syn. "Very much so."

"I remember him." A grin tugged at Syn's lips as her brown eyes lightened just a bit from the fear that had filled them earlier. "He'd sit a few tables over when we had lunch with another bodyguard. I always noticed how he watched you. All of us did."

Amara stared back at her in surprise. "You never said anything."

"Of course not." Syn rolled her eyes as amusement lightened her expression. "We were all totally jealous and completely lusting after that hard body."

Amara lifted her hand quickly to the ear that held the earbud, but she knew it was too late as she heard the snickers coming through the link. She couldn't hear Riordan speaking though, and she prayed he wasn't listening.

"I could have done without that information." Riordan definitely didn't need it, but she lightened the protest with an attempt at a grin.

Syn sighed heavily, her hands linking together at her knees.

"We were all totally jealous," she said a bit wistfully then. "The few times we saw your gazes meet, we could tell there was something there, Amara. Silent but incredibly deep. I've never seen that before, and we all agreed that was what we were searching for ourselves."

There was an edge of regret in Syn's tone though, as though she felt she'd never find it. And perhaps she was right, Amara had never needed Riordan to declare himself to her, or for her. She'd known how he felt, she realized. Her father wasn't right to demand that he deserved to know who was sleeping in her bed. He didn't. She would have told him when she was ready to, when she was ready to share Riordan with the world and accept that he wasn't just hers.

She'd been greedy, she realized. Allowing others to know meant that when they were out, other women, or her father, or a myriad of other people would demand his attention. The fact that they'd kept their affair secret ensured she didn't have to do that.

The time for it would have passed, she knew. The moment she realized she was pregnant, she'd also realized how dissatisfied Riordan was with the secretiveness and how dissatisfied she had been growing as well.

"I don't like your father," Syn sighed when Amara didn't respond. "I just think you should know that. He nearly got us all killed by skidding into the coffee shop and grabbing me the way he did. His friend should have shot him as he threatened."

"He and Ilya have a complicated relationship," Amara told her with a slight smile. "They've been friends forever. Since they were boys actually."

Syn snorted at that. "They didn't sound too friendly, I have to tell you. They sounded like they wanted to kill each other."

Amara leveled a rueful look at the other woman. "As I said, complicated."

Her lips pursed thoughtfully for a moment. "Are they lovers?" she asked.

Amara nearly choked on the strangled laugh that nearly emerged and shot her friend an amazed look. "Do they act like lovers?" Now this was funny. She'd never had a woman ask if her father was gay.

Syn only shrugged. "Sometimes it's hard tell."

"Miss Delaney?" Riordan chose that moment to step over to them. "The comm link I'm wearing is very sensitive and I should warn you, Ivan heard every word."

That was amusement in his voice. Amara could hear the muttered curses through her link, but she'd been ignoring them. She hadn't expected Syn to go in quite that direction or she would have covered the link at her own ear again.

Syn merely rolled her eyes. "He'll survive. As long as he keeps any weapons out of my hand that is. I'd enjoy shooting him, I think." She gave her head a little toss before sitting back on the couch and throwing Amara a subtle little wink.

How could she have forgotten Syn's habit of pricking the male ego every chance she had? It was one of the things that made her so fun to be around. Though Amara doubted her father would see it that way.

"Ivan's on his way up," Riordan told them then. "Miss Delaney, would you like a drink before they arrive? I have a feeling all of us may well need one."

Syn shot him a mocking look before grimacing. "Sure," she drawled. "But just to be social. You might want to leave the bottle out for Resnova and his dragon though. They may well need it before I'm finished."

And Amara had a feeling Syn wasn't talking about the insults she could deliver.

chapter twenty-one

Amara had been certain her abduction and the torture inflicted on her had been due to one of her father's enemies. Even he was certain that was where the threat lay. For six months, she knew, he'd worked with his contacts in that shadowy underworld to uncover the person, or persons, responsible. But Syn had a far different story.

One Amara listened to in silence as she felt those shadows in her mind shifting, twisting together warningly.

"The first intern to disappear was Shelly Mitchell. She worked with assistant DA Parrick." Crimsyn turned to Amara, her expression tight with renewed fear again. "Do you remember her?"

Amara nodded, swallowing tightly. Shelly was young, filled with dreams, and newly engaged.

"She was supposed to go on vacation with her fiancé. She was supposed to be back the day after you were abducted. A week later her body washed up on some beach in Jersey. She'd been shot in the head. Her fiancé still hasn't been found."

Inhaling a shuddering breath, Syn pushed her fingers through her hair as Amara and the five men who sat around the room watched her silently, waiting.

"The day after Amara's rescue was announced, I had to work late to finish up a brief for ADA Parrick. I only live a few blocks from the office, so I normally walk. That night though, I took a cab." She linked her fingers tight and stared at them as her hands lay on her knees. "About an hour after I arrived home I heard my lock being picked." Her lips trembled. "I called nine-one-one but the call wouldn't go through, so I slipped from my bedroom to the fire escape and hid on the little ledge to the side of it."

She'd been hiding there, she explained, as she heard her apartment being ransacked, and through the small opening she'd left as she reclosed the window, listened to the two men as they went through her home. They were searching for information on where to find her because someone was certain she saw something, and might remember it.

They wanted her dead, she'd heard them say, just like that Mitchell girl, then they'd find a way to take care of that Resnova bitch. By killing Amara, one of them stated, they'd take care of the threat and seriously weaken Ivan Resnova as well.

" 'Two birds with one stone,' one of them laughed. 'Eliminate the threat and distract Resnova long enough to destroy him. But first, we have to make sure this Delaney bitch is dead. Then no one can tie the girls together or tie them to the boss,'" she recalled. "As I was waiting for them to leave, they opened the window, checked the fire escape rather quickly and when they ducked back in they left the window open. That's when I heard one of them say they'd just wait for me to call nine-one-one about the break-in. They'd have one of their officers take care of me then. And if I used my cell phone to call anyone for help, they'd track me with my phone."

A shocked laugh left Crimsyn's lips as she looked up again and stared back at all them in amazement.

"One of their officers," she repeated, the fear and outrage she felt reflected on her face. "When they left, I took what I could fit in my backpack, left my phone there, and ran." She was trembling as she stared at her hands again, then into the gas fire Ilya had lit as she spoke. "They've nearly caught me twice. And now, they're in Boulder. I was too scared to call your cell because they could've had a way to track the call." She looked back at Amara. "I was waiting for you to speak to me, thinking you must know who I was, but someone was always with you. I don't know what's going on, Amara. Or why. But Shelly's dead, they tried to kill you, and if they'd managed to grab me, they would have killed me too. That I know."

Two birds with one stone . . .

"Let Resnova's men get close. The prized stud he picked for his bitch daughter will be with them. Kill them. She'll never breed again . . ."

The memory swept over her. She knew the voice. As she listened to Crimsyn answer her father's and Riordan's questions, whispered voices began to emerge from those hidden memories.

Questions. Her abductors had questioned her, and they hadn't liked her answers. In a fit of rage, one—he wore a mask, but she could see his eyes—had pulled her from the floor by her hair and threw her into a chair. There, he'd hacked her hair off as she fought to remain conscious while he'd laughed at her. Laughed at her because her father and her lover seemed so proud of her pretty hair.

Her lover.

Who had known Riordan was her lover? Even her father hadn't known. But even more important, who had known she was pregnant?

"Why didn't you try to contact me?" her father's voice was a low, brooding sound of anger. "You obviously knew who I was."

"A Russian mobster?" Incredulity filled Crimsyn's voice. "The only redeeming quality you have is your obvious love for your daughter. It's also considered your only weakness. Besides, you were a target though I have no idea why." Crimsyn snorted with an edge of disgust. "You and him." She nodded to Riordan.

Two birds with one stone—her father and her lover. Why?

She would never breed again . . .

The memory, as faint as it was, played through her mind over and over again.

She knew those eyes. She remembered thinking she knew his eyes. The way he stared at her, their color.

What was that color?

Staring at her hands as they lay in her lap she tried to remember, to force the memories from hiding.

She could feel them so close, teasing her, tormenting her.

Terrifying her.

She listened to the questions her father and Riordan threw at Crimsyn, listened to her replies. There wasn't much more information that her friend could give them though. She'd been waiting on Amara to contact her, thinking she'd have answers instead since she was so heavily guarded.

She felt like a failure. She'd failed to keep her unborn child safe, failed to remember the bastards who killed her baby, who nearly killed Riordan. And she knew the answers were there in her memories, just waiting for her to find the key to unlock them.

Why couldn't she remember? Everything else was coming back. Everything but those hours between her abduction and her rescue.

Goddammit, Micah . . . we're losing him . . . Don't you do this to me, Rory . . . The words echoed through her head and sheer terror nearly stopped her heart.

Riordan.

She'd tried to warn him that he was targeted, but she'd been in so much pain and trying so hard to keep him from seeing it. He had to get away from her.

She looked up at the man running beside the carrier they'd strapped her into. Eyes like Riordan's. His voice harsh, scraping.

He'd been there. Micah had been there.

Amara could feel her heart racing now, panic, hope, building inside her.

"They said they'd get two birds with one stone . . ."

Crimsyn was telling her father again. "They wanted you as well. But there was nothing Shelly, Amara, and I had worked on that involved you. ADA Parrick never mentioned you."

"Parrick can't touch me and he knows it," her father snorted in contempt. "I warned Amara about working for that bastard."

He had. Her father had warned her that Parrick was a bastard who refused to play by the rules.

A memory flashed through her mind, too quickly to catch details or know what it meant. Three men, two with their backs to her, but Parrick was there. A door barely opened and Parrick glancing up as they walked by . . .

Oh God.

She, Crimsyn, and Shelley. The other two with her, but they weren't paying attention. Amara had just glanced at the door. It had been opened just enough.

But she remembered the ADA's expression. Parrick had looked sick to his stomach as their gazes met.

She remained silent, still. Her father would just kill Parrick, she knew him. He'd never allow the assistant district attorney to live. He'd sworn he'd kill whoever hurt her. She'd heard him, several times.

The memory flashed again. The men turning, turning as Parrick's head jerked up.

Faces. Who were they?

Just that fast, it was gone. Had she seen their faces?

"Amara?" she heard her name called, but the past held her, the memory of a moment out of time held her as she fought to remember if she'd seen the faces of the men with the assistant district attorney.

"Amara!" Her father snapped, but his voice simply joined the memories clashing in her head now. A jumble of visions and voices that made no sense, that she was unable to separate.

"Amara?" Riordan touched her. His hand on her shoulder, its warmth sinking into her skin and causing her to jerk from her chair.

Staring around the room frantically her gaze met Noah's . . . *God no, brathair, don't leave me* . . . brathair. Brother. Riordan had said his brother Nathan had died.

Did he know?

She watched Noah's gaze narrow, suspicion gleaming in them.

"We were together," she whispered, turning to Crimsyn and seeing the expression of fragile hope on her face that Amara had actually remembered something. "You, Shelley, and me. We were at Antonio's. You and Shelley were arguing over the work schedule."

"Shelley wanted a few days off unscheduled." Crimsyn nodded as she rose to her feet. "We were heading out."

"I saw a meeting," she whispered. "We passed a door, it was partially opened."

Crimsyn looked confused then. "We did?"

"Who?" The single word, so quietly spoken, terrified her.

"I don't know." She was lying to her father now. God help her, he would never forgive her for lying to him. For protecting him. "I saw a meeting. One of the men looked scared. So scared, it frightened me."

It was the truth. That sick look on Parrick's face as he looked up at her and as the two men started turning.

Then, she'd brushed it aside. She hadn't seen who he was with, so what did it matter?

And she should have known better. She knew she should have known better. She was her father's daughter, she'd grown up with such lessons drilled into her mind. Watch everything. Discount nothing. But she'd just wanted to leave. Riordan was waiting on her just ahead, his gaze pulling her, reminding her of their plans that evening.

The promises he'd made of all the sexy things he was going to do to her when Elizaveta and Grisha left for Russia. He was going to make her scream for him to take her, he'd promised her.

"I thought it was nothing," she whispered, trying to breathe through the knowledge searing her.

It hadn't been nothing.

Parrick's expression should have warned her of that. She should have never forgotten what she'd seen. She should have told Riordan. She should have called her father. But she'd forgotten about the meeting. And she hadn't known when Shelley had disappeared. She was supposed to be off work anyway.

"Riordan, get her out of here," Noah told his brother.

It wasn't an order, but the suggestion was firm, indicating that at one time, Noah had given the orders. "Ivan, call your contacts at Antonio's. Those rooms have to be reserved," he reminded her father. "Get the reservation lists from two weeks before her abduction. Let's see who's on it."

That would take more than a night, Amara consoled herself as Riordan's hand lowered to her back and led her from the room. Led her away from the suspicion in her father's eyes.

Oh, Poppa knew she was lying. He knew, and the look on his face promised her he'd be talking to her very very soon.

Brathair.

As Amara and Noah had looked at each other, Riordan heard the word as though in the lightest whisper. Barely there. More sensed than heard as he felt a sensation he'd only felt a few times in his life. Each time he'd felt it, Amara had been involved.

When she'd been abducted. The few times something had drawn him from the near coma after he'd been wounded rescuing her. When Noah had told him about the miscarriage. And again, now.

Brathair.

The warning look Noah shot him wasn't lost on him either. For some reason, somehow, Amara knew Noah was the brother Nathan whom everyone believed was dead. And that wasn't something he'd ever told Amara. Just as he hadn't told her about the miscarriage.

But she knew. That sensation he'd felt? It was the one his grandpops had often warned him about. The sensation that accompanied that moment when a Malone touched the soul of the woman who owned his own soul. That moment when Irish eyes saw past reality and into the heart of true love. The woman who loved. The man who loved. That moment their souls touched.

Checking her room quickly, he returned to the entrance, nodded to Micah who stood with Amara, then pulled Amara in and closed the door firmly before sliding the lock in place.

He watched her for long seconds as she moved to the gas fire and stared at the flames. The way her pants hugged her slender hips and pert ass, the line of her back beneath the sweater. His dick was so damn hard, he wanted nothing more than to throw her to the bed and tear those clothes off her. The need to touch her, to feel that bond again, deeper, stronger, was almost overwhelming.

"What happened in there?" he asked her, knowing what had happened, feeling it to the depths of his being.

"Nothing happened." Her voice was low, uncertain. "I told you what I remembered."

"Did you?" Stalking to her, he gripped her arm, pulling her to face him, and saw the truth in her eyes, her uncertainty and fears. And she broke his heart. "What did you remember?"

Her lips trembled for a second. "Brathair." The word was but a whisper of sound. "I heard him call you brathair as you died. You died, Riordan. . . I felt you die . . ." Her beautiful eyes filled with tears. "I felt you die and I wanted to die with you . . ." Her voice broke, a ragged sob that sent a jagged slice of pain across his chest.

"God, Amara." He jerked her into his arms, his head bending to her, his lips against her ear. "Never say that word again," he murmured for her alone. "Ever."

She nodded as he spoke, knowing the secret, sensing the danger in it.

Her voice had been low enough that this time no ears

could have heard what she said. He couldn't chance the word ever being heard. Noah couldn't chance it. Dead men didn't talk, but he knew in that moment that his heart had stopped on that chopper, a dead man had forced him back. His brother, as well as the bonds that held him to the woman in his arms now.

Slender, silken arms held tight to him, quiet sobs tearing past her lips as he tried to shelter her, to protect her from the memories. Memories he knew were far more destructive to her personally than that single word.

"I should have told you," she cried out then, shuddering his arms. "The day I saw that meeting, I knew something was wrong. I saw his face, the look on it as the two men with him were turning. I saw the fear and that look of horror . . ."

Her fingers clenched in his shirt, tightened in it as her body drew tight from the pain he could sense lashing at her.

"Who?" He knew when she'd told her father that she didn't know who was at that meeting that she'd been lying. And her father had known it too.

"Poppa will just kill him." The fear she felt that her father would act out of rage filled her voice. "It was my fault. My fault Shelly died. My fault you were lost to me . . . my fault . . ."

That fucking bond. He felt her in a way he'd never felt another human in his life. Inside him. A part of him. Sweet heaven, Grandpops had been right.

"It wasn't your fault." He held her, fought his own rage. He couldn't let her sense it, couldn't let her know he could become far more of a monster than her father ever thought to be. "Not Shelly. Not me." He kissed her temple. "Not our child."

The wail that tore from her throat cut through his soul like a jagged blade. But she knew. She'd remembered what she'd lost in the hours she'd spent at her abductors' hands.

She'd known, and she'd held it inside, until now.

"They knew." She tore from his arms, her arms wrapping around herself, hands clenched into fists as she stalked to the other side of the room and turned back to him. "They knew I was pregnant. They knew, and they meant to cause the miscarriage. They knew you'd come for me, and they meant to kill both of us. Kill us. Weaken Poppa . . ."

Her hands tunneled through her hair as a helpless grimace twisted her expression. "And I don't know why, Riordan. I don't know why. But when I saw his face at that meeting . . ."

"Who, Amara?" She knew.

Riordan could feel that knowledge feeding inside her, building, memories sliding slowly, insidiously through her mind. Even as she stood there watching him, the expression on her face filled with misery, he could sense the dawning feelings of betrayal and pain. And the remnants of terror.

That terror would break him. Her terror, the inky darkness and pain she couldn't fight, couldn't escape. Because he'd left her alone. Unprotected.

"The private rooms of the restaurant. The door was just open," she whispered. "I saw his face, and I wouldn't have paid any attention, but when he saw me, I saw the fear. He looked sick with it. Because I'd seen him.

But, I didn't realize what it was at first. I wouldn't have even remembered seeing him, but the two men with him were turning . . ." Her lips were parted, disbelief and betrayal filling her expression. "It was John Parrick, the ADA I sometimes interned with, but it was who he was meeting with. I saw one of the men he was meeting with. And . . . it's not possible, Riordan . . ." She shook her head slowly. "It's just not possible . . ."

He stared back at her, waiting, knowing she needed the time to let those memories become clear enough, to allow herself to be certain enough, to give him the name he needed.

Confusion filled her expression before she gave her head another hard shake.

"None of it makes sense," she cried out, a sob tearing from her. "It just doesn't make sense."

"Who?" he snapped.

He wanted that name, he wanted to know who to go after, whose blood to spill for the horror she'd suffered and the loss of the child she carried. Their child. A part of the overwhelming emotion and bond they shared. The tiny life they'd created together, would have loved together.

She couldn't do it.

Amara stared back at Riordan, knowing she couldn't say that name, couldn't accuse him without staring into his eyes, facing him with it.

He'd helped raise her. He'd been a part of her life, helped save her life when she was only a child. She couldn't sign his death warrant without knowing, without seeing his eyes, his expression when she demanded to know why.

Her father had raised her to be stronger than this. She'd faced the loss of her memories with more strength than this. She hadn't hidden in her room and refused to face life then. And she wouldn't hide in her room now and let others make the accusation to one of those who had guarded her for so long.

Why guard her? Why defend her as a child, only to betray her now?

"No!" The word was a guttural growl from Riordan, causing her to stare back at him surprise. "I won't let you do whatever it is you're considering. Don't even say it."

She blinked back at him, staring into those incredible eyes, and realized the part of her that had always felt him. From the moment they met, she'd known him, had somehow sensed what she was going to do, what she was going to demand.

It had been there the moment they met. It had snapped into place with their first kiss. A sense of knowledge, a bond that ensured they'd never be alone.

She hadn't been alone during those horrific hours she'd been held by her abductors either. He'd been there. She'd felt him.

"I have to face him," she whispered painfully. "You know I have to, Riordan. I have to face him. You know I have to."

Because he was such a part of her life. A daily part of her life. Always with her father, always watching over them.

"Amara." The demand in his voice was impossible to miss.

Dominance, that male intensity when faced with the certainty that a woman wasn't going to be swayed. She'd faced it before, with him. And with it, that spark of hunger and heat that she couldn't help but respond to.

It had always been this way with him. From that first meeting to the night before he left for England. He made her respond whether she was angry with him or simply challenging him.

He made her ache for him.

"I have to," she stated again, firmly, her head lifting, her shoulders straightening. She had to. Period.

She had no other choice.

chapter twenty-two

There she was. Riordan couldn't help but stare at Amara with a mixture of pride, lust, and pure love.

God, he loved her.

Until that moment, that second, even he hadn't realized how much she was a part of him.

That didn't mean he'd let her endanger herself so easily.

"No." He reached her in a few steps and pulled her against him, staring into eyes that gleamed with stubborn, female determination. "You'll tell me, and I'll take care of it, Amara."

"No, I won't." She pushed against his chest, her eyes narrowing on him, her features flushed with anger, with arousal.

Damn her, the things she did to him, they made him crazy, they made him *feel*. For years he'd fought to not feel anything. To ensure that nothing could touch him inside. And then Amara. He'd been helpless against her.

He was still helpless against her, but not so damn helpless he'd allow her to endanger herself.

"You will!" The growl that tore from his throat was a dangerous sound as he well knew.

Dangerous, and hungry.

Before she could challenge him again, he lowered his head and covered her lips with his, stealing her protests. And it was like gasoline to fire. The most potent, most intoxicating liquor to hit a man's head.

She made him drunk on lust. Drunk on the need for her and the overwhelming emotion she pulled from his soul. He was a man used to controlling his emotions, his needs, but there had never been any sense of the steely control he used to possess since the moment he'd met this woman.

Parting her lips, his tongue swept in, tasted her. The moan that whispered from her only fueled the need. The hands that buried in his hair to hold him to her made him crazier for her.

His.

She was his.

He tore at her clothes, at his own, as his lips held her captive. Buttons popped free, seams tore. And he'd be damned if he cared. Nothing mattered but getting to sweet, silken flesh and possessing her senses as she possessed his.

To mark her soul as she marked his.

"I won't lose you again," he all but snarled as he pulled back and swung her into his arms. "Never again, Amara."

She couldn't lose him again.

The room spun as Riordan lifted her into his arms

and strode to the bed. Laying her on the blankets, his lips covering hers again, she was distantly aware that he was working his boots and his jeans off even as she struggled with her own.

What made her wear so many damn clothes? Now she remembered why she liked dresses and skirts so much better around Riordan. It didn't take near as long to undress. If she had to undress at all.

As the jeans and silk panties cleared her feet to be kicked aside, those amazing lips moved from hers, along her neck and jaw, spreading sensations that stole her breath and pulled another of those low, pleasure-tortured moans from her lips.

Sensations raced across her flesh, shot to her nipples, her clit. Each touch, each scrape of his teeth and lick of his tongue, had her arching closer, desperate for more.

And just as desperate to show him the same pleasure.

Pushing at his shoulders, struggling beneath him, she was well aware he went to his back because he wanted to. Even as he did so, he pulled her over him until her legs straddled his waist and his lips captured one far too sensitive nipple.

"Riordan." She breathed his name out on a moan, her eyes closed as pleasure washed over her.

The draw of his lips on the sensitive tip, the lash of his tongue, was exquisite. She could feel each pull on the tight bud in a burst of sensation at her clit.

Tilting her hips, she moved against the hard contours of his waist, the bunch of muscle, the stroke of heated male flesh against the bundle of nerves had her hips shifting, moving against him. It was the lightest touch to the swollen bud of her clit, a tease and nearly more than she could bear.

Her breath caught as his hands stroked from her hips, along her back, to her shoulders then to her hips again. Callused flesh rasped against her softer skin, caressed and excited each nerve ending. Each draw of his mouth and scrape of his teeth on her nipple sent her senses spiraling out of control.

What he did to her . . .

He made her high on sensation, and she loved it. The sensitivity of her body, the pleasure of his touch, that edge of pain he liked to give her.

His hands caressed her hips, then the curve of her rear where they clenched in the flesh, parted them, and sent a heated surge to the sensitive entrance they revealed.

The spill of slick heat from her pussy was a slow stroke of increased hunger. A cry slipped from her as she thrust closer to rub against the tight abs beneath.

Her pussy ached, clenched. The need for him was growing by the second in ways it hadn't when he first took her. It was like a fire, a flame licking over her, inside her, demanding him.

His lips moved from one nipple to the other, sucking and drawing at the tight tip, licking over it as he held her in place and ignored the desperate cries she couldn't hold back.

"Please." The moan was torn, pleading, as she tried to lower her body, to get closer to the fierce length of his cock that brushed against her rear. "I need you."

His hands clenched on her rear again, his teeth scraped her nipple. She could barely breathe. Heat rushed through her body as her pulse pounded through her veins, thundering with excitement, with the knowledge of the intensity of sensations waiting on the horizon.

When he drew back, her breath caught at the loss of his mouth against the sensitive bundle of nerves.

"Ride me," he demanded, the wicked, sensual look on his face causing her stomach to clench in reaction.

Her breathing increased, the drugged fervor overtaking her. Oh God. That suggestion nearly had her coming from the sound of it alone.

Strong hands gripped her hips, pushed her lower, until the slick folds of her sex met the throbbing crest waiting to penetrate her.

"Riordan." His name slipped past her lips, a breathless cry of searing need and hunger as he controlled her movements, forced her to ease against him rather than take him as she wanted. As she needed.

"Easy, baby." He ignored her desperate movements, the plea in her eyes staring up at her, the gleam of sapphire fire between thick black lashes holding her gaze. "Ride me slow and easy."

Slow and easy? Slow and easy would kill her.

As the first fiery stretch at her entrance began, her lashes dropped further. Her fingers curled against muscular biceps and her head tipped back. Sensation, striking and intense, lashed at her, stealing her senses, her breath.

She barely heard the cry that parted her lips. A sound she'd never made before, even with Riordan. She'd always been quiet, always been aware her bodyguards would hear her pleasure, and report it.

It didn't matter now. She belonged to him totally, but even more, she knew he belonged to her.

Each push inside her tender flesh had her crying out

for him, feeling him in agonizingly slow degrees as he took her, inch by inch. Impaling her with the broad shaft in heated strokes of pure ecstasy.

How could it be this good, this hot? How can any man's touch sap protest, steal the senses, and chain a woman's desires as he did hers? No, he didn't chain them. He mesmerized them. Owned them.

"Feel how good it is, baby," he groaned, hips lifting to push deeper inside her. "So sweet and tight. The way you grip me."

Deep, involuntary spasms of her inner muscles had her clenching on the thick shaft easing inside her.

"Ah fuck . . . Amara." His hips jerked, slamming his cock deeper and dragging a ragged cry from her lips.

Tightening her thighs on his, Amara pushed into the thrust, taking more. Demanding more.

"Damn, baby," he groaned, his expression tightening, a grimace of pleasure pulling at his face as she strained to take more. "That's it. Take all of me."

Her pussy rippled around the impalement, taking him, crying out with the pleasure, the heat of each stretching penetration of her body.

"Give me all of you then," she cried out, her fingers tightening, nails digging into his upper arms. "Let me have you, Riordan." Her hips flexed, inner muscles clenching. "Let me ride you . . ."

The guttural curse that tore from his throat came as his hips arched, burying his cock inside her, and then he let her have her way.

She was beautiful. Black curls framed her face as the blue gray of her eyes darkened, narrowed. Her body undulated, driving the fist-tight sheath of slick silk up and down his cock.

Clasping her hips, he let her have her way, let her ride him, impaling herself with the tortured length of his erection.

Fuck. It was good. Fist tight. Heated.

She worked her pussy over his erection, tightening, clenching, rippling over the sensitive head and throbbing shaft, pushing him closer to release.

Never had he seen anything, anyone, so beautiful.

His Amara.

And she rode him like a dream.

Sensual, sinuous movements, rising and falling, her gaze heavy lidded and locked with his, seeing into him as he saw into her.

She was consumed by him. He filled her, penetrating her in ways that went far beyond the physical, beyond anything she could have imagined existing. The rush of pleasure, of sensual heat and pure sexual sensation was more than she could bear. With each stroke she could feel that edge, the whirlwind of ecstasy growing nearer, stealing her mind, taking a part of her soul.

"Riordan," she cried out his name, allowing him to guide her now, allowing his hands to lead her, to keep her from flying apart when it took her.

"I have you, baby," he groaned. "Mine. I have you, Amara."

It struck with such force, with such overpowering intensity, she was afraid she might have screamed his name. The pleasure coalesced, imploded, and sent her spiraling into waves of exquisite ecstasy.

She writhed within the grip of it, pushing into each thrust, feeling his body tighten and hearing him groan her name as his own release rushed over him.

The world tilted until she found herself beneath him, her legs pushed back, her knees bent over his arms, and him hammering inside her. Desperate, driving strokes that threw her deeper into ever-growing waves of desperate rapture.

"I love you." She gasped the words she'd fought to hold back, to keep to herself.

She gave him that last measure of herself as he tightened above her, his lips burying at her shoulder as he marked her again. A mark she knew she wouldn't bother to hide should it show. A physical mark that did nothing to compare to the mark he placed on her soul.

And all she could do as she lay in his arms was cry. For what she'd lost, for what she'd nearly lost, and for the loss that was coming.

Minutes, hours passed—Amara didn't bother counting time. It was still dark, the light from the gas flames flickered through the room, casting Riordan's features in shadow but doing nothing to hide the gleam of his sapphire eyes.

Lying next to him, turned to him, Amara felt the ragged shards of everything she'd tried to hide, tried to hold back, ripping through her. "Our baby," she whispered as his thumb brushed against her cheek. "They took our baby, Riordan."

"They'll pay for it."

And there wasn't a doubt in her mind that someone would indeed pay. She didn't try to stop the tears this time—there was no strength left to hold anything back.

Lying against his chest as he pulled her to him again, his hand stroking her back, her arm, she let the tears fall, let the pain free. It was the only way she could do what she knew she had to do, tell him what she had to tell him.

He was her only chance to find a reason why. Why someone so close to her had betrayed her. Betrayed her and her child.

"They knew," she whispered as he held her to him, his arms tight around her, his head lowered over hers. "No one should have known I was pregnant but myself and Poppa."

But there were those who could have gotten that information if her father hadn't been incredibly careful. And there were just a few, a very few, who could have gotten it anyway.

"Amara . . ."

"The men who abducted me. I don't know who they were. They were masked. But I saw the eyes of the one who cut my hair, heard his voice. He knew Poppa would send you after me. He knew I was pregnant, and each blow was meant to kill my baby, Riordan. He said my death, the baby's, and Poppa's chosen stud for me, would weaken him. It would weaken him, then they could take him down. But, he also said if I wasn't so damn nosy it would have never happened."

"You saw the man who beat you, didn't you? That day in the restaurant?" He couldn't hide his fury from her, she realized. She could almost taste it.

"You can't kill them yourself, Riordan. It's why I

wouldn't tell Poppa." She drew away from him, drawing the sheet to her breasts and staring down at him. "I won't be the reason either of you risks prison for me."

Those blue eyes were like fire in his dark face. "Prison?" Incredulity filled his voice. "Have you forgotten who your father is?" For a moment, an amazed laugh nearly escaped—and would have if the hurt and fear hadn't flashed so bright across her expression. "Amara, baby . . ."

"I won't risk you carrying that crime for me." Her voice broke on a sob. "The law means something to me, Riordan. I couldn't bear it if you and Poppa took vengeance rather than justice. You have to swear it to me."

It meant something to her. Yes, the law meant something to her, because she'd grown up under the shadow of where her family had come from and how her father's family had amassed their fortune.

A fortune that allowed Ivan Resnova to walk away from the bloody legacy he'd been born into. A man who walked in the shadows of both worlds, the criminal and the just, never really stepping fully into either no matter his desire to live free of his past.

She knew the horrors her grandfather, Ivan's father, had committed. Knew the consequences of them and as a child had nearly died as a result of them more than once. And her conscience simply couldn't countenance murder.

There was a difference though, Riordan had learned, between murder, retribution, and justice. Sometimes, the only justice was the one that came swiftly, without fanfare, and with no chance of freedom. And he'd never give those responsible for hurting her a chance to do so again. If Ivan or Noah didn't beat him to it.

Riordan could only stare up at her, fury pulsing through his veins as he fought the vow he knew she was going to ask him to make.

"You're asking for the impossible," he finally told her. "Whatever your father does, I'm afraid I can't stop him. And I can't promise I won't help him."

Her face crumpled. Tears ran from her eyes in slow rivulets as she covered her face with her hands and silent sobs shook her slight body.

"Goddammit, Amara, you can't ask this of us." Surging from the bed, he grabbed his jeans from the floor and pulled them on.

Dressing took only moments, but he was aware of her moving from the bed. Silently. Finding her clothes, she dressed as well.

"Then I'll do it myself," she told him, her voice hoarse from her tears.

God! He was a second away from plowing his fist into the wall.

"What the hell do you want from me?" he growled. "That was my child too, Amara. My child and my woman, and they nearly took both of you from me. Do you want me to just stand aside and allow that to happen?"

"No!" she cried out, jerking her sweater over her head before facing him. "I want you to stand with me. Stand with me and let me face the man who took our baby and nearly killed you. I want you to let me face him." She was all but screaming. "Then I want him and the bastards he was meeting up with turned over to law enforcement. I won't have you murder a man for me. Not you or Poppa."

Anger filled her face, but determination defined it. She wouldn't tell him a damn thing if he didn't agree to her demands, and he knew it.

She was the most stubborn, independent, aggravating woman he'd ever known in his life.

Clenching his teeth, Riordan jerked his shirt on as she glared at him, her lips set in a firm line, arms crossed over her breasts.

He could find a way to make this work for both of them, he told himself. Noah would never allow his brother's wife to be in harm's way, and Amara need never know that a very private arm of the law had taken care of the bastards determined to see her dead.

The agency that gave Elite Ops their power had given the other man full authority on this mission. Ivan was essential to several operations they had underway now, and may have in the future. He was their eyes and ears into organizations they'd have never known about otherwise.

He could discuss this with him and Micah, come up with a plan, and then give Amara what she asked. Neither he nor Ivan would pull the trigger, but the threat would be eliminated.

"We can't do anything until the storm's over anyway." He forced the words past his lips.

Her head lifted as she took a trembling breath before she said, "He's here. In the house."

Riordan felt his blood freeze. In the next breath, he swore the rage filling him had it boiling.

"Say that again," he demanded, furious. "I know I didn't hear you correctly, Amara."

"I said, he's here, in the house," she snapped, face flushed, not even bothering to hide her anger. "Now will you help me, Riordan? Will you promise me you won't let Poppa kill him and you won't kill him yourself?"

In the house.

The bastard was there, believing himself safe because Amara's memory of the kidnapping and the loss of her child had been forgotten. No one knew Amara was aware of who had beaten her so horribly yet.

And if he was here, he would know who the others were.

Pushing his fingers through his hair furiously, he restrained his need to force every person at the estate, except those he knew hadn't been a part of it, into a room and begin interrogating them one by one.

Micah had taught him some interesting tricks over the years where interrogation was concerned. And he wouldn't have a problem using them.

Until he stared into Amara's eyes and saw the knowledge she would carry, that he could be just as cold blooded, just as merciless as her father.

She loved the man she called Poppa. Loved him as a cherished, well-loved child, but she once told him how she had cried over the years for the choices she'd suspected he'd made to protect her. Choices that had nothing to do with the law.

"Everything," he ground out then, turning for the bar for a drink and wishing he could drink enough to still the ice he could feel trying to take over what little conscience he had left where the enemy was concerned.

"Tell me everything, Amara. And by God"—he turned back to her, one finger stabbing in her direction—"you better not leave so much as a breath you know they made out of it. I want to know it all."

chapter twenty-three

He'd told her he wanted to know it all.

He'd been insane.

Standing in his room more than an hour later as Amara showered, Riordan recounted the information to his brother. The assistant district attorney, Parrick's meeting. She hadn't seen the other two men, but as the bastard sliced her hair off, she'd seen his eyes and recognized his voice, and he'd laughed at her.

And as his fists had plowed into her fragile stomach, he'd gloated. Because he'd known she was pregnant.

Standing by the fire, staring into it as his brother and the man they both called a friend, silent behind him, he had to force himself to call back the rage filling him.

Tobias and two other members of the team were ensuring the bastard stayed in place as this meeting played out. Ivan was waiting in his office, waiting. Ivan didn't wait well. He'd taken Riordan's only bottle of Irish whiskey as he stormed out of the room, dragging Crimsyn Delaney with him.

Amara had demanded that she be allowed to face the man who tried to kill her first, and the betrayal that filled her eyes, her voice, still echoed in Riordan's head. That son of a bitch had helped raise her, helped protect her. And he'd laughed as he'd nearly killed her.

"I'll have a team sent out for Parrick before Ivan's told to ensure he doesn't beat us to him," Noah said into the silence. "We'll get the identity of the third man and have him picked up as well and taken to the mountain."

The mountain. The base of operations, inside a mountain located just outside the small town in Texas both of them had been raised in. Riordan had lived there all his life and had never known that a top-secret military installation had been built inside one of the rising formations of the national park there until the year Noah had come to town.

"What will be done with them?" He asked his brother as he turned back to him. "I promised her neither Ivan nor myself would kill them, but God help me, Noah."

His teeth clenched to hold back the damning words.

"They'll be interrogated," Micah answered, his expression, his voice, reminding Riordan of the hardcore Israeli Mossad agent he had been years before. "Once we have everything, you know how it works. We don't pass sentence or carry it out except under the most extreme circumstances. But once their guilt's proven, Riordan, they're not given the chance to walk away from it."

He was one of the few people outside the agency who knew how Elite Ops worked. It wasn't always pretty, and justice was determined by guilt or innocence. Guilt didn't walk way.

He gave a sharp, brief nod. "Ivan won't like it."

His gaze met Noah's in concern. If Amara's father killed in front of her, it would destroy her last fragile hope that her father wasn't the monster others made him out to be.

"Ivan will agree to it," Micah disagreed. "Once he knows the lengths his daughter has gone to keep him from killing someone in vengeance, he'll give her the illusion needed. But no doubt, he'll be there when the sentence is carried out."

"I'll be there as well." Riordan knew he'd have to be.

He had to know that once this was over, there was no doubt that the bastards behind this could ever strike out at her again.

Noah simply nodded. His expression solemn, regretful, but that regret was an older brother's affection for a man he'd helped raise, one he still tried to protect whenever possible.

Riordan hadn't needed protecting for quite a few years now, he consoled himself. He'd found that steel core of Malone pride and savage determination years ago, and it had only hardened in the years since.

"Bring her downstairs after she's showered," Noah told him. "We'll be waiting for you in Ivan's office. Let's finish this."

Finish this.

Blowing out a hard breath, his head turned toward Amara as he heard the bathroom door open. She stepped out, dressed in well-worn faded jeans, long-sleeved dove gray shirt tucked into the low band, and ankle boots.

As their gazes locked she pushed the sleeves to her elbows then clasped her hands together, staring back at him miserably.

She'd had to face too much. That thought tormented him. The abduction, the loss of their baby, the knowledge that a friend, a person as close as family, had betrayed her, weighed on her slender shoulders.

"Don't leave me like that again, Riordan. Like you did before the abduction," she said as he walked toward her.

Determined. Stubborn. That was his Amara.

"No worries," he promised, a growl in his voice that he couldn't hold back. "The next time you try to make me promise to keep our relationship a secret, I'll just paddle your ass." He cupped the side of her face gently. "You sure you want to do this?"

"I'm sure." Her answer was as confident as the look in her eyes was heartbreaking. "Let's get it over with so I'll stop tormenting myself with it. Before I start crying again."

She'd cried enough as far as he was concerned.

"I love you, baby." He whispered the words against her lips, feeling her quickly indrawn breath as surprise lit her soft gray-blue eyes. "What? You hadn't figured that one out yet?"

He was amazed that she hadn't. The day he awoke in the hospital, even his Grandpops had known.

"I hoped." Such a wealth of emotion filled her eyes, reached out to him, held him and made him so damn hard it was all he could do to not throw her to the bed and fuck her until she was too tired to make this demand of him.

"I loved you from the first look, before I ever kissed you, before I ever touched you," he swore against her lips, his gaze holding hers. "Now stay close to me. We do this and then we secure him. Don't risk yourself."

She nodded quickly as he drew back from her, wishing he'd chosen a different time to proclaim his love.

"Your education in romance etiquette is sadly lacking," she told him as he drew back. "Declarations of love are supposed to come when you're not in a hurry."

"It should have come long before this," he told her, his tone heavy with regret. "Long before. Come on now, let's get this over with."

Letting him take her hand, Amara tried to tell herself that everything would be fine as they left the bedroom and headed for the stairs.

Noah and Micah waited at the bottom of the staircase; Tobias and two others from Riordan's team waited at the door to her father's office.

This was the hardest thing she'd ever done. To face this man who had been such a part of her and her father's life and to have to face that he'd betrayed her so horribly.

The fact that anyone had betrayed her to that depth shook the very foundations of her life. Never at any time would she have considered it possible that she could be hurt so horribly by someone she knew.

"He's in the office," Noah said quietly as she reached the bottom of the stairs. "Your father's having his evening drink now."

Yes, her father liked to enjoy a drink in the evening with the few friends who had come out of Russia with him. They'd sit around the fire, discuss security, or any problems that arose. They were his confidantes, his friends. It was one of the rare times during the day that her father wasn't armed.

It was one of their rules. They locked any weapons they carried in Ilya's desk in the main office while they were talking. They were friends. They trusted one another. There was no need for weapons, her father often said, when a man was with well-trusted friends or family.

Entering the ante office where Ilya usually resided, she let the memories of that night play through her mind. The beating. His eyes. His voice.

"Your father never understood the past," he snarled down at her. *"The past is never forgotten, bitch . . ."*

The past.

A time when brother had been turned against brother, husband against wife. When the Resnova family had been torn into so many pieces, ripped asunder to the point that the lives lost far outnumbered the survivors.

Stepping to the door in front of Amara and Riordan, Noah gave a firm wrap with his knuckles.

He was armed, as were Riordan and Micah and the others behind them.

"Enter," her father called out, his voice not exactly relaxed, but his normally jovial disposition had been strained since her abduction. And she could still hear the anger from the meeting with Crimsyn.

Not that she'd found her own former light-hearted attitude.

Opening the door, Noah stepped inside first, his hand settled carefully on the weapon he wore at his thigh. Tobias, Sawyer, and Maxine flanked her and Riordan, with Riordan guarding her side carefully.

Amara watched her father stand slowly as Ilya watched them curiously from one of the chairs in front of the fire.

"Amara?" Her father frowned. "Did you remember more?"

But he knew. She saw his expression, the heaviness in it, the grief.

"I did." She let her gaze turn to the men who sat with him.

Ilya and Alexi.

There was such concern in their expressions. And love. How could she see that in his eyes?

Slowly, Ilya rose from his chair beside her father, protectively, as Alexi did the same.

"Why?" she whispered, staring at the man who had stolen such precious life from her.

Her baby.

"Amara?" Her father drew her attention back to him with the snap in his voice.

"Why, Alexi?" she asked as she fought her sobs and her rage as shock filled his face. "You were there. You beat me. Cut my hair. Why?"

"No . . ." he whispered, his expression slack now as her father and Ilya stared from her to Alexi.

"You did!" she cried out, fists clenching at her stomach. "You knew I carried Riordan's baby. You knew he and Poppa loved my hair long. You said my and Riordan's death would weaken Poppa. Why?"

Riordan held her securely to him as she screamed out the last word, restraining her, holding her back when she would have flown at him.

"Why?" she screamed again.

And he just stood there.

Comprehension filled his gaze before he dropped his head and stared at the floor, saying nothing. The glass in his hand dropped to the rug, the amber stain of the liquor spreading across the fine material.

Silence filled the room.

Her father's silence. Ilya's silence.

"Are you sure?" Her father sounded almost broken.

"I didn't see his face." Shuddering, she refused to take her gaze from the other man. "I saw his eyes, I heard his voice. And he laughed"—she sneered at the memory—"laughed that I would never survive the night to tell my poppa. And Riordan wouldn't matter because he would die as well."

And he nearly did. Riordan was almost taken from her forever.

"Look at me!" she screamed when he continued to simply stare at the floor. "Damn you. Look at me."

And still, he stared at the floor.

"Ilya." Her father's voice was like a lash of fury. "Please secure Alexi in the back room. . . . Before he dies by my hand."

Alexi flinched.

Catching his arm, Ilya jerked him away as the steel door to a secured room opened on the far side of the room.

"Ilya." Alexi's voice sounded strangled.

"Silence," Ilya snapped. "Say nothing to me."

They disappeared into the room, and the sound of the door sliding closed was the only sound they heard for a long moment.

Then the sound of a single gunshot had a cry tearing from Amara's throat. She tried to jerk away from Riordan's grip, her gaze going to her father's hard face, his dark blue eyes, as he watched her.

"No!" she cried out.

"I did not kill him," her father stated, his Russian accent heavier than normal in his voice. "He would have never lived out the night. No man in this house that has watched over you would have allowed him to live."

The steel door opened and Ilya stepped out, a gun held loosely in his hand, his face still and unemotional. Even the tattoo at the side of his face was still for a change.

Amara could only stare at him in shock.

"I lost my family at the hands of the men who followed Igor Resnova," Ilya stated. "My brother, my baby sister. I will not allow anyone involved in the torture of the child I have protected in their stead all these years to live. No man will strike this family and not know my wrath."

Her heart was pounding in her chest, racing out of control as she stared at her father and Ilya.

"I'll have to notify the proper channels, Ivan," Noah stated then. "But I doubt there will be any problems."

She swung around to the other man, her lips parted in disbelief.

"Amara." Riordan drew her back to face him, his voice hard now. "Come on. Let's let your father and Noah deal with this."

Let them deal with this?

This was how they dealt with it? This was what she'd wanted to prevent.

"Amara?" Ilya drew her gaze back to him. "Had your child lived and a friend threatened to take him or her from you and you knew justice would never convict him, would you not ensure they were stopped?"

What could she say? She had wanted to kill him herself when she remembered, wanted to die inside because she loved him and couldn't make herself believe he would do something so horrifying. Even as the memories of what he had done had torn through her, she hadn't wanted to believe.

"Would you not do anything?" he snapped, causing her to flinch. "Would you not do anything to protect your child no matter the cost or the actions you had to take?"

She couldn't answer, because she knew she would. She knew she would do anything . . .

The tears that filled her eyes and began spilling to her cheeks she couldn't explain, or understand.

Lifting a hand, she turned from them. She was barely aware of Riordan wrapping his arm around her and drawing her away, pulling her from the office, a curse sizzling from his lips.

"Riordan, don't leave her alone," her poppa ordered as they reached the door. "Stay with her."

"Fuck you, Resnova," he snapped furiously. "God-damn it."

He all but carried her from the room, leaving her father and Ilya with Noah and Micah as Tobias and Maxine followed her and Riordan back up the stairs.

They were quiet. No one was saying anything. And she hadn't expected that. There were no protests, no demands for explanations. Even Riordan was surprisingly quiet despite his anger and what he'd said to her father.

They were too quiet. And that didn't make sense. It wasn't like them.

"Your father's a damn head case," Riordan growled as he pulled her into the family room and to the couch in front of the fire.

The heat from the flames felt weak, though she knew they weren't. At any other time she'd be warm there.

"Stop babying me, Riordan," she breathed out heavily fighting back the tears, well aware that she was letting him baby her.

"I'm not babying you, I'm protecting you." The offended male tone of his voice had her looking at him doubtfully.

"No one wanted to hire me at the DA's office," she told him as she drew in a shaky breath. "No one knows the man I know Poppa to be." She lowered her head and stared at her hands. "Could he have done it, and could I have lived with it, he would have killed Alexi himself."

"No Amara, I don't think he would have," Riordan said, his voice low. "I don't think he would have."

She didn't argue the point though. She still hadn't gotten over the fact that Ilya had killed Alexi. Just that fast, with no more emotion than it would take to squash a bug.

They were friends. All their lives—her poppa, Ilya, and Alexi. This didn't make sense.

She rose to her feet, wandered to the fireplace and stood staring into the flames.

"Why did he wear a mask?" she asked absently frowning into the flames. "He knew I'd recognize his eyes, his voice. Why wear a mask?"

"Why have you abducted at all?" Riordan snapped as Tobias and Maxine stepped into the room to provide additional security.

Something simply wasn't sitting right, and he was damned if he could figure out what.

He knew Amara couldn't take much more. The attempts against her, the nightmares, the slowly emerging memories, and now the knowledge that a friend had betrayed her.

"He was there when Igor Resnova tried to take me away from Poppa," she said, that childhood terror reflecting in her voice. The night the cold, austere grandfather became a monster. "They wore masks then too. Just as they did when they abducted me. Four men, wearing masks, with guns. They shot the bodyguards. They were demanding to know where Grisha and Elizaveta were."

Amara could see it all now. She'd been packing to go to England where she'd learned her father had sent Riordan. Micah had come to the penthouse. He was supposed to be there the next morning because Riordan had sent for her.

"You didn't leave me." The memory was shattering her. "Micah was going to take me to you."

She stared back at him, the memories flooding her mind now as she fought to make sense of too many things, too many events.

"They came for me the night before I was supposed to leave. They were going to kill Elizaveta and Grisha."

She shook her head. "Why kill them? Why would it be important to get rid of them if they were there?"

"You heard them say they were going to kill them?" he questioned her, his voice harsh. "Be certain Amara. Is that what they said?"

"Get rid of them," she whispered. "Find them and get rid of them if they were there."

But her cousins hadn't been there. They'd been delayed in their return from Russia by their mother. She'd insisted Elizaveta stay to attend a ball with her.

"Once they dragged me from my room, they knocked me out. I awoke in that room with six men standing around me. All masked."

Just as they had been masked as they beat her, laughed at her.

And familiar to her. Not that she knew them. She had known Alexi's eyes, his voice, but he too had remained masked, and he'd known the others.

She paced to the other side of the room aware of Riordan watching her closely, his gaze narrowed on her. Whatever he was thinking, or watching for . . . she turned her back to him and closed her eyes, as she felt him.

She knew she did, just as she'd felt him for the past six months before he'd returned to her. His warmth, the strength he always carried with him, every part of him wrapping around her.

"You feel it, don't you," he stated softly. "That's all that kept me sane after I learned you'd been taken, Amara. That sense of you. That assurance that you were alive and waiting for me to rescue you. That was all I had to hold onto."

And she'd reached out to him. As those fists had slammed into her stomach over and over, and she'd felt the life she'd carried inside her drift away, she'd held onto that sense of him as she'd never held onto anything, or anyone else.

"They wanted to weaken Poppa," she said then, turning back to him. "If they killed me and you, they would weaken him. How would killing you weaken him?"

Because he'd done something no one else, even Riordan, had managed to do. He'd managed to identify men within Brute Force who were still part of the former Russian mafia Ivan's father had once controlled.

But Amara didn't know that. As he watched her, the slender line of her back filled with tension, he felt the pieces slowly coming together.

Whoever had taken Amara had known of their relationship, had known she carried his child, and had known he'd come for her. They'd intended to kill her and him, and ensure that Ivan was hampered in his search for a mole who had been a part of his organization since he'd come to America.

The slow bleeding of resources, information, and targeted accounts had finally caught Ivan's attention several years before. When he'd seen what was going on, he'd taken the problem to his contact within the Elite Ops.

Ivan had been part of the Elite Ops network for years. Not as an agent, but as an asset who allowed their investigations to reach certain levels within the Russian government that they'd had difficulty entering without him.

"What were you doing besides protecting me?" Amara turned to him and he saw the suspicion in her eyes.

She remembered the nights she'd awakened as he worked on the secured laptop in her sitting room. The contacts he'd meet with as she worked, or during the functions she'd attended.

She'd been getting suspicious though even before the abduction.

"Several things." He sighed, moving past her to check the French doors that led to the gardens.

They were locked just as securely as they'd been earlier.

"The Brute Force Agency isn't just personal protection. It's electronic and cyber security as well. Your father's had several problems within the organization that my team's been working on since we arrived."

Tobias and Maxine were part of those investigations as well.

Suddenly, the sense of being exposed, of Amara's vulnerability within the estate, began to nag at him. And as he let the information play out in thoughts, he had a hell of a bad feeling that something wasn't adding up with Alexi.

"What have you found?" He could feel her grief, her fear.

She'd tried so hard to protect her father and Ilya from the fallout, only to face Alexi's death.

He stilled, his gaze narrowed on the deepening shadows within the snow-shrouded garden. He was all too aware of Ivan's past and his conflicts in Russia when Amara was but a child. During that final confrontation with her grandfather, her father had depended on only two men.

Ilya and Alexi.

They'd been as close as brothers. Throughout the blood years of the father's reign over the family, Ivan's battle to wrest power from him and the slow, methodical dismantling of the criminal enterprise, the three men had worked together without so much as a rumor or hint of what they were truly doing.

Something was very wrong.

Turning quickly from the doors, he moved for Amara, only to draw up short. Rage gathered into a knot in his gut, threatening to explode through his being at the sight that met his eyes.

chapter twenty-four

It wasn't Alexi.

Riordan stared at the man holding a gun to Amara's head, and saw the realization in her eyes as well as the terror.

"It's hard to imagine it was really this easy," he said, his voice so like Alexi's that it was easy to understand how Amara had mistaken it. "I've been waiting for months for the moment that Ivan or Ilya would put a bullet in his head. It was a very pleasant surprise to have it happen so soon."

The same odd gray eyes, the same voice, same height, same hair. Alexi's older brother lacked the empathy and warmth his younger brother's expression always carried though. Andru lacked a lot of Alexi's qualities actually.

He hadn't expected the other man to surprise him so easily though.

"Yes." Danny sighed with glee as he stared back. "Contacts do amazing things for your eyes. All I had to do was sit back and wait. I knew the little bitch would remember eventually. And I knew it would be Alexi she remembered. Not his brother Andru."

Andru was going to die, Riordan decided in that moment. Seeing the fear and the memories in Amara's expression, he knew right then and there that he'd kill Andru.

Danny, the quiet, seemingly content servant that Andru had masqueraded as, had been a damn good ruse. He'd managed to fool all of them. Riordan had suspected whoever they were looking for was a close associate of the family's, but he'd been looking at security, not the various cousins and relations who worked within the house.

He damn sure hadn't suspected the unassuming servant who delivered Amara's tea every evening to be a threat.

"Tell me, Amara?" Andru asked as he caressed her temple with the barrel of his gun. "Did you know your father chose this man for the specific purpose of grandchildren? What was it he told Alexi? Oh yes, the two of you would make strong children. Did you tell him of the grandchild I stole from him?"

The sound that slipped from her lips could have been mistaken for a cry of pain. Andru damn sure mistook it as one. But Riordan saw the flash of rage in her eyes.

Carefully, he allowed the knife he kept tucked beneath his jacket sleeve to drop to his palm. The leather-encased handle was easy to grip, the blade was deadly sharp.

"No. I didn't," she answered him, the anger hidden in the softness of the response.

Andru's arm tightened around her neck, the gun barrel pressing tighter against her temple.

"How do you think you're going to do this, Andru?" Riordan sneered, shaking his head at the other man's foolish daring. "The gun's not silenced. You'll have not only Ivan and Ilya out here the minute you pull that trigger, but my men as well. You might kill Amara and me, but you can't kill all of them."

He'd be damned if he'd let that bastard kill Amara. To disarm him, he first had to find a way to get him to lower that gun from Amara's head.

Andru smiled at the question. "I don't have to kill her. I just have to kill you."

The weapon moved, the barrel turning on him. Amara's snarl of fury would shock him later, as would the fact that she somehow managed to throw him off balance. His arm slipped from around her neck and she ducked. The knife flew from Riordan's hand as Amara gripped Andru's wrist, pushing the weapon away as the sound of a gunshot ripped through the room.

His first thought was Amara.

Jumping for her, he jerked her from the other man and pushed her to the floor as he cleared his weapon from the small of his back and watched Andru drop to the floor.

Blood pooled from his head, half his face blown off, leaving him crumpled on the floor as Riordan's head jerked to the doorway.

"Alexi?" Amara breathed out in shock. "Oh God. Alexi!"

Standing with Alexi were Ivan and Ilya, their expression inscrutable as Noah and the other agents rushed past them, weapons drawn.

"I'll kill you," Riordan snarled as he pulled Amara to her feet and held her firmly against him. "God as my witness . . ."

"It was not Ivan's doing," Alexi stated, his voice tortured, his expression lined with grief. "When Ilya came into the room, he listened to my suspicion and did as I asked to make it appear he had killed me in rage." Alexi stared at his brother's body for a long moment before shaking his head. "I knew the only way Amara could have believed it was me there was if it had been Andru. There could have been no one else."

He stepped to the body, his hands hanging loosely at his sides, the weapon gripped in one hand firmly.

"I believed him dead," Alexi said softly. "A man should not have to kill his brother once, let alone a second time in his life. I believed him dead in Russia." A grief-torn smile curved his lips. "He would have killed her when she was but a child on the order of Ivan's father. I believed the bullet I put in his chest to have killed him as we escaped the house that night. I ensured this time there would be no escape."

He'd blown half his brother's head away.

Holding Amara to his chest, Riordan could feel the shudders tearing through her.

Amara could feel herself shaking, could feel the disbelief, the clash of memories breaking through the veil that had hidden them and surging into her mind. The abduction, the beatings, the rescue.

She held onto Riordan, though her shock at seeing

Alexi alive had her desperate to just sit down before her legs gave way.

"I really need a drink," she whispered. "Desperately."

Seconds later Micah pushed a glass into her hands as Riordan eased her to the sofa and Alexi threw several logs on the fire.

Ilya, Grisha, and Elizaveta dragged the body from the room, and Tobias and Maxine hurriedly directed several of the servants who came running to clean the blood from the floor.

There would be no report, no law enforcement would be called. Noah would see to it that Andru's death as well as the assistant DA's questioning was taken care of and kept silent.

"He was one of the men meeting with Parrick at the restaurant," Amara stated, watching as the two older servants, men who had been with her father for as long as she could remember, cleaned up the mess Alexi had made of his brother's head. "The other was also at the farmhouse they took me to."

"Our initial report on Parrick came in as you left the office," Noah said, speaking to Riordan as Amara tried to make sense of everything that was happening. "From what we know so far, Parrick was contacted by Andru and one of the men we identified after Amara's rescue. Andru was going to kill Ivan and Ilya and take over Ivan's businesses. The young girl who died, Shelly Mitchell, and the attempt against Miss Delaney were merely insurance in case Amara recognized Andru that day."

Amara finished the drink, barely aware that Riordan took it from her hand as her poppa sat gingerly next to her.

"Amara?" He touched her cheek gently, his gaze concerned. "I'm sorry, sweetheart."

She looked up at him, frowning. "Why? How could you have stopped it, Poppa?"

He always blamed himself, she realized. Anytime the past touched their lives, or she was reminded of it, he took the blame firmly on his own shoulders.

For so many years she had believed her poppa existed on that shadowed fringe between what was legal and what wasn't. But the night Andru had taken her child, he had told her the truth. "I would have stopped this had it been possible. I would have never let this touch you."

And she knew he wouldn't have let it, had it been possible. This one time though, he'd been powerless to stop it.

"You should have told me the truth all these years," she whispered as he watched her, regret and anger filling his face. "Andru knew an American agency aided you in tearing down your father's organization. That you have worked with them all these years. You should have told me."

Because she had always wondered, always feared her father could be dragged back into the past he'd fought to keep them clear of. That knowledge would have reassured many of her fears.

"To keep you safe, I would withhold that and more from you," he sighed. "It was always to keep you safe."

As he spoke, Ilya moved to his side, drawing his attention.

Sighing, her father rose, his gaze going to Riordan.

"Take her upstairs, Riordan. Let her rest," he said softly. "We'll deal with the mess here."

She let Riordan draw her from the room even though she knew she'd probably learn a hell of a lot more if she stayed. The problem was, she didn't know if she could handle any more right now. And she knew she needed just a moment alone to assure herself that Riordan had indeed fought his way back from the dead for her.

Because she'd felt him die the night he pulled her out of that hole. She'd felt his life slip away, and the pain, the soul-jarring agony of it, had been more than she could bear.

She needed to know, all the way to the depths of her being, that he was indeed there with her. That death hadn't stolen him from her as well.

Just for a moment.

chapter twenty-five

She gave him no more time than it took to lock the door before she turned on him, enraged.

"You lied to me!" One finger went up, stabbing into his chest as he stared back at her in surprise. "You lied to me, Riordan."

The fury on her face was something he definitely hadn't expected. Taken aback, he simply stared at that pretty little finger poking into his chest.

"I haven't lied to you." Frowning, he gripped that imperious little index finger and set it back from his chest. "I don't lie to you, Amara. And if you don't stop accusing me of it, we're going to have words."

"You said no one died," she snapped, furious as she turned from him and paced several feet away before turning back again. "You died, Riordan. I felt you die. I felt you leave me. . . ." Tears filled her eyes. "And I wanted to die with you."

That whisper, so broken and filled with pain, was more than he could stand.

Moving to her, he touched her cheek gently, brushing away the tear that escaped.

"Only for a moment," he said softly. "I came back to you, Amara. I fought to come back to you. I'll always fight, even past death, to come back to you, baby. Don't you know that by now?"

"But you didn't tell me," she cried out, the tears falling faster now. "You didn't tell me. And you wouldn't listen to me. I told you to leave." A sob tore from her chest. "I told you he was waiting for you. He was waiting to kill you."

"By God, if you think I'll walk away from you, ever leave you in danger, then you have a piss-poor opinion of what I feel for you," he charged, grabbing her shoulders and jerking her to him. "Never, Amara. Never in this fucking lifetime will I allow you to remain in danger. Never will I allow anyone to steal this from us."

His lips covered hers before she could respond, before she could argue. God help him, she was the most argumentative woman he'd ever laid his eyes on. She was the sweetest, the most generous woman he'd ever known in his life, and that intangible something that reached out to him, locked his soul to hers, and filled him with a heat that would never be denied. Could never be denied.

As their lips touched, desperation, hunger, renewal. It all fed into that kiss and so much more. His lips consumed hers, and she gave in turn. Lips, tongues, hungry moans, and a desperation to know they belonged right there, in that moment, overtook them.

Tangling his fingers in her hair he deepened the kiss, sipped at her lips, caressed, tasted, and drove himself crazy with the need for more of her.

God, he had to have her. Now.

Pushing her the final few feet to the bed, he silently cursed his throbbing cock, the imperative need driving him and a hunger he couldn't seem to fight. His shaft was iron hard, pulsing. If he didn't get their damned clothes off and get inside her, he was going to go insane.

Lifting her to the bed, he pushed her to her back and followed her there. There, his lips consumed hers as he toed his boots off, aware that somewhere she'd lost her cute little pumps.

They tore at each other's clothes, throwing them out of the way, not caring where they fell. He knew he was going to come in his damned jeans if he didn't get them off.

He was sweating by the time he managed to lever himself up to stand next to the bed and shuck his jeans. Throwing them aside, he moved to come over her once again when she shifted and, pushed him to his back, her kisses moving to his chest.

"You'll fucking drive me crazy," he groaned as her hot little lips found the flat, hard disc of his nipple. "God. Amara."

"I remember," she whispered against the sensitive flesh. "Everything you taught me, Riordan. I remember it all now," and it was the only warning he was going to get.

His stomach clenched at the memories of exactly how well he had taught her. And as her lips and tongue began caressing lower, her hand smoothed to his thigh.

His balls clenched in anticipation as his cock seemed to swell further.

"Like that?" she asked with a temptress voice as her fingers slid between his thighs to cup the taut sac of his balls.

"Dangerous, baby," he growled.

He watched, barely able to breathe, as she moved between his thighs, her fingers stroking his erection.

Ah hell. He could barely fucking breathe as he watched her head lower, her tongue reaching out and curling over the head of his dick.

"Fuck! Amara!" Every muscle in his body tightened as radiant fingers of sensation flashed from her tongue through his balls.

Then, she destroyed his mind.

Her lips parted, her sweet, hot mouth sucked him in, and he lost his damned mind.

Her hands stroked his thighs, her delicate fingers cupped his balls as she played, massaged, and tormented. Then the heat of her mouth consumed him as she sucked him inside. Her tongue licking and stroking . . . destroying him with pleasure.

She sucked the head and her tongue rimmed it as her hand moved from his balls, she stroked the shaft and destroyed his fucking mind.

Suckling, licking, her mouth worked over him like a dream, like a temptress, a seductive little imp intent on stealing the last shred of control he could possibly possess.

"Enough." Desperate, lust beating a wild tattoo in his brain, his fingers clenched in her hair, he drew her mouth from the pulsing head of his cock and pushed her onto her back.

A gasp parted Amara's lips as she found herself beneath him again. Dazed, intoxicated by pleasure, she watched as he moved between her thighs, pressing them apart, his head lowering to the smooth, waxed flesh of her pussy.

"My turn," he growled.

His head lowered to the tormented bud of her clit as her hands clenched the blanket beneath her.

Sensation exploded through her senses, streaked over her nerve endings. She was burning, lost in a storm she had no idea how to control, no desire to control. With each touch, each lick, each suckling kiss given to the tight bundle of nerves, the need for orgasm built until she felt lashed by each sensation.

He sucked her clit into his mouth, tongued it, held her hips steady as she twisted against each fiery lash of exquisite pleasure. She lost her breath, desperate moans parting her lips and whispering in the air around them. He teased and tormented, built each touch, each burning fork of extreme sensation until when she exploded, the cataclysm was destructive, imploding inside her until she was wracked with such pleasure she wondered if she could survive it.

Then she knew she couldn't.

Before the violent clash of ecstasy could ease, he was rising over her, pausing at her breasts. There, his lips and tongue played with each hard nipple in turn as he lifted her thighs to his hips and the steel-hard crest of his cock pressed between the swollen folds where his lips had played but moments before.

Senses on fire, still caught in the release she swore had destroyed her, Amara felt possessed, taken over by her need for more. She moved against the wide flesh pressing into her, crying out, gasping as she felt the stretching invasion.

The flared crest eased into the entrance, the bite of the penetration only making her hungry for more.

"Look at me, baby." The demand was a rough, guttural groan. "Let me see those pretty eyes."

She had to force her eyes open, to stare up at him.

Almost of her own volition her hands lifted, her fingers clenching in his biceps, the power and clenched strength beneath her touch adding to the hunger driving inside her.

"I love you, Amara." A tight grimace contorted his face as the words had her jerking against him. "You're mine. Say it," he demanded. "Tell me you're mine."

He wanted her to talk?

Oh God, she could barely breathe.

"Tell me, Amara." Hoarse, demanding, he stared down at her, the rich sapphire of his eyes burning into her. "Tell me."

"Yours." The cry tore from her as his hips bunched, the head of his cock nearly retreating. "I love you, Riordan. Oh God . . . I love you . . ."

A strangled cry tore from her lips as the sudden shift of his hips buried him partially inside her. Stretching her. Sending a streak of burning pleasure cascading through her senses.

She was crying his name. Breathless, ecstatic cries that refused to be contained with each hard thrust until he was buried fully inside her. The hard length of his cock throbbed against her inner walls as he paused, motionless.

"Please . . ." She was begging, needing.

Pulling back, he pushed inside her again, a single hard stroke that buried him full length inside her, and he didn't stop. He began working his erection through the clenching tissue, each thrust a stroke of pleasure/pain she found herself up against. Each impalement assaulting sensitive, pleasure-ridden flesh with such extreme sensation she became lost. A creature of his pleasure. A creature of her own pleasure.

Lust was a driving, overriding hunger that tore through her senses and left her clinging to him. Love was a bond, a steadily growing flame that melded them to each other.

"More," she cried out, demanded. "Harder. Fuck me, Riordan . . . harder . . . oh God . . ."

He began pounding inside her. Hard jackhammer thrusts that sent such an overload of ecstasy exploding through her that she was helpless against it.

Her orgasm destroyed her. Then remade her. It shook her body, shattered her senses, and swept through her like a raging torrent. Light exploded behind her closed eyes, swept through her with a blaze of white-hot sensation and violent shudders of release.

"I live for you." Riordan's vow rang in her ears as he tightened above her and she felt each heated pulse of his own release inside her. "God help me, Amara, I live for you."

Languid, shuddering aftershocks of ecstasy trembling through her, her gaze locked with his, she felt that vow to a depth of her spirit that she had no idea existed.

"Always," she swore in turn. "Always, Riordan. I live for you."

It went beyond love. It went beyond death. Beyond heart.

The souls of two were bound, until they were indeed one. Feeling with a love outside their own, loving with a spirit bound to their own.

Caught within each other.

epilogue

It wasn't over.

It should have been over, but then, it should have been over, finished, the day he'd killed his own father.

Standing between Ilya and Alexi, friends when he'd been certain he had none, brothers in a way, when the only brother he'd had was murdered by his father, Ivan reflected on the past, the sins of the father, and a present he was no longer so certain of.

"Noah and Elite Ops still have the ADA in their custody," Ilya said softly. "They also picked up your cousin, Petrov Goreski, the one who accompanied Andru to the meeting at the restaurant. According to both, this was Andru's plot alone. To kill Amara when he learned of the pregnancy, and Riordan as well. He would then make it appear you had killed yourself, allowing your cousin Petrov to claim your estate."

Not that such a thing could happen. Ivan had ensured

it would never be possible for the Resnova fortunes to ever be used as they had been before him.

"What of the girl?" he asked.

Crimsyn. Syn. Red-gold curls, a fierce gaze, a body a man could spend hours enjoying and still not be sated.

"Sawyer and Maxine will be watching her for a while," Ilya stated. "She'll be returned to New York, resume her life, just as you ordered. We'll make certain of her safety, Ivan. Just in case."

Just in case the gut feeling all of them had that this wasn't over was indeed true.

"How did he hide beneath our noses so well?" he murmured, knowing the truth just as the others did.

They didn't answer the question, though there was really no reason to. Each of them knew. They had believed Andru to be dead, along with Ivan's father and the others who had attempted to murder one fragile, innocent child.

His child.

No older than five, petite and filled with innocence, Amara had been, and still was, the bright star in his world. And that was something his father couldn't tolerate. Ivan's heart and soul had to be just as blackened, just as evil as his own. And such evil didn't love. Especially a child.

And now, that bright star was grown, and had another hero other than her poppa, and a life she needed to embrace outside his world.

And that meant he would be alone.

For a second, bright green eyes and red-gold curls flashed against his mind's eye. Sleek, silken limbs, breathless cries . . .

"I want to know every breath Andru has taken while he's been on this estate. Everyone he spoke to, looked at, shared space with," he ordered with icy fury. "By God, I want to know if anyone, anywhere, even suspected his deception and God help them if they participated, because they'll die. And get that woman out of my estate and back home. Now."

With that, he turned on his heel and strode from the steel-lined room, confident Ilya and Alexi would take care of the details. They would see to it that Andru's body disappeared, and they would see to it that the woman was gone.

That the temptation was removed . . .

Coming soon . . .

DON'T MISS THE NEXT BRUTE FORCE
NOVEL FROM #1 *NEW YORK TIMES*
BESTSELLING AUTHOR

LORA LEIGH

DAGGER'S
EDGE

AVAILABLE IN SEPTEMBER 2018
FROM ST. MARTIN'S PAPERBACKS